"All of us have in our veins the exact same percentage of salt in our blood that exists in the ocean, and therefore, we have salt in our blood, in our sweat, in our tears. We are tied to the ocean. And when we go back to the sea, whether it is to sail or watch it, we are going back from whence we came."

-John F Kennedy

Feb. 17th, 1995

It was night and they were still a mile from shore when a young man dressed in the waterproof oilskins of a fisherman stepped through the wheelhouse hatch into the cold air of a winter storm. The steel hulled fishing boat rolled side-to-side in the waves of the mid-Atlantic. All boats roll and steel boats roll the most. This boat, he knew, rolled more than any other. He faced aft, into the on-coming sea and watched waves taller than the boat follow their path. The closer they came to shore, the taller the waves grew. The bitter wind carried a salt spray that stung his face as he turned to the rail and leaned out, peering ahead, trying to make out the inlet. He stared into the dark while leaning on the rail, waiting for his eyes to adjust to the contrast from the brilliantly lit deck of the boat that was now laden with mounds of dogfish. A soft glow from inside the wheelhouse cast shadows on the windows of the Captain, standing at the helm, and another 'sternman' pulling on oilskins. Minutes passed and the swells grew until they evolved to rolling surf. The boats' diesel engine picked up speed when it slid down a wave, surfing, then wallowed heavily as the wave passed. He felt the boat lift on a wave, the diesel raced, the boat surfed, and a violent heave of the deck he had been standing on pitched him cart wheeling. He slammed into the deck and was buried in the shifting mound of fish. The boat listed drastically and he pulled himself from the pile. He knew the boat was unbalanced and fought to get the weight off the side the boat was leaning on. Another impact and he expected to be slammed to the deck again. Instead, a cold rush of water filling his ears, nose, and mouth. He tumbled, weightless. Dark surrounded him and he didn't know which way was up. Another wave propelled him further from the boat and he felt his head hit sand. A bubble came from his mouth and he saw it head for his feet. He was upside down and underwater. Mordecai knew to kick off the heavy rubber boots that would fill with water and drag him down. Paralyzing cold assaulted his effort but fear was more powerful as he used his feet to get out of them and swam for the surface, following the bubble. He broke the surface of churning foam. The skin of his face felt the rush of colder, wind-driven air. Treading water in the frothing inlet of Ocean City, Maryland, he turned, scanning between waves breaking over him, until he saw the fifty-foot, fishing vessel

Desire, right side up, and floating twenty yards away. He swam for it, with long, powerful strokes, kicking and breathing through the icy water. His heart pounded and his lungs burned with the mixture of salt and oxygen. He swam with every bit of strength in his being to get back on that boat, out of the water, behind the steel shelter deck that would cut the wind. Lifting his head to view his progress, he saw he was even further away. The outgoing tide, clashing against incoming sea, the 'washing machine effect' referred to by the old-timers, churned around him. The Atlantic fought to claim a victim, to have him as her own. He looked to the breakwater jutting out from the amusement park of Ocean City, then to the sand dunes of Assateague Island. He was right in the middle of the inlet and being swept out to sea. Even if Wolf, at the helm, could know where he was, see him, there was a sand bar between Mordecai and the *Desire.* Mordecai knew there was not much chance of the deep draft boat re-crossing the bar and coming to him. So he had to decide, here, at this point where fishermen exchanged the sanctuary of the harbor for the wild of ocean, which shore he would swim for. The lights of the amusement park were clear, the dunes of Assateague dark. But which was closer? In which direction would he fight less current? The cold was immobilizing, muscles resisted. At this intersection between what was developed by man and the wild, Mordecai felt his mortality.

July17, 1988

A small, wooden skiff floated in the tidal pool surrounded by smooth brown rocks. The water was clear and blue green, swirling the dark brown of moss which clung to the rocks below tides edge. The moss exposed above the tide, dried into a stiffened, brittle crust. A dozen or so boat lengths away, beach goers watched two twelve-year old boys work the water around the skiff. One had long, dark hair that flowed past his shoulders and protected his face and neck from the sun. The other had a short crew cut that let his head and neck turn red in the sun. The boys worked silently except to grunt from the strain of lifting heavy mounds of moss into the skiff. The sun baked their bare backs as the two lean bodies hunched, then straightened. The valuable moss would be sold at the dock, dried out, and resold to be used as a gelling agent in cosmetic products.

Flip pushed his hair from his eyes and looked at Mordecai. "We gotta get you out of the sun. Your head looks like a medium-rare burger."

"Guess I should've wore a hat."

"This tide's pretty much done. We got a decent load. Let's head in."

"All right, then." Mordecai laid his rake on the pile of moss and stepped out of the skiff.

"Hold on till I get it started." Standing in waist-high water, Mordecai held the rail of the skiff as Flip yanked on the pull-start outboard. "C'mon, girl." Flip muttered after a couple unsuccessful pulls.

"No rush, Flip. It's not like my dick is about to fall off." Mordecai shivered.

"I'll bet it's tiny." Flip answered as he worked a combination of choke and throttle.

"It is right now, anyway." Flip pulled again and the outboard sputtered blue smoke as it came to life. The smell of two stroke exhaust mixed with the pungent aroma of the sea. Mordecai pushed from the bow as Flip guided the stern with his rake, keeping the propeller clear of rocks until they were in deep water. Mordecai pulled himself back in as Flip dropped the sputtering engine in reverse and the skiff bobbed slowly in the light chop of a southerly breeze. There was a sliver of deck space for Mordecai to stand on between the heavy pile of wet moss and he steadied himself by holding onto the rail. He didn't mind being the guy that jumped in the water to push the skiff out. He didn't have a skiff and Flip did. There was a job that needed to be done and if it required getting wet, he was happy to be there to do it. 'What man of the sea wouldn't?' he reasoned.

The skiff plodded through the water, past the sailboats in the channel and past the yacht club. The wake it cast rippled against trawlers tied to the fish pier. Mordecai looked up at the much larger boats, with nets strung up in the rigging. They cast tall shadows like giant birds over the water. The bright colors of the painted wood hulls contrasted against bleeding rust stains of the steel ones.

"I wonder what it's like to work on one of those boats," Mordecai said.

"It's hard," Flip answered, brushing hair off his face. "They get fish that are bigger than us." He dug in his pocket, pulled out a crumpled pack of Winstons, "Hey, there's Andy." Flip pointed to one of the large boats with men on deck unloading fish. "Hey Buttflakes!" Flip called with a laugh and gave his brother the finger. "Look what we got." He pointed to the pile of moss. A teenage boy on the trawler fastened ropes around plastic totes, which were then hoisted off the trawler. He turned, smiled and gave his little brother the finger back. "*He's* making money!" Flip said to Mordecai. A deck hose pumped seawater across the larger boat's deck, where it spilled out the scuppers and back into the harbor. Andy grabbed it and compressing the end with his fingers, shot a spray of water over the two young boys in the skiff. Cold, saltwater rained on them and cooled their sun kissed skin.

Flip pulled two broken cigarettes out of the pack. "Crap, he got my butts wet." He tore the filter ends off, and handed one to Mordecai while fishing for a lighter in his pocket. "Think they'll still work though, if the lighter isn't soaked."

"Your dad ever figure out you're stealing his butts?" Mordecai asked.

"He's too drunk to notice," Flip muttered. He lit his cigarette and handed the lighter to Mordecai.

"My parents would ground me forever if they knew I smoked."

"They'd freak if they knew you were out in a boat, too. And with me." Flip smirked, took a haul off his cigarette, and inhaled. "Since when you're not allowed to hang around with me anyway? We been friends for two years now; since we were kids."

"I don't know," Mordecai lied. That morning, Mordecai and his father had driven to the harbor—the center of the town's commerce—for the mandatory (and enforced) monthly crew cut at the barber shop. "There'll be none of that hippie crap in my house," Mordecai's father would insist. A short way down the coastal section of road, called the Driftway, they'd seen Flip thumbing a lift toward the harbor.

"That's my friend, Flip," Mordecai had said. "Can we give him a ride?"

"Kids are lazy today. When I was your age I had to walk to the next farm to get water for the animals." Mordecai had heard the stories of milking cows, plowing fields and other aspects of life on the farm in rural Nova Scotia enough to know the loss of that farm was an emotional scar that ran across his fathers' pride. "Kids need to learn self-reliance and not always be expecting a free ride."

Mordecai had watched Flip in the rearview mirror as they drove past, dust from their Buick swirling around him as he walked along the side of the road.

Two years earlier, Mordecai Young and Francis Xavier 'Flip' Murphy became fast friends one sunny summer morning. They were both altar boys and had just served the 7a.m. Sunday Mass at St. Mary's in the far end of Scituate, Harbor. "What are you doing with the rest of the day?" Flip asked Mordecai as they pulled off the gowns altar boys wore. Mordecai and his father had ridden their bikes to the church. Mordecai looked out the window to where his father kneeled at the base of a statue of Saint Joseph.

"Don't know" shrugged Mordecai. "Maybe lift weights. Get pumped up. Think I'm gonna play football this fall." Mordecai made a scrawny, bicep-muscle-pose.

"Football, huh?" Flip made a face. "If I'm going to lift something, I want there to be a point to it."

"What's a better point than getting muscles?"

"Getting paid is a better point."

"I get paid, got a job, makin' *big* money."

"Yeah?"

"Yup."

"What, ya got a paper route?"

"Uh, yeah." Mordecai suddenly felt a lack of manliness. "How are you going to get paid for lifting?"

"I'm going out in my skiff to haul my ten pots. You want to get strong? I'll show you something."

"Tenpots?" Mordecai looked at Flip befuddled. "What are tenpots?"

"Lobster pots, dummy." Flip looked at Mordecai, his face showing he couldn't believe this kid didn't know what he was talking about.

"I'm not that good at swimming. I don't know."

"The idea is to stay in the boat. But, if you don't think you can handle it,-"

"I can handle anything." Mordecai responded defensively.

"C'mon, then."

The two boys walked out to their bicycles leaning against the side of the church by the front steps. "Hey Dad," Mordecai called to his father praying in the court-yard "I'm going with my friend, Flip." His father waved to acknowledge, looking deep in thought at the base of Saint Joseph.

Crossing the short bridge over the *Satuit* brook, the two boys were untying Flips' fifteen foot skiff at the lobstermen's' dock floating in the very back end of Scituate Harbor and less than a quarter mile away a few minutes later. Flip stepped to the stern, pulled a lever and swung the outboard down into the water. Mordecai stepped into the skiff and staggered as he felt the rolling, floating motion. "Never been in a skiff?" Flip smirked. He dropped the outboard in gear, gave it some throttle in reverse and Mordecai stumbled. He reached for the rail to catch himself as Flip switched the transmission to forward and again gave it some throttle. Mordecai's motion was going the other way. He missed the rail and fell, flopping onto the deck and spilling a five gallon bucket of smelly, bloody fish. Fish blood splattered his face.

"Gross!"

"Hey! We need that bait! Scoop it back in the bucket, quick. I need it bloody, fishes better."

"You mean *touch* it?"

"How else you gonna' get it back in the bucket? I gotta steer."

Mordecai squeamishly picked up a slimy, blood and oil covered fish and dropped it in the bucket, feeling as though he was going to vomit from the smell. "Oh, c'mon. They're not gonna bite, they're dead." Again feeling his manhood challenged, Mordecai fought his revulsion to the strong odor of the fish and fired them into the bucket, his sneakers slipping in the slick mess coating the deck. He felt wetness seeping through the shoulder of his t-shirt and saw the foul red stain inches from his face.

"Oh my god. Why does this shit got to smell so bad?"

"That's a good smell. Lobsters like it." Using his hands to pick up fish, Mordecai teetered and feared he would slip and land in the disgusting mixture again.

Finally getting all the fish back in the bucket, Mordecai made his way up to the bow, grasping the rail hand over hand the whole way. The sun was bright, the sky clear and blue. Mordecai looked at the suntanned skin and sun-faded clothes of fishermen heading out in their well-worn boats. Pleasure boats also floated by; sparkling white sailboats carrying pasty white skinned people clothed in new looking crisp white clothes. Suddenly Mordecai felt lucky to be where he was. He wasn't some namby-pamby going for a sail. He was covered in fish blood, like a grown man going to work the sea.

Flip steered the skiff to a buoy floating a few yards from the breakwater that guarded Scituate Harbor from the sea. "Take that gaff." He pointed to a hockey stick with the blade sawed off and a metal hook protruding from the end. "Hook onto the rope coming off the buoy and pull it in." The skiff rocked and bobbed in wake cast from boats motoring by in the channel a hundred yards away. Mordecai reached out with the gaff and missed the buoy. Flip stood in the stern with ease and worked the tiller to keep the skiff from drifting past the conical piece of red and blue painted Styrofoam. Mordecai fought to stay upright and on his third try, hooked the line floated up by the buoy. "Pull it in the boat." Flip told him and Mordecai did. A brown, mossy seaweed with a thick odor of the sea, grew from the rope and Mordecai's hands slipped on it when he pulled.

"How heavy is this thing?"

"As heavy as it feels." Flip came forward and grabbed the rope from Mordecai, pulling it hand over hand until the box of wood slats came to the surface. "But it gets easier once you get it started." Both boys grabbed it and pulled it aboard. Kelp and seaweed hung from the inch wide spaces between the inch wide wood lathes the trap was made from. Mordecai saw what looked like a miniature, twine net going around a wire hoop in the center of the pot. Flip twisted a latch on top of the pot and flipped the hinged door open. Inside, with claws bared and tails flapping, were five lobsters. Flip took a metal gauge from another bucket and reaching into the trap, pulled out the largest of the five. He put one end of the gauge in the lobsters' eye socket and measured the length of the lobsters shell. "That's a keeper!" he smiled and put the lobster on the deck. He reached in again and pulled out the next biggest lobster and threw it over board.

"Why didn't you measure that one?"

"Got eggs on it. Can't keep it." Flip pulled out another lobster and showed Mordecai the mass of dark eggs clinging to the underside of the tail. The next two lobsters were so small Flip didn't even bother measuring them and tossed them over. He reached into the bait bucket and grabbed three fish. "I go with a pogey and two herring." He put the fish in a mesh bag that he hung on a nail in the trap, slapped the door shut, and turned the latch. "Watch your feet." He said as he slid the trap off the rail. The wet rope coiled on the deck ran past his feet as Mordecai watched the foot and a half tall, two foot by three foot lobster pot sink to the granite ledge bottom and land amidst the scattered rock, kelp and seaweed ten feet below. He looked back at Flip who was using a tool that looked like a pair of pliers to put rubber bands on the lobster's claws. Flip dropped the lobster in a bucket he covered with a seawater dampened rag then motored over to the next buoy floating several boat lengths away and the routine was begun again. This time, Mordecai gaffed the buoy on the first try and pulled the trap to the surface himself. Again Flip came to the rail and they both pulled the trap in.

"This is fun." Mordecai said.

"You want to make real money you should come mossing tomorrow."

"Yeah?" Mordecai thought for a second. "Is it as fun as this?"

"Only one way to find out."

With the ten pots hauled and baited, Flip turned the skiff under the noon sun, and gave the outboard throttle. Summer light sparkled on clear, blue water. Moving toward the dock at the far end of the harbor, Mordecai didn't want the ride to end. "You got a fishing rod?" Flip asked.

"Yeah, I got a fishing rod."

"Bring it tomorrow. We'll go striper fishing before dead low tide. That's the best time for mossing, but the outgoing tide is good for fishing."

"Why is it best for mossing?"

"Because that's when you can get at it."

"Why is outgoing best for fishing?"

"You ask a lot of questions. Why don't you just see for yourself?"

"All right." Mordecai was already excited about what the next day would bring.

"Dead low is eight-thirty."

"How do you know that?"

"It's always in my head cuz it's an hour later every day."

Mordecai rode his bike the two miles home that afternoon, excited to tell his parents about his adventure on the water with his new friend, and the potential to catch a striper tomorrow. But on nearing the driveway at *Ford Place*, he thought of something. What if his parents wouldn't let him? If they didn't like the idea of two ten year old boys out in a skiff without adults, they could say no. That would make him look silly to his new friend. So he decided to say nothing and went to his room to check the Zebco fishing rod he used to catch sunfish in Greenbush Pond. In his room, he held the rod with the line tied to a chair. He bent it over and imagined he was out in the skiff, fighting a giant striper and impressing his friend with his skill.

He could hardly sleep all night. When the sun rose the next morning, he was up and getting dressed. At six am, he was well ahead of schedule for the ride to the harbor. He slipped out of the house without waking anyone, with his fishing rod, and walked out to the shed that housed his bicycle. With fishing rod in one hand, he set out for the harbor, eager, his heart full with the anticipation of the catch.

The July sun had climbed in the morning sky when he arrived at the lobsterman's dock after a 15 minute bike ride. A large truck was backed up to the ramp leading down to the dock and a crowd of men in rubber boots, jeans, t-shirts and ball caps bought plastic totes of herring and pogeys. Some of the men were joking, laughing. Others were glaring at each other, clearly not friends. Mordecai watched as men used three foot long metal hooks with handles on one end to tow the plastic totes down the ramp to waiting boats. The men would then untie and begin moving across the harbor water. Seagulls would dive onto the herring in totes left unguarded, flying away with fish or swallowing them whole. Noticing the commotion of flapping birds stealing their bait, men would run over swinging the hooks at the birds and scatter them. Two men began shoving behind the bait truck. The other fishermen hardly noticed, as though it were a usual thing. Mordecai sat on his bike and looked over to where Flip's skiff floated. He knew he was early and would just have to wait. He looked at his wristwatch and his stomach growled. It was six-thirty. He wished he had thought to eat breakfast.

At seven am he looked at his watch and wondered if Flip had forgotten, then saw a boy on a bicycle with a fishing rod and a brown paper bag. Flip pedaled across the parking lot and kicked back on the brake sending the bike into a skidding slide, stopping next to Mordecai. He looked at the fishing rod Mordecai was holding. "What are you going to do with that?"

"I thought we were going to do some striper fishing."

"Not with a freshwater rod." Flip started laughing as he saw the look on Mordecai's face drop. "You're gonna get spooled with that thing."

"Spooled?"

"A fish will take off with all of your line, and probably snap the rod." Mordecai looked at Flip's rod and saw it was twice as long, thicker, and with a beefier reel. "C'mon. Might as well bring it, but we'll take turns with mine."

The boys parked their bikes and walked down the ramp, onto the dock and over to the skiff. Flip jumped in the skiff, lay his rod down on the deck and dropped the outboard into place. He grabbed the bait bucket and walked back up the ramp to the truck and Mordecai saw the men in the back, wearing bright orange overalls, put fish in the bucket. Flip walked back to Mordecai waiting at the skiff. "Fresh herring, next best thing to live bait." He smiled broadly. "We should get a keeper." Flip pulled the line that held the skiff to the dock, bringing it to him and climbed in. He put the bucket down, pulled out the choke on the outboard, twisted the throttle lever and pulled several times on the starter cord. When the outboard sputtered to life he nodded to Mordecai who undid the line going to the dock and threw it in the skiff while Flip concentrated on working the choke to keep the faltering two-stroke running. Mordecai reached for his fishing rod on the dock, turned and stepped for the skiff. Only the skiff wasn't there. In a few short seconds it drifted as many feet from the dock. But Mordecai had already stepped up and out in his haste to get going. He saw Flip turn and look at him just as he hit the water. Mordecai felt the water go over his head, dropped the Zebco and reached for the dock that was now above him. His left hand felt the dock then he felt two hands grab his right hand and pull him up. His head broke the surface to see Flip, looking down at him and pulling him by his right hand. Flip let go so Mordecai could get both hands on the dock and climb from the harbor. Standing on the dock soaking wet, Mordecai realized his fishing rod was gone. The two boys looked at each other. "How's the water?" Flip asked.

The skiff puttered across the still harbor while Mordecai shivered in his wet clothes. "Are you sure you don't want to go home and get dry?"

"I'll dry out soon enough. It's summer time, I'll be ok." There was no way he intended to pedal his bike home wet and defeated. He would need the time to dry out to avoid having to explain wet clothes to his parents who must have noticed he was gone by now. He would tell them he woke early to fish in the pond, but he doubted they would believe he fell into that shallow water. He stripped off his t-shirt and the summer sun warmed him. Wet sneakers and shorts weren't so bad, he thought.

Flip cut the motor and let the skiff glide toward a large outcropping of rocks by the entrance to the harbor. He used a small knife to cut a herring into four chunks and slid one onto the hook on the end of his line. Casting it toward the rock, he said to Mordecai who watched. "Stripers like rocks and anywhere the water swirls around something."

"How come?"

"They look for bait fish that tumble in the current." He looked at Mordecai. "Kind of like you." Mordecai could only grin, sheepish. There was a sharp tug and Flip let his finger off the line. "Look, it's a run." Flip whispered excitedly. Mordecai watched the line be taken from the spool for a few seconds then Flip hit a lever on the reel and yanked the rod back. The rod bent over and Mordecai heard the drag screeching as the fish peeled off line. "I think it's big!" Flip almost shouted.

"Get him, Flip!" Mordecai leaned on the rail and watched. When the drag stopped letting out line, Flip lowered his rod end and reeling as he did, then stopped reeling to pull back on the rod again. He did this twice then looked at Mordecai.

"You want to fight him?"

Mordecai nodded, trembling as Flip handed him the rod. Immediately he felt the strength and power of the fish, pulling against the rod, the butt end pushing into his hip. The drag started screeching again as more line was pulled from the reel.

"Let him take it. Tire him out." Flip told him. Mordecai held the rod back, bent over in a U. "Now real as you lower the tip." Mordecai did and felt himself gain some line on the fish, only to have the fish take out at least as much again. "Stay with it. Work him." Mordecai's heart pounded. He had never been so excited. He watched the line move in an arching turn to the right, then an explosion of thrashing in the water twenty yards in front of the bow.

"You see that!" Mordecai yelled as he was cranking on the reel.

"Yup, he's coming to the surface, bring him in, he's getting tired. Looks like a good one too." Flip stood by the rail with the gaff. After another minute of reeling, Mordecai saw a flash of silver in the water along side the boat. He pulled on the rod and reeled. Flip reached down into the water with the gaff and the fish sizzled more line off the real, the drag howling. "Guess he's not done yet. Stay with him." Mordecai did, continuously pulling and reeling. The butt-end of the rod pushed deeper into his hip, sweat beaded on his forehead and his arms burned. Again there was a flash of silver below the surface beside the boat and Mordecai pulled as he reeled. Flip leaned over the side taking the line in one hand and gaff in the other. He reached into the water with the gaff and made a sharp, quick motion. He let go of the line and used both hands on the gaff. "Give me a hand with this!" Mordecai dropped the rod, his pulse hammering, and grabbed the gaff with Flip just as the large fish came above the water. The moment it came out of ocean and hit air, the fish hung like dead weight on the end of the gaff. Together, the two boys pulled it into the skiff. Mordecai stood, breathing hard, feeling his heart pound and watched the gills on the fish flap open wide, exposing the soft tendrils of red inside. Blood ran from the gaff wound just behind the gills and Mordecai noticed it was the same color red. The blood pumped onto the deck almost in the same rhythm as Mordecai's heartbeat. Flip took a yard stick from the back of the skiff and ran it along the fish. The fish was an inch longer. "Keeper!" Flip exclaimed and the two high fived. Mordecai was speechless as he watched the exhausted fish thrash on the deck then lie still, opening its' gills in a desperate attempt to breathe out of water. A thin stream of blood ran across the deck. "Well, what do you want to do?"

"I don't know. What do I do?"

"Well, you can keep him. Sell him. Or let him go." Mordecai thought about it and his stomach growled.

"Would he live if we let him go?" Flip looked at the fish, slowly working its' mouth. The blood no longer pulsated from the fish, but came much slower, thickening in the July sun. He shook his head

"Probably not. He's lost a lot of blood." Flip gave the fish a nudge with his foot. "Think he's dead."

"Then I guess sell him; if you don't want him."

"We'll get twenty, maybe thirty bucks for him at the Tavern or one of the restaurants in the harbor."

"Then that's what we'll do." And with that decision Mordecai felt himself become a fisherman.

"You want half a fluffernutter sandwich?" Flip offered reaching into his brown paper bag and pulling out a sandwich in a plastic baggie.

"I'm starving." Mordecai answered. Flip tore the sandwich in halves and handed one to Mordecai.

September, 1992, a group of sophomores sat on the bleachers in the high school gym, waiting for the teacher. Three ropes hung suspended from the rafters. Several senior boys from the basketball team were shooting baskets. Mordecai and Flip watched the taller boys set each other up for lay ups and saw the girls watching this as well. Mordecai saw Kerri Cole, whom he considered the prettiest girl in the school, and long the object of his desire, look over at him and Flip. From beneath blonde bangs, her furtive glance asked Mordecai, 'Well can't you do something to impress me?' Mordecai knew he couldn't shoot baskets to save his life. "Flip, I think Kerri looked at me."

"Ya, right."

"No, she did!"

"If you say so. I think she's watching the jocks."

"We gotta' upstage these clowns. They're no better than us." Flip shook his head and laughed.

"Oh, boy, I can see the gears turning. So what's the plan, Einstein?"

Mordecai looked around and saw the ropes hanging nearby a lone hoop at the other end of the gym.

"She's going to watch me swing on a rope up to the hoop and slam dunk. C'mon."

"What?" Flip asked, incredulous as Mordecai stepped off the bleachers, picked up a basketball and handed it to Flip. "I'm gonna' get a running start, then when you see me take off, toss the ball towards the hoop."

"You're gonna fuck it up, but okay." Flip took the ball and walked over toward the hoop.

"Just get the toss right, you'll see."

Mordecai grabbed the rope and eyeballed the distance to the hoop. It looked like it might work. He looked over at Kerri, caught her curious gaze and decided, 'Fuck it. It *has* to work now. She's watching.' He took off running, holding the rope in both hands and swung up towards the hoop. Flip underhand tossed the ball toward the basket. The ball floated in front of Mordecai, the timing perfect, as was the throw. Mordecai deftly handled the ball with one hand but misjudged the amount of scope, or length of rope needed to reach the basket. He also over-estimated his own strength to hold his body weight with one arm. He reached for the basket as he swung. Everything had gone so perfectly; the girls were watching, Kerri was watching, everyone in the gym was watching. There was no way he was going allow that ball to go anywhere but through the hoop, but the hoop was just out of reach. He reached, stretched, at the full height of the swing, and lost his grip. The ball slammed off the backboard as Mordecai cycled his legs in the air. The slam dunk mission aborted, he at least wanted to save face by landing on his feet. But his trajectory had tossed him at an angle. Arms and legs flailing, he saw the hard, wood floor coming at him. A sickening crack echoed through the gym as Mordecai crumpled onto the gym floor. He writhed in agony, pulling his right leg out from under him. His ankle was bent at a grotesque angle. The other students looked at each other, and cringed. Piercing, debilitating pain shot through Mordecai. He wanted to stand and walk away from the attention he had just so desperately tried to gain, then forgot about it as the pain pulsated from his leg.

"Dude" Flip said. "Are you all right?"

"No! Definitely not!" Mordecai writhed, and tried to hold his ankle. He could feel it swelling and holding it did nothing to help. "Oh no!" he fought back tears. Crying was the last thing he needed now. The only way he knew to salvage the situation was to hang tough and not look like a pussy. Phys Ed teacher Drew Coughlin had seen enough sports injuries in his twenty years at Scituate High to know something had happened by the atmosphere around the students as soon as he stepped into the gymnasium. Mordecai saw him evaluate the situation at a glance, then dispatch Kerri to the principle's office. "We'll need paramedics." Mordecai heard. "Try to relax," Drew Coughlin told him. But Mordecai knew relaxing was the last thing that was going to happen as he spent more agonizing minutes, lying on the gym floor, hearing his classmates explain to Mr. Coughlin how Tarzan tried to stuff a basketball. Firemen arrived and carted Mordecai away to a waiting ambulance while his classmates began warming up with calisthenics.

Stuck on crutches and in a full length cast, Mordecai was confined to bed for a week. He could get himself to a bathroom, but not much further. After one week he could get around the house and out in the yard. Stepping into fresh air, he felt the warm, late September sun surge through him with a charge of frivolity, laden with promise. He crutched over to where his ten speed bike hung from pegs in the shed, and he pondered. After a week stuck in the house he was desperate to be anywhere outside. If he could get to the harbor, a ten minute bike ride, he could get in a skiff, maybe catch Flip and at least go for a ride. He reasoned that he could still haul pots with his arms. He had forgotten the Percocet he swallowed a half-hour earlier. Had he considered that, he may have realized what artificially bolstered his confidence. There was little that could stop him. He would simply remove the right pedal from the crank, and slip his left foot into the opposite toe-clip pedal and let his right leg dangle in the cast. He would only need one leg to pedal. The wheels were off for storage, but they were a snap to put back on with the quick release hubs. Just release the brakes, drop the axle bolts into their slots on the forks and rear of the frame, put the chain on the back sprocket, clamp down the hub release levers, and the modified bicycle was ready to roll. He put his crutches across the handle bars and thought he would just remember to swing wide around anything he had to. He got his cast leg over the frame and gave himself a push down the driveway. Sittting on the seat, with the bike rolling, he got his left foot into the toe clip and was under his own power. Exhilaration flowed through him with the freedom of mobility. He was high. This was what it meant to be alive. He pedaled out of the driveway to the street he grew up on. He followed the flat pavement to where *Ford Place* met *Country Way*. A few hundred yards up *Country Way*, things were going smooth when he turned right to go up the hill that began *Stockbridge Rd.* He cranked harder on his left leg as he began the climb. 'Should've thought to hit this with a little more speed.' He realized as he huffed up to the half-way point of the hill. Crutches across the handlebars, he couldn't reach the shifter levers to down shift, he had to make the top in that gear, or he could swing around, roll to the bottom of the hill and try again with more speed and momentum. A car was coming up the hill behind him. Mordecai was swerving, trying to keep his bike going in a straight line as he lost momentum. The cast on his right side swung awkwardly. The car gained on him as he fought to keep his balance. Three quarters of the way up the hill, Mordecai heard the car pull out to go around him, and slowing as it did, but Mordecai was at stall speed and losing his balance. He counter steered and swerved toward the car. The crutches, extending two feet from either side of the handlebars, caught the car windshield and swung the handlebars hard right. The car had slowed to nearly matching Mordecai's speed, the driver hesitant to speed around the wavering rider. Mordecai's left leg bounced off the passenger side door, but he didn't go down. The impact knocked him into an arcing turn that sent him careening back down the hill. Adrenaline, terror, and the amazed relief that comes with the realization of surviving a close call, rushed at him as he hurtled down the hill, still on the bike and picking up speed. That was the end of his ambition, he would be happy to get home in one piece. The bike continued to pick up speed as it rolled. Mordecai wanted to just roll home. But a car pulled out of a driveway in front of him. 'Not now!' he thought as he reached for the brakes and squeezed. The brake levers closed all the way to the steel bars, but the brakes didn't grab. Terrified, he realized he had forgotten to reset the brakes after putting the wheels back on. If the car pulled out quickly enough, he reasoned that he could slip behind. At the bottom of the hill, he was going way too fast to jump off. The car pulled out partly onto the road, saw Mordecai bearing down the left-hand side of the road, cast dangling, and stopped. Mordecai slammed into the passenger side of the car just behind the front wheel and was launched over the hood to land with a smack in the street. He felt pain in his broken leg. Remarkably, that was the only damage he had other than some minor abrasions on his shoulders. He hadn't even hit his head. He tried to pull himself up as the elderly driver exited his car. "Are you all right, son?" The old man looked as if he was about to have a heart attack. Mordecai felt sharp pain in his broken leg and as he tried to pull himself up, saw that the cast was snapped. He and his bike lay crumpled in the street. Other cars were stopping and Mordecai felt the embarrassment of that day in the gym creep back. He desperately wanted to pick up the bike, smile and wave at the crowd gathering, tell them he was all right, and vanish.

The bones that had started to mend re-broken, Mordecai was confined to his bed for another week. His parents were not happy with his stunt and another phone call that their son had been taken, again, to the emergency room via ambulance. Mordecai knew the look on the EMTs' faces when they realized they were responding to the same foolish kid who tried to slam dunk from a rope, and now crashed his bike in a cast, was a preview to the reaction his parents would have.

When he was well enough to get back to school, his mother decided she had had enough of accidents and didn't want him having a mishap getting on or off the school bus. Despite his desperate pleas for her not to do so, Mrs. Young called the high school and made arrangements for the station wagon school bus that drove the special needs kids, to come pick him up as well. On one October morning, the first trip for Mordecai, he sat in the passenger seat of the bright yellow, station wagon school bus. He felt ridiculous, embarrassed, and on display. To his horror, the bright yellow car rolled right down *Front Street*, to pick up a boy who lived near the harbor. He saw Kerri crossing the street in front of him with another girl and get into a Camaro. He faked a sneeze and pulled his jacket over his head. "God Bless you," said the middle-aged woman driving.

"Thanks." Mordecai responded as the car rolled past Kerri. "It's real important to me not to spread germs," as he pulled the jacket back down. 'That was close' he thought.

"I'm sure your reluctance to spread germs has nothing to do with those cute girls crossing the street." the driver added.

'Why can't this happen to somebody else?' Mordecai thought as the station wagon school bus rolled through Scituate Harbor, and Mordecai was vigilant for classmates who might recognize him. Approaching the end of the harbor, the bright yellow car drove past the fish pier. It was just after sunrise, clear, bright, and Mordecai saw a fishing boat steaming across the harbor towards the eastern horizon. He stared at the boat silhouetted against the glare of rising sun reflecting off water. It occurred to him that he would rather be heading for the horizon than the spectacle of the kid who broke his leg in gym class being driven to school as if he were retarded. For the next six weeks, that was the favorite part of his day, cruising past the harbor for the brief glimpse of the boats steaming out to begin their day.

He was not allowed to leave the house except to go to school as punishment for his foolhardy stunt on the bike. So he spent his afternoons lifting weights in the cellar. He could stand on one leg and do sets of curls, sit on the bench for military press, and lie back to do bench press. Between sets, he would catch his breath and stare at the cellar wall, where his imagination took him far beyond the grey cinderblock. In his mind he would see the sun bouncing off blue water, and sense the intoxicating salty-sweet, smell of ocean. As soon as he was able, he would be back on the water with his friend.

In mid November, Mordecai was finally out of his cast, the broken leg still tender and not ready for long walks, but he could ride a bike. So one Saturday morning he took one of his brothers bikes and pedaled to the harbor. The cool fall air had a bite he wasn't ready for as he rode down streets lined with the fallen autumn leaves. The sky and water at the back float dock were far darker than he remembered. He saw Flip standing at the boat ramp. "Hey Flip. I'm back! We going out?" Flip looked at Mordecai as though he had two heads.

"Out? The Skiffs' coming out. That's it till spring."

Mordecai watched as the skiff was hauled out of the water on a trailer behind Flip's father's car.

"Oh. Ok." Mordecai shifted his weight off his sore ankle and tried to stand as though he were completely healed. "Well, what are you doing today, you want to hang out? We could fish for flounder from the pier." Flip shook his head, then grinned at Mordecai.

"Spending the day with the girlfriend. I'm dating Liz Flaherty." Flip lit a smoke. "Want one?" Mordecai took the cigarette as he considered this in astonishment. How could he have not known this? He hadn't seen Flip at his locker for a week. Their school lockers were just two apart. Flip lit Mordecai's cigarette with his Zippo lighter while his father sat in the car, waiting for Flip as salt water ran from the skiff and trailer in little streams. The water trickled down the ramp and back to the harbor. "Been getting a little." He winked.

"All right, Flip!" The boys high fived. "Good for you. She was in my math class. Man, she's a good looking girl."

“Yeah.” Flip nodded. “I gotta get going. She’s waiting on me. I’ll see you in school Monday.” With that he climbed in the car and was gone. Mordecai sat on one of the concrete blocks lining the ramp and looked at the yellow and orange of leaves that floated on the black water of the harbor. The cigarette tasted harsh and he flicked it at the autumnal flotsam and jetsam.

“Now what am I gonna do today.”

May 6, 1994, Mordecai sat in the bleachers of the football stadium while Flip, Liz, Kerri Cole and the rest of his classmates graduated from Scituate High. Mordecai saw Flip and Liz exchanging smiles. The warm spring air stirred with a light breeze and Mordecai felt hopeless and alone. Kerri was on the tennis team and her blond hair shone against the blue of her graduation gown. Aside from playing tennis, Mordecai decided she must have been getting sun at the beach as he watched her smooth tanned legs step on the stage. Friends and family of classmates were also in those stands watching the ceremony. Mordecai winced at the alarmed and confused looks on their faces as he saw them realize he wasn’t going up on the stage with his classmates to receive a diploma. He wished he was basking in the success of achievement with Flip, Liz and Kerri. But at this point, he had never even spoken with Kerri, just watched her from afar. Mordecai never understood why he couldn’t find success at academics. His teachers noticed that he wasn’t dumb, but he never seemed to understand instructions. A guidance counselor suggested he be tested for an auditory condition that affects how an afflicted person interprets information. Mordecai believed his hearing was fine, and didn’t want the attention of being a student with a condition. The weekend after his eighteenth birthday, he went to a local community college and took the test for his grade equivalency diploma.

Sitting on the bleachers at graduation, Mordecai knew that no one could see his GED, only that he wasn’t where his peers at Scituate High were. He wanted to get out of the spotlight of his defeat and go have a few beers on the beach with Flip as they planned. With the end of the ceremony, Mordecai tried to slip out unnoticed ahead of the crowd when the marching band started playing, but he stood while everyone else was still sitting and he felt conspicuous as he made his way off the bleachers, feeling the weight of all those watching the drop-out make his way to the parking lot.

Flip came out to the truck where Mordecai waited, pulling off cap and gown as he approached. "Sorry, about the wait." He offered tossing cap and gown in the truck bed. "Feels good to get that shit off me. Thought I was gonna roast during that speech. Pulled it off soon as I got off the stage then my parents asked me to put it back on for pictures. Fuck, enough of this shit already."

"Well, you're a grad now. They're proud of you." Flip nodded slightly. "Congrats bro, you did it."

"You should have been up there with us. You're smarter than half the kids they gave this bullshit diploma to."

"Don't mean shit without the diploma though."

"At least you got that GED, it's the same thing."

"I guess." Mordecai looked at the palm of his hand and started picking at a callous. "So what are you going to do?" Flip shrugged.

"Got a site on a gill-net boat, commercial fishing, full-time, staying in Scituate Harbor, I guess." Flip lit a Camel and blew smoke out his window as they drove. "Don't plan on much beyond that for now. What about you?"

"Guess I'll keep working for this builder as long as he can keep me busy. I like being outdoors, but I think he's more interested in having me be a lumper than teaching me carpentry." Flip drew on his smoke and looked at Mordecai.

"Maybe you should think about fishing."

"I remember going out on the ocean with one of my fathers friends. I got sick as hell. And they said it wasn't even that rough." Mordecai shrugged. "Guess it's not like a skiff in the harbor out there. Maybe I'm not cut out for it."

"Liz has some parties she wants me to go to."

"Oh." Mordecai thought about the spectacle of being the only kid to not graduate at a graduation party. "I thought I'd just go hang down at the beach"

"C'mon, man. Come to the party. It'll be more fun with you there."

"Not for me, thanks."

"Why not?"

"Don't know how to say it." Mordecai said while fighting emotion. "Think I'll just go to the beach." Flip said nothing and dropped Mordecai off at Pegotty beach. Mordecai walked across the sand to stare out over the ocean while standing at water's edge. A thin wisp of smoke rose from a distant speck as a ship traveled across the horizon. He wished he could disappear like that ship.

Two years passed and Mordecai bounced from job to job. He washed dishes, painted houses, worked banging nails, whatever he could find, but never found what he truly loved. There was a moment, while working on the construction of new condominiums abutting a golf course, he stood atop the chimney of one of those new condo's. High above the construction site, the landscape stretched out before him. In the distance, he could see the ocean. It inspired in him a longing for wide open spaces that he couldn't explain.

On a balmy spring afternoon, Mordecai was throwing a football with one of his brothers in the yard at home when he saw Flips' fathers' big Chrysler pull into the driveway. Dressed in cut-off jeans, a tie-dyed t-shirt and sandals; Flip walked from the car with a plastic bag in one hand and two lobsters in the other. "Hey Flip. What ya got?"

"Some cod fillets and a couple bugs. I know you're parents like seafood."

"I like having friends that can make them happy." Mordecai tossed the ball to his brother who caught it and ran over to examine the creatures from the sea. "Maybe this will help out with my status around here. Not too popular with the parents since school didn't work out."

"Hey, I'm here to help."

"C'mon in. My Mom will be glad to see you." The pair walked into the house where Mrs. Young was getting ready to start cooking dinner. "Hey Mom, Flip has something for you."

"Oh. Hello Flip. How are you?"

"I'm well, Mrs. Young." Flip extended the bag of fish. "Brought some cod fillets."

"Brought lobsters, too" chimed in Mordecai as he began filling a pot with water.

"Oh how sweet." Mrs. Young kissed Flip on the cheek. "I remember when you and Mordecai were altar boys together." Flip and Mordecai exchanged looks. "You boys looked like two little angels."

Who are going to smoke a fat joint soon as we leave. Mordecai thought. But plans for a quick exit to smoke and cruise with his friend faded when Mrs. Young asked, "Well Flip, would you like to stay for dinner?" Flip looked at Mordecai and Mordecai shrugged.

"Yes, Mrs. Young. I would like that. Thank you."

"Mr. Young will be so pleased to have fish. It's his favorite." Mrs. Young called to her husband in the living room where the voice of Jerry Falwell boomed from the television. "Richard? We have company." Mordecai was adding the two lobsters to a pot of boiling water when Richard Young walked into the kitchen. His expression of interest in who may be visiting fell from his face when he saw Flip.

"Oh. Hello Flip." He looked over to where Mordecai was at the stove. "Lobsters? Really?"

"And fish." Mordecai included. Richard Young looked at Flip and his long brown hair that tumbled almost to his shoulders.

"You catch those today, Flip?"

"They were swimming just a few hours ago." Flip answered. "Couldn't get anymore fresh." Mr. Young looked as though he were pondering a miracle.

"To look at you, Flip; I'd guess you were just back from Woodstock, or some other, psychedelic, 'love-in', rather than working on the ocean."

"Why thank you, Mr. Young." Flip smiled. "We try to fit in as normal people when on land."

During dinner, Mr. Young said nothing; consumed with the delicacy before him. Mrs. Young talked about Flip and Mordecai when they were altar boys. "You boys were so cute then." She sighed. "Of course, Mordecai doesn't seem so interested in church anymore." Mordecai gave Flip a look signaling he knew what was coming. "I wish Mordecai would consider one of those nice catholic schools. But I guess you can't make someone want what's for their own good." She looked at Mordecai, then at Flip. "Are you thinking about college, Flip?" Her look was hopeful, as though

Flips' aspirations may influence her son. "Find a nice girl and settle down?" Mordecai saw her glance sideways at him.

"I think there is plenty of opportunity for someone who is willing to work hard." Flip spoke after wiping his mouth with his napkin. "I'll keep fishing for now. After all, there are a lot of fish in the sea." There was a sound of metal scraping on ceramic as Mr. Young cleaned his plate with his fork. Mordecai prepared himself for a story from the long-lost farm in Nova Scotia.

"Thank God for that." Mr. Young said as he looked up for the first time since the meal started. "Is there anymore?"

Mordecai left with Flip in the big Chrysler after dinner. They drove to the point at Peggoty beach where the road took a sharp left to go up and around Scituate's Second Cliff. Flip pulled over and started rolling a bone on a Frisbee. The days were getting longer and the sun was still in the sky in early evening. The waters of Massachusetts Bay sparkled before them. "I don't know why my parents think I don't want a girlfriend, a future, or a life. It's like they think I want to be a loser."

"I guess they don't understand that school isn't for everybody." Flip looked at Mordecai and shrugged while breaking up the weed over the Frisbee. "They *are* schoolteachers."

"Yeah, that's true." Mordecai looked out over the vast expanse of ocean beyond the hood of the Chrysler. "They don't understand being happy as a working man."

"Well are you happy?" Mordecai thought about that.

"Doesn't mean I want to live with my parents my whole life." Flip licked the glue on the paper and smirked.

"Well your old man was happy with the fish." Flip stuck the joint in his mouth and reached for the lighter. "I thought he was going to lick the plate."

In late May, the house Mordecai was working on was finished and he was laid off. That spring he had started a small lawn mowing business out of an old Chevy pick up, and was satisfied to be his own boss until drought turned the lawns to patches of dead grass. Then the transmission on the pick up went and there was no money for a replacement. His status in the family was already low and getting lower. Ultimately, he took his mothers' suggestion of bagging groceries at the Angelo's Grocery in Scituate Harbor- his parents had made it clear he was to find somewhere else to live if he didn't find steady work. Bagging groceries paid minimum wage and meant wearing a tie to work, which his mother saw as the most dignified option for her drop-out son.

The tie was hot and uncomfortable around his neck. He hated wearing it and wanted to rip it off every time he got outside. Bagging groceries for suburban soccer moms was not the freedom of outdoors he longed for. Sometimes they re-arranged the groceries in the bag from how he did it. He tried to like it, but couldn't wait to get outside for the walk home each day. The time dragged. He would look at the clock and watch its agonizingly slow pace.

Three weeks into the grocery bagging job, Flip and three other fishermen in tall rubber boots came into the store and started filling up carts with groceries. They fanned out through the store with purpose, yet with a casual sort of contentedness with their stature. One grabbed paper towels, plastic cutlery and paper plates, tossing them to another pushing a cart. Another used his arm to wipe over a dozen cans of tuna off a shelf and into a basket he then dumped into a cart pushed by Flip. Their cut-off flannel shirts and sweatshirts exposed muscled and tanned arms. The other shoppers regarded them with fascination as though they were 17th century pirates. The fishermen's carts were overflowing with groceries as they approached the register. One of them tossed the items of his cart to another fisherman who gracefully caught each item and placed it on the registers conveyor belt. Mordecai noticed everything these guys did; they performed as a smooth efficient team.

Flip walked over to Mordecai as he bagged the groceries. "What's up, brother?" he said, grasping his hand firmly in greeting.

Mordecai grinned. "Not much. This job sucks. I feel like loser on display, like the woman with the beard at the carnival or something."

"Yeah, we got to get you on a boat, man. You don't need this shit."

"Really! You think you could get me a job with you guys?"

"We'll find something for you. Come talk to me when you are ready to make some money."

There were four carts full of groceries to be wheeled out to the pick up. Mordecai grabbed two bundles and walked with the fishermen across the parking lot. A tall blond fisherman Mordecai guessed was a few years older than him, said "First thing I'm gonna do with this steak is put it in a Ziploc bag with a bottle of Italian dressing. Let that sit on the ice in the hold and we'll have some well marinated meat."

"That's the only way you're going to get your meat marinated," answered another wearing a red bandanna on his head. "You aint much to look at but you can cook."

"Can you believe this shit?" the blond guy looked at Mordecai. "Haven't even left the harbor and he's starting already." He looked back at the fisherman in the red bandanna, "It's not smart to fuck with the cook. Besides, who would want to be pretty on a boat with you, you pervert." The fisherman all laughed as two handed groceries to two in the truck. Mordecai tried to help but the four fishermen had the bundles packed before he could join in.

"Then I guess you have nothing to worry about."

"All right" Flip said to Mordecai as the others climbed in the truck. "We got to get these on the boat." Flip climbed in the bed of the truck, and sat on an overturned fish tote.

"Wish I was going with you" Mordecai said.

"You might, eventually. It's up to you." Flip looked at Mordecai. "You want to be a fisherman, or do you want to carry groceries for little old ladies."

"Hey! We're not little old ladies" exclaimed the fisherman behind the wheel of the truck and they all laughed again.

"Just something to think about." Flip said as the truck pulled away. Mordecai waved and turned to head back across the parking lot and resume bagging groceries. He thought about being on a boat with Flip again and enjoying the ocean. He turned before he entered the store and had a view of bright blue harbor water beyond the parking lot. On the other side of *Front Street*, and behind the bank, the water of the harbor invited memories of mossing in the skiff.

One of his mothers' friends exited the store with the manager carrying her groceries. Mordecai was about to say hello when the manager began scolding him for chatting with friends when there were groceries to be bundled. "You might not be worth keeping around if you don't straighten out your act," he said to Mordecai.

"Fuck you. I quit," said Mordecai and dropped the tie in the parking lot.

It took Mordecai half an hour to walk home from the store. Walking up *Ford Place*, he saw clothes in the front yard, then his mother come out the front door with what looked like his hockey equipment.

"We are not a flophouse for the unemployed," she shouted as she saw him come up the street. "Take your things, or we'll throw them away. If you don't leave, I'm calling the police."

Mordecai was not entirely surprised. He knew his parents would have a reaction when they learned how he lost his job, but still, was in shock.

"Mom, could we talk? That job wasn't,.."

"You can tell it to your father. He'll be home any minute now."

"Dad? Does he know about this?"

"You'll see when he gets here." With that she stormed back into the house and Mordecai heard the click of the door lock. He began sorting through his things, trying to figure out what he needed most and what he was able to carry, when his father pulled up.

"Mordecai, what are you still doing here? We want you to leave, now! No more of your immature antics are going to be tolerated here."

"Dad! What are you talking about?"

"I'm talking about the direction you're heading. Your loser friends, you can't even keep a job." Richard Young pointed at Mordecai. "You're heading for skid row, and I'm not going to enable you by letting you live here."

"Dad, that job sucked. I can do better than bagging groceries."

"But you aren't! You just quit with nothing else to go to. You think you are too good for honest work, just like you thought you were too good for school. And it's because we let you think you will always have a roof over your head being a quitter. Well that's not how it works."

"Dad, I'm trying,.."

"You are going to have to learn to try a lot harder. And I want you off my property."

"I need to figure out,…"

"Don't make me call the police. You're twenty and I'll do it." Mr. Young abruptly turned and strode across the lawn toward the front door. He quickly took the front steps and twisted the door handle. It was locked. He stood for a moment with his back to Mordecai, then slowly raised his hand and knocked. He turned and looked at Mordecai. Mordecai briefly hoped that the feeling of being locked out would create some sympathy. That somehow he would be able to pick up his things and bring them back inside.

"I told you to leave!" his mothers' voice rang out from inside the front door.

"It's me." Mordecai's father answered and the lock turned and the front door opened. "He's leaving." Mordecai heard his father say as he stepped through the doorway followed by the door shutting and again the lock turning.

Shock became nervous energy. With shaking hands, Mordecai quickly tossed some clothes in a trash bag. He never felt so alone as at that moment, in the front yard of the house he grew up in. A police car pulled up in front of the house. With a police officer watching him gather what he could carry, Mordecai thought, 'Does this happen to other kids, or just me?' He took stock of what he needed most, and left the rest in the front yard. Leaving part of himself behind with the hockey equipment, dress clothes and other items he could not take, Mordecai started walking. He knew another kid from his class that lived with another family while finishing school. But it was known that kid was the product of a family where the father was a vicious drunk and people understood. How he would explain his estranged status for losing a grocery bagging job was beyond his reach.

Mordecai began walking the mile and a half to Flip's parents' house, casting his head down as cars passed, hoping to not be recognized. He desperately hoped no one would stop and offer him a ride. That hope ended when a yellow camaro pulled over and stopped next to him. Behind the wheel was Kerri Cole. "You want a ride?" she said as she looked at the trash bag slung over his shoulder.

"Uh, no thanks, just out for a walk."

"You take your trash for a walk?"

"Oh, this? No, uh, This is for a yard sale. My buddy is having one."

"My mother loves yard sales! You've got to show me where." Kerri leaned over and opened the passenger door. Mordecai sat in the passenger side with the bag on his lap.

"Well it's not today."

"Oh, when?"

"I don't know yet. Just wanted to have the stuff there ahead of time, so I'm ready when there is one."

"Uh huh." Kerri looked at the bag. "So where are you going?"

If you could drop me off at the end of Gilson Road; that would be great.

Flip lived in the basement of his parents house on Gilson, which he had converted to an apartment. Flip was just getting home as Mordecai walked up the street, and Mordecai saw him watching his approach, trash bag over his shoulder. Mordecai was mulling over how he would explain. When Mordecai told him what had happened, Flip said, "What? That's nuts. You can do better than that crappy job."

"Gonna have to now." Mordecai looked at his feet as the weight of his situation pressed on him.

"What the hell is wrong with your parents? I can see you're trying."

"I don't know." Mordecai was afraid to look up. He felt his lip quiver and fought to not cry in front of Flip. Flip looked at the trash bag in Mordecai's hand. "That all you got?" He took the bag from Mordecai. "Follow me." Flip took him inside and showed him a couch. "You're welcome to crash there," he said. "Tomorrow, we'll see about getting you a site on a boat."

The next morning he heard Flip come out of his room. Mordecai greeted him from the couch. "Good morning."

"Morning sunshine. What are you going to do today?"

"Don't know. Find a job I guess."

"Be on the pier when the boats come in this afternoon. Take my fishing rod and you can cast for stripers while you wait."

It was five a.m. He had a whole day to kill. He heard Flips' truck leave then put his shoes on and grabbed the fishing rod in the corner.

He walked the mile and a half from Flips parents' house on Third Cliff, to the harbor. As he walked, he remembered that bike ride to the harbor for his first day of striper fishing. He tried to find the solace of home in that memory. But it seemed to him a long time ago and he felt homeless and alone.

He walked down quiet *Front Street,* until he arrived at the more busy fish pier. As he walked onto the pier, the mixed smell of herring, diesel and ocean hung in the air. The bark of gulls echoed over the mellow hum of a diesel engine. He sat on a piling and watched fishermen get on their boats, untie and head out, across the harbor for the open sea. Two boys, about ten and twelve, were already casting into the harbor. He picked up errant herring spilled out of totes of bait lobstermen dragged across the dock. He found an old, rusty knife next to one of the pilings and cut the herring into chunks. He baited his line and cast it out. The sun rose and he watched it. One of the young boys hooked a fish and Mordecai watched him fight it, thinking about the day he caught his first fish in the skiff. He watched the boy reel in a foot and a half long, 'schoolie' striper and let it go. Then the other boy hooked up, fought and landed a fish a little bit larger. *That's a good sign,* Mordecai thought. *At least the fish are here and biting.* A fishing boat rumbled to life and a man let go the lines holding her to the pier.

"Bye, Dad" the boys called and waved to the man on the boat.

"You boys be good, and don't stay too long. Your mother will worry." He waved and stepped through a door. Seconds later, a dark puff of diesel smoke plumed from the stack and the boat backed away from the pier. Mordecai reeled in his line. The bait had a crab clinging to it and it was half eaten away. Mordecai walked over to the two boys as the younger one hooked up again.

"Hey, what are you guys using for bait?"

"Herring" said the older boy as he baited his hook.

"Really" Mordecai was confused. He was embarrassed to ask but had to know. "I'm using herring and haven't had a bite." The boy baiting his hook glanced at the herring chunk in Mordecai's hand.

"That's salted herring for lobster bait." He scowled. "Stripers won't bite that." The boy looked at Mordecai.

"You need fresh herring for stripers," chimed in the younger one as he pulled another schoolie onto the pier. "Don't you know anything?"

Mordecai walked away from the two boys. 'Stripers won't bite the bait that lobstermen preserve by salting. It's much more difficult to fool a savvy striped bass than a scavenging lobster.' He realized that he was already learning.

Most of the guys Mordecai knew who worked as fishermen came from families that fished. There were always children of fishermen in his class throughout his schooling in this coastal New England town. Like most people in his town, Mordecai saw fishing as something kids were born into.

Mordecai watched the boys continue to fish and catch then release stripers. After another hour, the boys exhausted their supply of fresh herring and left. Mordecai sat on the pilings and watched fishermen that weren't fishing mend nets on boats tied to the pier. The men talked and laughed as they tied twine into the mesh. "Well if it wasn't for theories fishermen wouldn't be worth a shit no how," he heard one say to another as both started laughing.

At noontime, an eighteen wheeler backed onto the pier. The men who climbed out of the truck used a forklift to unload large, square, plastic vats from the trailer. They set up a scale by the winch at the edge of the pier. Another half hour went by and Mordecai saw a fishing boat chugging down the channel, with Flip in bright orange overalls uncoiling a rope on the bow. The boat pulled to the front of the pier, and men, also in bright orange rubber overalls were on deck to tie up. Mordecai looked over the edge and saw a pile of grey fish on the deck. Tourists from the Clipper Ship Inn, across the street had walked over to look at the boats and catch a glimpse of fishermen working their craft. They gawked at the "saltwater cowboys" and the stacks of fish being unloaded. Flip climbed up the ladder leading from the boat to the top of the pier and saw Mordecai.

"Hey, you showed up! That's the first step. Attaboy!" He then turned to the people crowding the pier. "Could you back up, folks? We've got to get unloaded and this isn't going to be a good place to stand." Mordecai walked back to his seat on the pilings about fifteen yards away. Flip stood at the winch and immediately started working the lever. Blue plastic buckets were hoisted off the boat and dumped into plastic vats. The tourists who let curiosity get the best of them, moved closer to the vat to see what was being dumped in. There was a wet, splattering sound as the bucket emptied its contents into the vat and a woman's voice shrieked.

"Told you that wasn't a good place to be," said Flip. Mordecai saw a woman walking away while wiping her face. There was a dark stain on her shirt. The buckets kept coming and Mordecai stayed out of the way. He didn't want to jeopardize his chances of getting a job by being a nuisance. He saw other boats coming down the channel and then there was a pause in the unloading as one boat pulled away from the pier to be replaced by another. Mordecai saw Flip leaning over the pier to shout at someone below. Almost all the other fisherman had similar builds—lean and muscular, like gymnasts. Flip waved at Mordecai, calling out, "Hey, the guy that's lookin' for help is down there" pointing to the boat. "His name is Tony Amato. The *St. Joe*'s not a bad boat, and he's a pretty good shit. Go talk to him. And by the way," he added with a stoned sort of giggle as Mordecai headed down the ladder on the front of the pier, "you'll be working for one of the phattest guys in town."

As Mordecai stepped from the ladder to the boat, he saw that Flip meant "fat," literally. There, sweltering in the summer heat, where the pier blocked the breeze but not the sun, was Tony Amato. One hand gripped the rail to help support his immense weight as he stooped to pick up a fish off the deck. With great effort, he tossed it into a barrel that was then hoisted up to the pier.

"Mr. Amato? My name is Mordecai. I understand you're looking for some help."

Several seconds passed as Tony, his mouth agape, studied Mordecai.

His first impression of me must not be living up to his expectations of potential help on a gillnetter, Mordecai thought. *How can he tell so fast?* He cleared his throat and said, "I don't have any experience, but I'm strong and I can learn fast."

Tony motioned with his hand, indicating that he understood, but his eyes were cast downward and his mouth still agape. Mordecai realized the man was so out of breath that he couldn't speak. "Tomorrow," he finally gasped. "Six o'clock."

"Okay. Six. See you then." Feeling no more words were necessary, Mordecai went back up the ladder to tell Flip the good news. "I start tomorrow."

That night, Flip's girlfriend Liz came over Flip's. Mordecai got up to leave so they could have some privacy. "Dude, don't leave. Watch the tube with us, she brought a movie." Liz looked at Flip and didn't say anything.

"Uh, I can pick up chips or something in the harbor." Mordecai offered trying to bow out gracefully.

"You're not walking all the way to the harbor for chips now." Flip gently pushed him toward the couch and Mordecai sat down. "You got a big day tomorrow."

"That's true." Mordecai answered feeling the anxiety for his performance the coming day.

"So kick back, chill out, watch a flick and you'll be fresh for your first day."

"Flip, can I talk to you for a second?" Liz suddenly more demanded than asked. The two of them went in Flip's room and Mordecai heard them arguing. "Why do you have to have a guy living in your apartment? What about us?"

"He's got nowhere to go and he's my friend. I'm not going to turn him out on the street."

"So you are putting your friends before us." Mordecai felt uncomfortable and really wanted to go for a walk to get those chips now. He figured he could easily kill an hour walking around the harbor, maybe play some video games at the arcade in the bowling alley. He was pulling his jacket on when Liz walked out of Flip's room and past Mordecai coolly. She left slamming the door behind her. Flip came out of his room and flopped on a recliner next to the sofa looking exhausted.

"You sure you don't want me to take off for a bit?" Mordecai asked.

"No point now", Flip lit a joint and held it out for Mordecai. "No nookie tonight." Flip exhaled smoke. "Fuck it, what's on the tube?"

Chapter 2
Tony and Ed

When Flip and Mordecai showed up on the fish pier at 5:45 AM, Tony was leaning on a car, with a pair of oars over his shoulder and a new pair of oilskin overalls in his hand. "I still gotta get the boat and Ed's not here yet," he said breathlessly. "You got time to get a cup of coffee or something. Here—these are for you." He handed Mordecai the pair of skins. Mordecai felt like a knight being given his first set of armor. At five foot four, four hundred pounds, and a long white beard, Tony looked like Santa Claus in fishing boots. Mordecai walked toward the coffee shop, admiring the new skins. He looked back at Tony as the man slowly made his way toward the skiff. It was low tide, and Tony had to negotiate the steep down-slope of the ramp that led to the float where the skiff was tied. Mordecai was curious to see how such a massive man could pull off this feat of coordination, yet he was afraid to watch. It was already 85 degrees at 6:00 AM, and Mordecai was afraid that Tony would have a massive heart attack or another physical crisis on his way out to the boat, and that would be the end of Mordecai's fishing career—before it even started.

He caught up with Flip at the Coffee Corner. "Hey, are you sure Tony is all right? He looks like he's gonna collapse."

"He's been doing this since before we were born, dude. Just hope you don't skunk out. You don't want to be the Jonah."

"The Jonah?"

"Yep."

"You mean the biblical prophet who was swallowed by a whale after being thrown overboard by his pagan shipmates?"

"That's the one."

"So if we don't catch anything, they throw my ass overboard?"

"No, they'd just never take you again cuz you're bad luck. Neither would anyone else."

Great. Mordecai thought. Fishermen, a superstitious lot, drew an analogy between being swallowed by a fish and the new guy keeping fish away. If he went out on his first day and didn't catch anything, he would be back to where he started.

Mordecai, taking his coffee and lunch, walked back to the fish pier with Flip. Mordecai was nervous, apprehensive. "Just go with the flow." Flip said as the two stopped on the pier at the point where they would go their separate ways. "You'll do fine." He gave Mordecai a light punch on the shoulder.

"Thanks Flip. See you when we get in?"

"You will at some point, I'm sure." Flip turned and headed off to join the captain of the *Desire* while Mordecai walked down the steep ramp to board the *St. Joseph.* The down slope was tricky for him. *How does the big guy do this?* The first mate, Ed Barrett, several years older than Mordecai, nodded and stepped aside so Mordecai could step aboard. At six foot four and three hundred pounds, Ed bore a distinct resemblance to the character of Hoss Cartwright on the TV western *Bonanza.* Mordecai smelled a salty, musty combination of diesel and fish. Light vibration from the diesel engine ran along the deck and through his feet. He leaned against a two-by-four that supported the overhead and felt the vibration in his back. Ed untied a single line and then started duct-taping pieces of plastic tarp to two-inch PVC pipes. The pipes ran through buoys stationed about midway along their eight-foot length, with window weights on one end and the plastic flags Ed was fashioning on the other. Mordecai put his lunch on a table in the center of the deck space behind the wheelhouse; he was ready to work when told what to do. But neither Tony nor Ed said anything to him, and other than a nod from Ed when he first came aboard, he was hardly acknowledged. *I'll have to show what I'm made of before I can expect that*, he thought.

The *St. Joseph* idled through the harbor, and Tony and Ed exchanged waves with the fishermen on other boats as they moved past. The engine emitted a steady hum until they reached the end of the harbor, where Tony throttled up and the diesel wailed from the exhaust stack. Ed strode up to Mordecai, carrying a pair of boots that were covered in black, oily grime and the orange dust from rusty metal. Without a word, he dropped them at Mordecai's feet. Mordecai kicked off his sneakers and pulled on one boot. A sudden sharp sting went into his big toe and he reflexively jerked his foot out. Stuck to his toe was a spiked, green ball—it looked like a crab apple with porcupine needles all over it. As he pulled it off, Ed yelled over the racket of the engine, "Sorry about that! Little joke I meant for the last guy who wore those boots! I forgot about the sea-urchin-in-the-boot gag!"

"Report all injuries to the captain," Tony said over his shoulder from the wheelhouse.

"Okay, I got a spine in my toe," Mordecai answered.

"If I see the captain, I'll tell him," Tony responded, turning back to the helm.

The sun was rising from the horizon, and it already was a clear June morning. The view of the coastline and ocean expanded as they left the harbor. The cliffs lining Scituate's coast ran southward, diminishing onto a horizon swallowed by the vast Atlantic. The beaches drifted behind them, and slowly, ocean surrounded the small boat. Mordecai leaned against the table and watched Ed tape the flags to the pipes then place the completed units in a barrel. "What are those?" he asked.

"High-flyers." Ed responded as he began pulling on his oilskins. So Mordecai pulled on the pair that Tony had given him. Tony walked out of the wheelhouse wearing an apron made of the same rubber fabric as the bright orange oilskins Mordecai and Ed wore.

"The captain doesn't fit into those dainty little oilskins anymore." he announced to Mordecai as he made his way to another helm on the side of the deck. "This is the starboard side of the boat. Facing forward, the right is starboard, the left, port." he said to Mordecai. Tony throttled up the boat again and guided the *St Joseph* to a high-flyer buoy in the bay, like the one Ed was preparing. Tony reached out with a gaff, pulled the buoy to him, wrapped the line from it into a groove around the cylindrical hauler, twisted a lever and they were hauling the first set.

The fish they were targeting that day was dogfish. Mordecai was fascinated—although at first, a little terrified. He immediately noticed the distinguishable shape of a shark when the first fish came around the hauler and was deposited in front of him.

He had been reaching forward to grab whatever came around the hauler, eager to show Tony and Ed that he was going to pick up on fishing faster than anyone they had ever seen, when he reeled back in horror at the open mouth of the two-and-a-half-foot shark. He stood motionless, not sure what to do. The fish writhed in front of him, tangled in a ball of monofilament webbing. The look on Mordecai's face set Tony and Ed laughing. "What's the matter, fella? Afraid he's gonna bite?"

"You didn't tell me we were fishing for sharks," Mordecai protested.

Ed stuck his gloved hand in the mouth of a dead fish, watching for Mordecai's reaction. "See? He ain't got any teeth. Not to speak of, anyway. Just a couple rows of real little ones that ain't gonna hurt ya." Ed twisted his hand in the fish's mouth, proving his point.

"That's why they have those horns on their backs," explained Tony, wiping away tears of laughter from his cheek. "That's their defense mechanism. They can't do much with those little choppers."

"Scared the livin' hell out of him, though, didn't they?" Ed said, and he and Tony had another good belly laugh.

Mordecai grinned sheepishly and then laughed along with them. These were good guys; he could learn to work with them.

The dogfish came around the hauler in clumps and thrashed about on the table, all wound up in the net. They had mildly abrasive skin, like sandpaper, that gave Mordecai's rubber gloves an excellent grip, but the motion of the fish's thrashing fought Mordecai's efforts. Mordecai's forearms and back muscles burned as he tried to work the pile mounding before him. The exertion of his awkward effort reaching into the pile of fish and mesh wore on him and he felt himself slowing. Ed, on the other hand, was firing fish out of the net, even as Mordecai wrestled with every one. Although it was a relatively calm sea, the boat constantly bobbed up and down and rolled side to side. Mordecai steadied himself by holding on to the table or to the vertical two-by-four that supported the overhead. Frequently, he found himself grabbing a fish, then dropping it to reach for the table as he started to fall. Eventually, he figured out how to lean against the table with his hips, freeing his hands to work with the fish.

Tony sat on the rail that ran along the inside of the hull, about a foot off the deck and on the other side of the table from where Mordecai stood. He deftly handled the boat, keeping the *St. Joseph* in position with wind and tide to cleanly lift the gill nets off the ocean floor. "You'll get your sea legs eventually," Tony said. "You just have to put your time in."

Tony explained that hauling a gill net required that the boat be held in a position directly over where the nets sat on the sea floor so the net could be gently peeled off of the bottom. "You gotta be careful the net doesn't 'part'—that means it rips or breaks—from being hung up on rocks, wrecks, and other objects on the bottom. Rocks and wrecks are favorite spots for fish but you gotta watch out for the nets. There's an old barge below us that sank in the fifties. I'm trying to haul the net without hanging up on it."

Mordecai watched Tony's skilled hands busily work the throttle, transmission, and hauler levers continuously, as he concentrated on retrieving his net intact.

The hammers of the hydraulic hauler made a loud, metallic clacking noise as they released the net—and fish it held—on the table. Ed worked flaking net in preparation to set it back out. He spun the twists out of the float and lead lines and then straightened out the mesh in between before pulling the section of net back into the net bin. Mordecai was showered by a light salt-water spray as the lines spun and untwisted in front of him.

Staying ahead of Ed required strength and dexterity. Ed showed him how to grab the dogfish by the snout and work the mesh down the fish, while Tony repeated over and over, "Control the fish! Don't let the fish control you." Mordecai worked the mesh down each fish as fast as he could only to have Ed pull the fish out of his hands as he flaked the net back.

"You gonna be any help at all, fella?" Ed said casually.

"I'll get it. I'll figure it out." Mordecai tried to sound confident but felt he didn't. Tony said nothing.

After a set was hauled on board, picked through and flaked out, Tony would swing the boat around and give Ed a signal. Ed threw the high-flyer buoy over, let it take some line, and then threw a steel weight over the side to act as an anchor. When the anchor went over the side, it took a few fathoms of line with it, and then the net started flowing over the setting bar, which looked like a goalpost with an inverted U for a cross-section, which separated the lines and helped spread out the mesh webbing.

Mordecai had taken two of the Dramamine tablets, but with the constant rocking of the boat, even on a calm summer day, he felt on the verge of vomiting ever since the boat left the harbor.

It was around noon when the fourth and final set went back in the water, and the *St. Joseph* turned west for the twenty-minute steam back to the harbor. They had a fair haul—several thousand pounds of dogfish and about a hundred pounds of mixed cod and flounder, which at the market price of a dollar a pound was worth about the same as a thousand pounds of dogfish. Mordecai watched the white lighthouse at Cedar Point grow larger. The sun was hot but the breeze over the water felt good. The air was so fresh. He hoped he had done well enough to work another day. As they idled down the harbor channel, Mordecai saw a half-dozen boats tied to the pier, waiting to unload. One boat, tied to the front of the pier, had a crew busy loading the fifty-gallon, blue-plastic barrels of dogfish which were hoisted to the top of the pier by the hydraulic winch. Mordecai could see the crew sending up barrels as the *St. Joseph* entered the harbor, and they still had a pile of fish onboard bigger than the *St. Joe*'s catch. Mordecai watched the individual boats pull up to unload, while still others came in. Some had more fish than the St. Joe's catch; some had less. He thought idly, *I see why it's called fishing and not catching*. The crews of boats with big hauls had big smiles; the crews with not as much were not so happy. After an hour and a half of watching the procession of boats file in to unload, it was the *St. Joseph*'s turn. The men pulled along front and tied to the pilings of the pier. The blue barrels descended, and Mordecai and Ed pulled fish out of the pile and threw them in. Mordecai pulled at a tail that was sticking out of the pile, but the fish was stubbornly stuck under other fish. "Top of the pile, fella," Ed said calmly. "Take the fish from the top of the pile. It's easier." He smiled at Mordecai.

"Yep, it's good to have help," said Tony, leaning on the table as Ed and Mordecai worked. Mordecai looked for the fish on the very top of the pile, and found that Ed was right. "Of course, watching is easier still," Tony mused. "It's nice to be captain."

After forty-five minutes of heavy exertion, lumping fish into barrels, the last of the dogfish went up, and Ed began spraying down the deck and checkerboards that were slick with blood and fishing offal, which Ed referred to as "gurry." He slid a five-gallon bucket of sudsy saltwater to Mordecai and tossed him a brush. "Hey Greenhorn, 4500 lbs, not a bad day, but it aint over." and the two started scrubbing while Tony idled the boat over to one of the vacant docks so that the next boat in line could unload. After a half-hour of scrubbing, Mordecai stepped off the *St. Joseph* to the dock. Eight and a half hours earlier, a greenhorn had stepped off the same dock, unsure of what he was getting into. That afternoon, he was salty, sweaty, sunburned, and covered in fish blood. But he felt distinguished. He turned to the *St. Joseph* as it pulled away and called to Tony at the helm, "Same time tomorrow?"

Tony regarded him, shrugged. "If you want."

Mordecai watched the forty-foot wooden *St. Joseph* idle over to her mooring, the wet wooden deck and boards, scrubbed and well-worn, reflected sunlight with the brilliance of a redeemed soul.

That night, Mordecai and Flip cruised the coast in the big Chrysler. Flip had a new pickup, but his father's car had room for six people, at least, so it was good to have the room in case they found what they were looking for. Flip and his girl, Liz, had been spending more time apart, and Mordecai hoped they would find a pair of girls who were unattached. They cruised the coastline, stopping at beach parking lots, looking for beach parties, and riding down Front Street to see the girls heading for the bars of the harbor. As they drove by the fish pier, Mordecai mused, "I wouldn't mind having my own boat." He pointed toward the tall gallast frames and rigging of the trawlers tied to the pier. "If I could afford it."

"Maybe you will." Flip sucked on a joint and handed it to Mordecai. "That's the best part about fishing." He exhaled his smoke, and it flowed past the steering wheel. "It's about the fish you haven't caught yet."

Mordecai felt the heat expand in his lungs, held it a moment, and then released the cloud to mix with that already glowing with the lights of the dash. He liked how that felt.

"What do you think it would take to get into a boat?" he said, excitement infusing his high.

"Depends on the boat." Flip took the joint. "And the permit. You can't just put any permit on any boat. There's rules to what goes where, even more now, but if somebody was getting out of it, selling a turnkey operation, boat and permit—who knows?"

Mordecai glanced in the rearview mirror at the boats. "I'll bet between the both of us, we could save up enough for a down payment."

"That wouldn't be a bad idea," Flip answered. He took a hit on the joint, held the smoke, and looked thoughtful.

The next morning, Mordecai sat on the dock with his coffee, watching the sunrise, as Tony and Ed rowed out in the skiff to where the boat lay anchored on the mooring. At first he wondered why they didn't expect him to go out in the skiff with them—then he saw why. The little skiff was nearly overwhelmed from the weight of the two men, with no more than an inch of freeboard showing above the water. "This short trip in the skiff is the craziest risk we take all day." Mordecai heard Ed mutter to Tony. Tony and Ed fired up the *St Joseph* and brought the boat to the dock and Mordecai climbed aboard with his back pack. "What's that for?" Tony asked.

"It's my lunch." Mordecai answered.

"Oh yeah?" Tony looked interested. "What's for lunch?"

"Sandwich and a soda."

Tony scowled. "All that for a sandwich?" He looked at Ed, incredulous. "And nothing for me?" He shook his head dismissively. "You hippie college kids and your backpacks. I would think you had a whole buffet packed in that thing." Tony looked at Mordecai. "Didn't Ed or Flip tell you the new guy is supposed to pack lunch for the captain?"

"No, I never heard that." Mordecai answered honestly as Tony turned to the helm.

"Somebody has to talk to you about honoring the traditions of this industry." Mordecai sat on the checkerboard wondering how he missed this piece of information.

Neither Tony nor Ed hid their passion for food and spent part of the day talking about the best way to prepare certain dishes or where to get the best take-out.

"Hey, Ed, you tried the Moo Shi beef at Tsing Tao lately?"

"That ain't no place to get Moo Shi, fella."

"Why not? I think they give you a pretty thick piece of meat there."

"No. Gotta go to the Beijing House for Moo Shi. 'Bout the only decent dish at Tsing Tao is the Szechuan chicken."

Looking at Mordecai, Tony said, "Oh, and he's the expert now! When he started on this boat, he was nothing but a Pu-Pu platter guy. All he knew was chicken wings and fried rice."

"And how can you be judge of anything, fella?" retorted Ed. "You pick it up around eight, microwave it around midnight and eat it when you're shit-faced!"

Mordecai didn't have much to do when not fishing. Flip was fishing on a boat that went farther out, so he was home later in the day. One hot afternoon after fishing, Ed asked Mordecai if he felt like having a few beers at the farm. Mordecai didn't feel right going back to Flip's place when he wasn't there, so going to Ed's for a couple cold beers and seeing the farm sounded like fun. Ed drove them both in his new Chevy pickup.

"You ever seen making hay?" Ed asked on the ride. "Me, my brothers and sister-in-law are the last people in Scituate who still cut and bale hay." Ed looked over at Mordecai with a wry smile. "Maybe you'll learn something." Mordecai was eager to experience this slice of Americana. Whether fishing or mowing hay, he wanted to feel a connection to those folks who came before him and who continued in these time-honored traditions. In this way, he felt that he could replace what he had lost with something else. Then the dry, dusty reality of it crashed into him.

"First we use a tractor to mow the field," Ed explained as he and Mordecai tossed hay bails up onto a flat bed truck. "Then the hay is left in the field to dry for two days." Ed pulled a bandanna from around his mouth to take a long pull off a gallon jug of water. He handed the jug to Mordecai who took a long swig. "Then a tractor tows the machine that rakes the hay into furrows."

Mordecai and Ed resumed walking behind a pickup, driven by Tom's wife, Deb, and tossed the hay bales onto the bed. "Then we got a tractor to tow the bailer; the last step."

"And hucking the bails onto the truck. Isn't that the last step?" Mordecai asked, sweat stinging his eyes. A dust cloud billowed from the baling machine and hung in the thick, humid air. "And there's no tractor for that." When Mordecai tried to wipe the sweat from his eyes, he only rubbed the dust in. Eyes burning, Mordecai used the inside of his shirt to wipe them. The cloud of dust expanded like shaving cream, clinging to everything—even the back of Mordecai's throat. Mordecai noticed Ed knew enough to wrap a bandanna around his mouth to keep out most of the dust. By the time Mordecai noticed, he was beyond thirsty.

"No, stacking the bails is actually the last step." Ed was laughing as Mordecai blinked, bleary eyed, and tied his t-shirt around his face and mouth. "See? You're learning something!"

"Learning what, 'Do you want to come over for a few beers' means." Mordecai said as he picked up another bale and tossed it at Ed on the truck. "Thanks for the heads up about the bandanna." Ed was having a good laugh.

"Don't have to thank me now." There were gallon containers of water on the front seat of the pickup, and Mordecai hit them again and again. Still, they worked in the hot afternoon sun, with mouths so dry that they couldn't make spit.

"So what's the story with the new guy brings the captain lunch?" Mordecai asked. Ed started laughing again. "What's so funny?" Mordecai watched Ed and his brother Tom double over with laughter.

"He told you to bring him lunch?" The truck stopped as Ed called to his sister-in-law. "Hey, Deb! Tony told him to bring the captain lunch!" The truck stopped as Ed, Tom and Deb took a break to recover from their laughter. Mordecai just stood there dumbstruck. Tom and Ed exchanged knowing looks and laughed again. They resumed moving, slowly, yet steadily and deliberately, filling the pickup over and over again. Several times Tom and Ed looked at each other and started laughing. 'Bring me lunch' Mordecai heard them say through the laughter and knew he was the butt of the joke. Still, it felt good-natured.

After they'd finished stacking the hay bales in a corner of the field and covering the pile with a tarp, Tom came out of the house with a cooler of frosty beers, which he set in the shade of a tree. They each took a beer and sat on the tail-gate of the truck. A cool evening breeze touched Mordecai's forehead as he felt the first cold beer wash the dust down his throat.

"Hey, Mordecai." Ed extended his beer. "Thanks for the help. You made the difference in getting this done." Mordecai looked at the beer Ed held towards him and they clinked bottles. He felt, he suddenly realized, a *connection.* Ed may have suckered him into being cheap labor at the rate of few beers for a couple hours work, but he'd ingested the dust of the land; now he held a beer with his sea-salt–encrusted forearms. He inwardly celebrated the connection to earth, sea, and hometown.

Ed cooked dinner for everyone. Then after eating they went out to the porch swing. Tom rolled a joint while Mordecai cracked another frosty cold Bud.

"How long you been fishing, Ed?" Mordecai asked

"Been over ten years now."

"You ever think of doing anything else?" Ed looked thoughtful.

"Yeah, sometimes I do. Fishing's not what it was." He handed the joint to Mordecai and exhaled smoke into the warm summer night. "I was just out of High School when I met Tony. The *St Joseph* was a charter fishing boat then. He needed a mate to bait hooks and untangle lines for the folks that paid to go recreational fishing."

"People paid to go fishing? What happened to that?"

"It was seasonal." Ed shrugged. "Nobody wants to pay to go out fishing in the winter. But gillnets were being set by lobstermen when lobstering got slow. Tony noticed the guys gillnetting could make money year round. So he put a net hauler on the boat after Labor Day a few years back, set gillnets and that was the end of charter fishing on the *St Joseph.*" Ed drew a deep breath. "And it was the beginning of the end for fishing in general."

"What do you mean? I thought we did pretty good today."

"On dogfish." Ed snorted. "They weren't worth anything few years back. The money fish was cod. But Tony wasn't the only guy to notice gillnets caught fish where draggers couldn't tow their nets. Lot of guys started setting nets on the bottom that before was a safe place for fish to be. Now the fish were getting pressure everywhere. There became nowhere safe for them to go. There's not near the amount of codfish around as there was before gillnetting." Mordecai thought about this and Ed looked up at the stars. "The dogfish will get caught up too, and the government will get involved and start regulating everything and they'll probably say that's it. No more fishing."

"So we're part of the problem." Ed kept his eyes skyward and thought for a moment.

"Guess we'll get our share while we can." He looked at Mordecai. "Might as well. There's no pension plan and it aint gonna last forever." Ed looked back at the stars. "And neither are we."

Mordecai was content with making a living aboard the *St. Joseph.* He hadn't forgotten about saving money for his own boat, but was waiting for a big haul and a decent paycheck to start a fund. As they were hauling, Tony and Ed listened to the ballgame on the radio and talked about the viability of certain teams for the World Series.

"I guess I'll wait 'til the World Series is over to quit drinking," Tony said.

"Why?" Mordecai asked.

"Because I want to have a beer while I'm watching the ballgame," Tony answered, looking at Mordecai as if he were from another planet.

"No, I mean, why would you quit drinking?"

"That's a good question," Tony reasoned. "I'll have to think about that."

"Oh, c'mon," Ed interrupted from the stern. "He'll just get to the World Series and then decide he'll quit after the Superbowl. Then after the Superbowl, there's the Stanley Cup, and by then, the Sox will have already been through spring training. He ain't gonna quit. Don't let him kid ya."

"He's full of shit," Tony said to Mordecai, and then he turned to Ed in the stern. "When did I ever care about hockey?"

It was afternoon, June 15. They hauled the end of the last set, and then Tony stopped the hauler and turned to face the sun. With his hands extended toward the water, as if he were addressing the waves, he began to sing in an off-key baritone. "Mo-o-on River! Wider than a mile. I'm crossing you in style … someday." He placed his hands on the rail and supported his weight with his arms as he gazed out at the sun-splashed water. "He's gone," Tony said quietly. "Died yesterday."

"Who?" Mordecai asked.

"The guy who wrote that."

"Who's that?"

"Henry Mancini," Ed answered. "But he didn't write the words. He wrote the music."

"I was close enough." Tony shrugged. "He knows what I mean."

"Wrote the music to eighty somethin' movies, they said on the radio this mornin'." Ed included while untwisting a bridle.

"He was one hell of a composer," said Tony.

Mordecai found it ironic that just as his own new life had begun, the originator of something beautiful had died. The *St. Joe* steamed across Massachusetts Bay, across the sun soaked water, and the diesel hummed. But Mordecai held those harmonious notes of Moon River in his heart and could imagine himself doing nothing other than being a fisherman. He thought of his father. 'What would he think of this life?' He remembered as an altar boy, learning of St. Joseph, the patron saint of workers. Would his father respect him for this? At the time, he thought the beauty of this journey, this experience, would never end. This time-honored way of life on the bay, as old as the founding of the country, had to sail on forever. It would continue even after they were gone, their spirits forever reflecting off the water, like God's fallen light.

Chapter 3
Philosophy, Fish, and the Fisherman

Mordecai stopped at a convenience store after fishing one hot afternoon to get a bottle of water for his walk back to Flip's house. On the newspaper stand, one of the local papers had a photo of a fishing boat not unlike the *St. Joseph.* It was settling into the water, sinking with a big pile of dogfish on her deck. The headline declared: "Fishing Boat Sinks Off Plymouth." He bought the paper and walked back out into the afternoon sunlight. What he read made his breath come short—the crew had loaded on an unusually large haul of dogfish—then a brief squall; gusty winds; the weight of the pile shifting; the popping of an old wooden plank; seawater pouring in. The crew had radioed a distress call and were rescued by another gillnetter that was fishing nearby. One crewman had the foresight to grab a camera from the sinking vessel and, immediately after stepping onto the rescue boat, turned and snapped a picture of the old lobster boat, converted to a gillnetter. The hull was underwater, and waves washed over the rail, with just the wheelhouse above. The *St. Joseph* had been caught in the same squall as it swept across the bay.

The sky had darkened with clouds that swept in from the southwest, turning sea and sky gun-metal gray. A puff of wind had carried the metallic scent of impending rain—a few drops, then a blowing deluge of rain and windswept waves. Tony had tied the buoy line off to the net they were hauling, saying, "Fuck it; let's go in." Ed had passed Tony the high-flyer around the hauler, and they'd fed the line and net back to the sea.

Mordecai folded the paper and threw it in the trashcan next to him, remembering the fear that had caught him and the relief that had come when Tony found the harbor. Though visibility had been hardly a few yards from the bow, Tony returned boat and crew to the harbor as if it had been a clear day.

The scent from the day followed Mordecai. He knew it was in his skin and was not something that could ever be washed off entirely. The barrels that hoisted the fish from the boats had rained drops of blood and the yellow fluid from the embryonic sacks of the pups that were born as the mother fish died. In this slick of salty brine, Mordecai had been baptized, and he let it run over him, knowing he would wash in the salt-water torrent from the deck hose. The odor leaked from his pores, and wherever he went, by this odor, people would know he was a fisherman. Salt clung to his skin as he looked at the lobstermen's dock at the back end of the harbor. The *St. Joseph* swung on her mooring in the light breeze, and bright orange and green flags of the high-flyer buoys fluttered in a ceremonious posture. He couldn't see the *St. Joseph* ending as the converted lobster boat had ended. *On second thought*, he mused, *maybe it's a noble death—the warrior struck down in battle, going to the bottom honorably with a heavy load of fish, after fulfilling its role—its purpose—to the end.* No, he decided, other boats sank; the *St. Joe* would not be one that did. To him, there was something hallowed about the boat. In its cracking paint and sun-bleached wood, he sensed hundreds of sunrises that had lighted the cliffs of Scituate, the white lighthouse at Cedar Point, and all that bathed in that radiant light. The same light reflected off the scrubbed boards of the boat and in the efforts of men who spent hours aboard. He was becoming less anxious about venturing into the unknown, away from firm, dry ground. Maybe St. Joseph would watch over him in a new occupation.

There were enough risks in fishing, Tony reasoned, that chasing the fish to unknown waters would only provide the opportunity to meet the fish on their level. "If the fish aren't there one day, that's all right!" he yelled over the metallic clacking of the hauler as it dumped empty mesh on the table. "They'll come back; they always do."

Mordecai shoved the piles of net down the table to Ed, who pulled on the float and lead lines and spread out the mesh in between. Even when there were no fish, the flaker still had work to do, preparing the net to be set back. Ed worked silently, and Mordecai felt awkward standing at the table with nothing to do other than pulling out the occasional strand of kelp or seaweed. "The secret lives of fish," Tony said. "We aren't meant to worry where it is that they go; we're meant to be content with those that have come to us."

Mordecai nodded, acknowledging that the old man was imparting wisdom. But Tony's face took on a look of resignation as he looked at Mordecai. Then he turned to watch his empty nets rise from the depths of the sea. Mordecai knew the old man believed the young man wasn't listening.

The nets were empty for the next five days, but Mordecai said nothing, and the men went about their routine silently. On the afternoon of the fifth day, Mordecai asked Tony where the fish might have gone.

Tony looked at him for a moment before answering. "You think I don't wonder?" He throttled the boat down, put the transmission in neutral, and turned from the controls. "Tell you what—let's ask." He grabbed a cod fish and gave it a couple slaps in mock interrogation. "Where are your friends, you little bastard?" he growled. "We got ways to make you talk." He stared at the silent fish for a moment and then placed it in a bin with the few others they had. "I think he's resisting," Tony said, and he returned to hauling the empty nets from the sea floor.

Later, while scrubbing the boat on the steam home, Tony straightened himself up for a moment and let the warm summer breeze wash over his sun- and salt-weathered skin. Mordecai stood next to him in the stern, trying to hear Tony's words over the drone of the diesel. "What you don't understand," Tony told him, "is that you don't need to understand. They will be back. You don't want to get caught up in that insatiable lust for more fish. If you do, there will never be enough."

They were tied to the front of the pier, waiting to unload the few hundred pounds of fish they had caught and waiting, along with a few boats at the pier, for the fish truck to return from New Bedford. Enthusiasm had dissipated with the catch and the men said little. Mordecai sat on a checkerboard with his arms folded on the picking table. A toy fire engine rolled down the table and bumped to a stop at his elbow. The winter before, a merchant ship lost several containers overboard in a heavy northeaster. At least one of those containers held toy fire trucks. Before they began washing up on beaches, fishermen found them in their nets. Mordecai decided Ed was reluctant to throw them back, as there were already several on the boat, and now this one showed up at his elbow. Mordecai turned it around and rolled it back to Ed, who pulled the little truck to the end of the table and extended its plastic ladder.

Then he heard someone say, "Hey, what's going on with McArthy?" He turned around to see another gill-net boat, the *Cathy Marie,* steaming down the channel in the harbor at full throttle. The *Cathy Marie* didn't slow as she passed other boats; she cruised down the channel with her deck awash and her stern under water. Two sternmen were on deck, bailing furiously and throwing dogfish overboard. The owner, Jim McArthy, was at the helm, looking intently at the front of the pier. When they reached it, the sternmen wasted no time in getting the tie-up lines around the pilings immediately, but the lines were not strong enough to hold up the boat with the weight of the water flooding her and the pile of fish on board. The forward motion of the boat, with the diesel engine pushing the bow through the water, had created enough water pressure to keep the boat afloat. At the front of the pier, however, without that water pressure, the *Cathy Marie* sank almost instantly in ten feet of water.

The captain of one of the larger draggers in the harbor came alongside, while another fisherman on the pier donned scuba gear and dove down on the submerged boat to secure strong ropes to her. The lines were then run through the powerful hydraulic winches on the dragger, and the *Cathy Marie* was raised off the bottom. With the boat secured alongside the large dragger, someone lowered a couple pumps, and the *Cathy Marie* pumped out to float on her own. She was then towed down to the back float—the dock in the back of the harbor—where a marine diesel mechanic was waiting to break down the John Deere diesel and flush the engine of saltwater. Within a few hours, the *Cathy Marie* was afloat and running under her own power.

That night, Jim McArthy bought rounds of drinks to show his gratitude, and he shared his story—the crew of the *Cathy Marie* had loaded on a catch of over twelve thousand pounds, an excellent haul. But the aging wooden deck was no longer water-tight, and as the boat was forced down by the weight of fish, water came aboard the boat through the scuppers and seeped into the bilge. This in itself was not unusual; pumps normally pumped out the water as it came in. But something had clogged the pumps, and the water in the bilge accumulated until the high-water alarm sounded. Jim saw that they were in trouble as soon as he checked the bilge. He cut the net they were hauling and headed full speed for the harbor, just a mile away. He'd thought about running her up on the beach less than a mile from where they were hauling, but opted to head for the fish pier, thinking the tie-up lines would hold her up at the pier.

"Damn good thing we weren't farther offshore when the bilge alarm sounded," Jim said. "If she'd sunk in deep water, we would've lost her."

The next day, Tony sat on the rail and across the table from where Mordecai sat on a checkerboard as Ed took the helm. "I'll be damned." Tony said. Mordecai leaned on the picking table to listen. "Things are on the beach." He looked at Mordecai. "We've been steaming right past them."

"Are we going to set our gear on the beach?"

"I don't know if we want to get sucked into it."

"What do you mean?" Mordecai had to ask. *They knew the fish were there, why not go after them?*

"Now everybody knows where the fish are. And you can believe that almost every boat in the harbor is going to set their gear in on the beach."

"Well, why shouldn't we get our piece?"

"In the end, it's about greed," Tony explained. "Greed can sink one boat, and it can sink an industry. It's the commons predicament."

Mordecai looked puzzled. "What?"

Tony leaned back leisurely as he gazed out to sea. "It refers to common land. Farmers of the region would graze livestock on land that was available for all to use. As no one owned the land—known as the commons—there was no mechanism for regulating how much livestock an individual herder could graze on the land. Eventually, the commons became overgrazed and were made off-limits to everyone."

Mordecai took all this in and tried to act like he was, at most, only casually interested, but he was fascinated. History, seafaring, and stories of how important fishing was to the founding of the New World all enthralled him.

"So you don't think it's a good idea to set on the beach?" Tony motioned toward the horizon and Mordecai saw at least six different boats, low in the water with nets on, heading for the beach.

"They have already hauled." Tony looked at Mordecai with a knowing smile. "Left early to get themselves a spot in there. The cat's out of the bag. There's going to be three hundred nets on the beach by 9 o'clock this morning." Tony looked back over the water. “Forget getting involved with that circus. We’ll find fish somewhere else, away from everybody.”

Over the days that followed, Tony expounded on fishing and its importance. He said that fishing had been central to the culture and economy of Scituate—as well as to all of Massachusetts—and surely helped ensure the survival of the New World by providing a life-sustaining source of protein for the first settlers, as well as economic vitality. They fished around Minot’s Light, two miles outside of Cohasset Harbor, and Tony mentioned that the two light keepers and the original lighthouse had been swept into the sea during a storm in April 1851. “Those two men knew they were doomed,” Tony explained, “but before they perished, they turned the lens to shine onto shore in the pattern 1-4-3—I-love-you—for their families on shore. The light pattern of the present-day lighthouse remains the same.”

Tony spent the better part of the morning telling stories. Mordecai learned that as early as the 1500s, European fishing boats sailed within sight of the rugged, unconquered New World to fish near its shores, and then sailed back to Europe. “As a matter of fact,” Tony said to Mordecai on a slow morning with few fish, “In 1621, when the non-fishing, freedom-of-religion–seeking Pilgrims were starving, ten British ships were profitably fishing for cod within sight of the hungry settlers.”

“Why didn’t they go fishing?” Mordecai had to ask.

“Maybe they hadn’t thought to bring fishing tackle.” Tony shrugged. “Sounds like they were too busy looking for God.”

“Well they must’ve found what they were looking for.” Ed contributed from the stern. “Pretty sure most of ‘em starved to death.” Ed chuckled. “Bunch a’ dummies.”

Of all the tales Tony shared that day, the story that most captured Mordecai’s imagination was of Nix’s Mate, a twenty-foot–high octagonal wooden structure built atop a forty-foot–square stone base on a low rocky island at the entrance to Boston Harbor. “The island was once a twelve-acre parcel where sheep grazed,” Tony said. “A ship had sailed into Boston Harbor with the captain dead. The mate was tried and found guilty of murder. Proclaiming his innocence to the end, the Mate of the dead Captain Nix prophesied that the island on which he was hung would one day be covered by water for condemning an innocent man." Tony shrugged. "Now it's completely covered at high tide. The monument was erected in the earliest years of the twentieth century to warn mariners of one of the harbor's most treacherous shoals. Legend also has it that this was where pirates were hanged, and their skeletal remains, in tattered cloth, left in iron cages on the island—for any passing sailor to see, the penalty for the nautical sin of piracy."

Tony's relating of the history of the area made Mordecai feel as if he was part of something bigger than himself, and he wished he could share that. He wondered if his mother and father would have the same enthusiasm for these roots that ran so deep. Would they be proud of him or recognize his effort to make a living among these men? He pondered this question on the mornings he waited on the pier for Tony and Ed to bring in the boat. Even though the boats were diesel now, Mordecai could sense what it must have looked like for generations of sailors who climbed the rigging to set sails in the masts. The atmosphere at the pier held these shadows of the Old World, cast by the rigging of the diesel boats. Mordecai felt a sense of nostalgia, but what he was really nostalgic for was a warm summer evening, when he, his father, and two brothers had gone to the fish pier to bait hooks with sea-worms and catch flounder. They had to share fishing poles, so when Mordecai wasn't fishing, he was content to walk the edge of the pier and look at the bright colors of the nets strung up in the rigging and of the painted wooden hulls that reflected a setting summer sun.

* * *

It was a bright, clear September morning as the *St. Joseph* steamed past the fish pier on her way out of the harbor. At the front of the pier was the *Michael Brandon*, a formidable, sixty-foot aluminum gillnetter. Hundred-pound totes of fish, stacked four high, were being hoisted from the fish hold to the Mullaney's Fish Market truck on the pier.

"How would you have liked to have been on that trip?" Tony asked. "They got in from Georges Bank at five this morning."

"I wonder how much they caught," Mordecai said.

"Twelve and a half thousand pounds of codfish is what I heard," Ed answered.

After more than a week of few or no fish—and the reality of a disappointingly small week's pay—this got Mordecai's attention. "How long were they out?" he asked.

"Five days. Two days for steaming back and forth and three for fishing," Ed said. "If they got here at five, then they probably started steaming for home yesterday afternoon."

Tony looked away, as if he knew what was coming.

Mordecai did the math. "Codfish is a little better than a buck a pound off the boat, right? So, say a buck—that's twelve and a half thousand bucks. What do you think he would take off the top for expenses?" Tony thought about it, but before he could say anything, Mordecai answered his own question. "Five hundred bucks?" Tony said nothing; he just looked at Mordecai. "So he must be sharing out on twelve grand. That's …" Mordecai's eyes lit with excitement. "Eighteen hundred bucks for five days!"

"You want us to drop you off on his boat?" Tony replied in a tone showing he was unimpressed. As they slowly passed, the captain and owner, Tom, climbed from his boat on to the top of the fish pier. When he reached the top, one disgruntled fisherman yelled at him, "You greedy fuck! You gonna leave anything for us?" But everyone on that fish pier knew that resentment didn't change the law of natural selection—a man could either make it as a fisherman, or he couldn't.

Tony's fishing philosophy was the opposite of resentment and was reflected in his time ashore while pursuing more simple pleasures. Mordecai was enamored of a man who would not be rushed and whose agenda was entirely out of sequence with the rat-race society. But this approach was doing little to help Mordecai save enough money to buy anything, much less a boat. Divorced from his wife and rarely in contact with his two kids, Tony had time on his hands and didn't mind driving seven or eight miles to get take-out from his favorite Chinese food restaurant. He'd meander along the New England back roads in his old pickup, pointing out that he really didn't have anything else to look forward to.

"Isn't that kind of far to go to get take-out?" Mordecai asked.

"Yep," Ed answered for him.

"Naw," Tony disagreed. "It's only a three-beer ride. It's worth it for the duck."

"Then they screwed him on the duck," Ed laughed from the stern. "Ask him."

"I used to get the half-duck," Tony explained. "But then, I guess they saw the four-hundred-pound guy enough times that they decided that they could sell him the whole duck. So the other day, I go up to get my half-duck and the Asian guy comes out and says, 'Oh, no, Mistah Amato. No more have half-duck. Only whole duck.' So I said, 'Fuck it. Just give me the whole fuckin' duck.'"

"So does he eat half one night and save the other half for the next?" Ed asked laughing.

"Ah, well," said Tony, shrugging his massive shoulders. "I'm not big on leftovers."

While Tony didn't mind the three-beer ride, he did mind the traffic that rode on his back bumper. The traffic was of a pace and way of life that he saw as an exercise in futility. He told stories about the big SUV that rode inches from his bumper the night before, with the driver honking and shouting obscenities. Tony would pull over and let it pass, then slowly cruise back out in the road and continue on—until it happened again.

"Why don't you just hit the gas?" Mordecai asked.

"You know, I was your age when I went to Vietnam. I came home a year later and a lot older. I'm gonna taste everything I want to taste and enjoy as much as I can while I'm on this earth. And I won't be rushed."

"Speaking of that." Ed directed the question at Tony while removing a lobster that got past Mordecai from the mesh. "How was that three pound lobster you took home last night?" Tony shrugged and looked sheepish.

"I don't know." He started laughing and looked to Mordecai a bit self-conscious. "You'd have to ask Louie the cat. I imagine he was a little tough." Tony motioned back at Ed. "I know I talk about food a lot but Ed is the guy who can really cook. I'm more of a take-out guy."

"C'mon now fella," Ed asked paying full attention to Tony. "What happened." Tony shrugged as if he didn't know what to say.

"Like I said. I'm not really much of a cook."

"What'd you do." Ed persisted.

"I fell asleep and the water boiled over for two hours." Ed started laughing.

"Well at least you didn't burn the house down." Mordecai contributed.

"And you remembered to feed the cat." laughed Ed.

Though Tony loved to talk about food, the only thing Mordecai ever saw him eat was the Snickers Bar Tony would send Mordecai to retrieve from the dashboard of the wheelhouse every day at noon.

Although the *St. Joseph* did not produce the big money like the steel boats that fished farther offshore, Mordecai could clearly see the personalities of Tony and Ed on the boat. The *St. Joseph* radiated contentment, and Mordecai knew there was wisdom in Tony's philosophy, but as the warmth of summer gave way to the chill of autumn, his youthful ambition began to take over. He had made a day's pay most days when they went fishing through the summer, but in the fall, the dogfish schools had been broken up by the fishing effort that targeted them. Before there was a dogfish market, fishermen went out of their way to avoid the massive schools of the valueless species, as they usually chased the "money fish" out of whatever area they came into. When fishermen targeted the large schools of dogfish, the schools broke up, with smaller schools spread all over the bay.

One morning at the coffee shop, Mordecai spoke to a tuna fishermen, who said there were still substantial numbers of dogfish in the bay. "There are enough that we have a hard time keeping bait," the fisherman said. "The dogs take the bait. It's costly, time-consuming, and a pain in the ass."

Like the other fishermen targeting dogfish, Tony had his gear spread all over the bay, trying to hit a decent school of fish. There were fish just about everywhere they hauled, but they weren't concentrated enough to get a decent haul out of one string of nets. Although they steamed all over the bay looking for fish, they only caught a few hundred pounds a day, which just covered fuel cost. Mordecai hoped that there would be a big cod run, like the ones Flip had told him about.

"Sure, there'll be some weeks where you might not make much—or anything—but then there will be the week when you make a couple grand," Flip had told him. It was a breezy fall day, and the two fisherman friends were walking Flip's dog, Dingo, on the beach. That day—spent strolling on the beach, drinking good coffee, and knowing nothing needed to get done—was a refreshing change from hustling to get through a day of fishing. It was a chance to let overworked muscles relax and recover from the daily abuse of picking fish and flaking net. They talked of the fish they would catch when the run returned; they imagined how they'd spend the money, talking about splitting the down payment on a boat, a fixer-upper. On such afternoons, Mordecai could convince himself there was a chance for a future.

But stocks of traditional groundfish species—cod, haddock, and flounder—on which the New England fishing industry was built were on the verge of collapse. In October, Tony gave up on targeting dogfish and instead, set the gear "on the beach," which was what Tony called the area about a mile from shore, where he fished for cod that came into the shallow water to feed on small lobsters and flounders. They were scraping up a few hundred pounds of cod a day, which for Mordecai was $45 to $60 a day. He approached each workday with a gambler's attitude, telling himself, "*Today will be the big haul.*" But day after day, there was no big haul; there was just a lot of work, picking and throwing back the abundance of various valueless species found in the shoal water—and each required a different technique to remove it.

Each species also had its own set of armaments that Mother Nature had bestowed upon it for its self-defense. Sculpins had heads like armor-plated turrets, with two long, sharp horns protruding from the top and about half a dozen smaller ones behind the head. A puncture wound from one of those horns was not only extremely painful but could lead to fish poisoning—the injured hand or finger would swell up and become infected. Mordecai found it amazing that such a creature was part of the food chain—he often found them in the bellies of other fish. Sea robins were about the size of a baseball. They would have been easy to pick out of the net, if not for their obstinate habit of clamping their mouths down on the mesh and puffing themselves until they were larger than the mesh that ensnared them. Skate wings—a flat, triangular-shaped, bottom-feeding fish with enlarged dorsal fins that acted like wings—were also easy to remove by clubbing them, pulling the mesh out of their mouths, and then pulling them through the mesh. Crabs were eager to devour whatever was caught in the net, and with their eight legs and two large claws, they easily became wound up in the lightweight mesh.

Because the men didn't want to pick through the outrageously disproportionate amount of "trash fish," they needed to be out early every day to get the nets hauled and cleaned before they became loaded with a smorgasbord of marine species. If the weather turned unexpectedly bad, that gear "on the beach" still had to be hauled, or it would be bait for the army of crabs.

As the weather became colder, there were fewer days that the *St. Joseph* could get out; when they did get out, there was little in the nets. For a stern man, pay was based on the value of the catch. In most cases, two stern men split a 30 percent share—15 percent for each—of the value of the catch, after expenses. But 15 percent of nothing was still nothing, so when the boat wasn't catching much of anything, there was no sense in burning fuel.

In December, having bought a new truck a year earlier, Tony gave Mordecai his old 78 Dodge pickup. Tony had a newer truck and the 78 was just sitting in his driveway. It was old and rusted but something Mordecai could get around in, and it was free. Mordecai found a room above a restaurant in Cohasset, where several other fishermen were living.

"Why the fuck you want to live there?" Flip asked. "Those are Cohasset Lobster maggots living in there. Most of 'em are drunks, don't drive, and live there because they can walk to Cohasset harbor."

"You've been great, Flip." Mordecai explained as he stuffed his clothes into a duffel bag. "And I appreciate your having let me stay here." Mordecai looked around the basement apartment then back at his friend. "But I should have my own place. Maybe it will help with getting things back on track with Liz if I'm not here."

"Bro's before ho's, Dude." Flip waved off the suggestion. "Besides, you could save money for a down payment on a boat living here. We both can."

"We will if we stay focused. And next year, we'll have our own boat." The two shook hands and for the first time, Mordecai left for a place of his own.

The Lioness Inn had been built in 1703 and had housed generations of sailors over the centuries. Mordecai didn't know the other fishermen who lived there; they were lobstermen out of Cohasset, the next harbor town to the north of Scituate. But as he walked down the narrow halls of that old building, he could smell the odor of the bait they used in their pots—the scent permeated the wool jackets and shirts that hung outside their rooms. When he returned to his room late in the afternoon, Mordecai could tell if they'd hung herring, or pogies, in their traps that day. In the darkness of morning as he dressed, he could hear their footsteps coming down the stairs, and he took comfort in knowing that he was part of a society of men who, historically, rose while others slept to venture out on the cold Atlantic.

His room wasn't much—small, with a bed and a bureau, and there was a bathroom down the hall that everyone on the floor shared—and Mordecai was happy to have his own little place. But by Christmas, he was wondering where the $100-a-week rent money would come from. To make a day's pay required two days of good weather—one day to get out and set the nets; an overnight period to let the nets soak, or fish; and the following day to haul them. A day's pay would cover a week's rent, but they just weren't getting the right sequence of successive fishable days. Each morning Mordecai drove to the harbor to see if they would be getting out. He picked up a Kingsize Snicker bar at a convenience store thinking it would be funny to upstage Tony with the oversize candy bar when the captain started eating his. But the candy bar sat on the bench seat of the truck waiting for a day when Mordecai would have the chance to play his joke while out fishing. And Mordecai had to explain to the landlord, for the second week in a row, that he'd pay the rent "when the weather breaks." He felt no one, other than his fellow fishermen, noticed that they didn't bring fish in at the end of the day. He felt his life had no purpose.

And when there finally was a break in the weather, and everybody went fishing, the dealers dropped the price of fish to near valueless. The fish dealers shrugged their shoulders and said it was out of their hands; that there was a sudden glut of fish on the market, and the market set the price. There was a moderate but brief protest from the fishermen, who noticed that the price of fish did not change at retail, but the dealers and fisherman alike understood that in the end, no matter what the fishermen were paid for the fish, they would take it—because it was all they had.

Christmas Day, Mordecai woke and sat in his room wondering what he was going to do. The morning was gray and soundless. So he climbed in the old Dodge and drove to the harbor, looking for signs of life from a friend or someone he knew. He knew Flip would be spending Christmas with his family, as would Ed. Driving down the empty streets, he felt the entire world had family they were with. He saw no one else on the desolate road. Driving by The Pier Restaurant on the edge of the harbor, out of the corner of his eye, he spotted a lone black pick up parked with its nose pointed toward the water. The round, bearded silhouette seated behind the wheel betrayed the identity of the sole of occupant. '*There's Tony!*' and he cut the wheel. The front tires screeched on the pavement at the sudden sharp turn as he narrowly missed the granite post marking the entranceway.
Mordecai pulled alongside and reached across the bench seat to roll down his passenger window. Tony's flannel shrouded arm hung out the window to dangle listlessly aside his door, his eyes fixed straight ahead as he watched the *St. Joseph* float on her mooring. Mordecai knew Tonys' father had that boat built in 1947, when he moved his family from the North End of Boston, to the shore of Scituate, where he could conveniently fish its rich waters. For a moment, Mordecai feared he was intruding. Tony never took his eyes off the water, and Mordecai wasn't sure if the Captain even noticed him pull up.

"Is this where the guys go who don't have any family?" Tony said without looking at Mordecai, his gaze fixed firmly on the boat. Mordecai gave in to a slight grin.

"I guess it is now."

"Good." Tony said. "I wasn't sure if I had the right parking lot." He pulled on his beard. "Thought I'd be the only one to show up again this year."

"Thought I may have the same problem." Mordecai looked down and saw the king-size Snickers bar on the bench seat. He picked it up and said, "Hey Tony" Tony looked over at him and

Mordecai tossed the bar to him. "Merry Christmas" The sun broke through a thin layer of grey clouds over the eastern horizon, and the two fishermen looked out over the water, comfortable, wordless, in a moment of Holiday cheer.

Two days later, Tony, Ed, and Mordecai headed out to haul the nets they had set the previous evening. As they steamed out of the harbor at sunrise, a cold wind blew out of the northwest. The temperature was in the low twenties, just cold enough to turn freezing spray that came off the bow to ice as they plunged through the choppy sea. The nets were a few miles offshore, but that was far enough for the sea to have built five foot waves in the distance from shore. Mordecai's tolerance for seasickness was at the point where he only needed Dramamine when the sea was rough. But on days like this, the Dramamine stopped working just a short distance from the harbor. The *St. Joseph* rolled and pitched as Tony reached with the gaff to grab the iced-up high-flyer buoy. They all stood at their positions on deck, with feet spread apart wider than usual, trying to maintain balance in the rolling of the sea. Standing on the deck in these conditions was tricky, and Mordecai needed to hold on to the table to keep from falling on the deck. He watched Tony grab the high-flyer and pull it through the roller that hung over the rail. He wrapped the line around the hauler in one deft motion, while balancing his four-hundred-pound frame on his thick legs.

Mordecai thought he might vomit—and no sooner did he get that feeling than his stomach acted on it. He should have known better than to drink coffee on windy mornings, but when he'd gotten up on that cold, dark morning, he'd wanted the comforting hot cup—it had gone down so well, but it sure was harsh coming back up.

"Just hang in there," said Tony. "The day will be over before you know it, and you'll be glad you made the effort."

"Just remember," Ed laughed from the stern, "if you taste hair, swallow, cuz that's your asshole."

Mordecai crouched against the checkerboard as he threw up and looked at Ed who stood like a monolithic fishing mechanism in the open stern, coiling the lines into a rope checker, with the freezing spray lashing at him. He was as impervious to the elements as he was on a calm day in July. And every time Mordecai retched, Ed laughed, until even Mordecai laughed at the funny sounds of his own vomiting. He'd been stoic enough to get on the boat that morning, and he wouldn't ask to be taken home before the nets were hauled. But if the nets were empty and they headed in early, that would be fine, too. The two-foot piece of steel railroad track came around the hauler, and Tony slid it down the table to Mordecai, who passed the track along to Ed, who placed it on top of the coil of lines in the stern. There was another seven or eight fathom of line; then the bright pink mesh wound around the hauler—and Mordecai smelled the fish even as he saw them. The net was loaded with cod! His hopes for an early day and a short bout of seasickness vanished as the codfish piled up in front of him. Codfish had been selling for about a dollar a pound, and he needed the money. Suddenly, he didn't feel as seasick as he pulled the fish down the table, and the men pulled them from the net. The cod were twisted and rolled up in the mesh. The trick to pulling them out was to unroll them from the layer of net in which they were wrapped; then to pull them through the square mesh they swam through into the net. Mordecai's back and arms ached, and his legs worked to keep his balance on the pitching deck. He found there was a big difference between picking codfish and the dogfish. Codfish had to be gutted and gilled on the boat, which required some skill with a knife. After each set, Mordecai and Ed cut the throat of the fish just below the gills and then made a lengthwise slice up the belly from the anus to about an inch short of the gill cut. After emptying the belly cavity, the guts were tossed overboard, where they were devoured by the gulls that followed the boats in anticipation of a free meal. Next the men reached in with as many fingers as they could behind the gills, grabbing hold of them tightly, and with a sharp tug, ripped them out of the fish.

Mordecai had developed his own "best way" to grab a codfish: he cleared the mesh away from the mouth, inserted as many fingers into the mouth as possible, and then, with his thumb clamped down firmly on the chin of the fish, used a pulling-twisting motion with his fish hand, while the pick hand slid the mesh down the body of the fish. The problem was that the rows of teeth in the fish made short work of his only pair of rubber gloves.

By the end of the first set, the fingers of his left glove were tatters of bright orange rubber, and the fingers on his left hand had rows of shallow slices down the length of them. His right hand, which held the pick, was tired but the glove was intact. He tried to switch hands but found that he was not ambidextrous.

At his best, he was only about half as fast as Ed, but he accepted that as the son of school teachers, he was not going to be as efficient as the experienced New England fishing and farm boy that Ed was. But he wanted to get better. He wanted it bad enough that he just puked on his oilskins and kept working. He picked fish as fast as he could, trying to ignore the pain of the icy-cold fish on his exposed, wet fingers. At first, his pride hurt more than his fingers, knowing that he couldn't keep up. Soon, however, his fingers became painfully frozen, and he started dropping and fumbling the fish even more.

"Why don't you go down below and git y'self another glove, fella?" asked Ed from the stern in his New England Yankee accent.

"Well, I don't have any more gloves, Ed."

"There's a bag of 'em down below. Go grab a left. I'm gettin' sore just looking at ya."

"Okay, thanks," Mordecai said. He noticed that Ed's gloves weren't in bad shape at all.

Mordecai moved through the wheelhouse and continued forward into the fo'csle. Inside the boat, warmth radiated from the diesel engine below deck. Mordecai found a bag of new gloves and pulled out a new pair. The warm, dry cotton lining of the new glove received his hand as comfortably as sliding into bed after a long day. Back on deck, Ed showed Mordecai how to grab the fish by sticking a middle finger into the fish's eye and hooking a thumb on its chin. It was more awkward for Mordecai's inexperienced hands, but he recognized that it was an acquired skill. *And I want no part of those damn teeth!* he thought.

After four sets of ten nets, they had twelve hundred pounds of fish. Mordecai's back, arms, and hands throbbed from the effort of picking fish from the net and getting them cut, gutted, gilled, washed, and packed in plastic totes—the totes each held a hundred pounds of fish.

While steaming home that afternoon, aching and sore, with cold hands and a wind burned face, Mordecai felt like a Viking, proud and strong for having braved the elements and returning home with a catch. At a dollar a pound, his share that day would be $180. *A week's rent, plus eighty bucks.*

Mordecai heard Tony talking on the radio, but with the noise of the Detroit diesel bellowing from the stack, he couldn't hear what he was saying. On the horizon, he saw boats swarmed by clouds of birds that were attacking cod guts that had been tossed overboard.

"Well, that's the nature of the game." Tony said to Mordecai from the wheelhouse over the noise of the engine.

"What's that?" Mordecai asked.

"Supply and demand." Tony said solemnly. "You didn't hear? The price went to thirty cents." Tony shook his head. "What can you do. They're getting them everywhere. The water has gotten cold enough and the fish have come in to spawn. That's all we're going to get for them." Tony shook his head again. "What can we do." and turned back to the helm. Mordecai's spirits sunk. He looked at Ed who said nothing but looked at the distant boats on the horizon and the swarms of birds that followed. Mordecai could sense that he had seen this before and quietly, stoically, accepted the hand they were dealt. Twelve hundred pounds would now bring $400. *And my end*, Mordecai thought dismally, *will be sixty bucks. Not even rent.*

Tony turned on the National Oceanic and Atmospheric Administration weather radio; the forecast was for northwest winds of 30 mph, with higher gusts and single-digit temperatures for the next few days. Much too cold to go out, they'd be forced to leave the nets on the boat.

The next day, Flip pulled onto the pier in his new pickup, with his dog, Dingo, sitting on the passenger seat. "Whatcha doin'?" he asked Mordecai.

"Looks like nothing," Mordecai answered. He could hear the first pangs of despair creeping into his own voice.

"Get in, dude," Flip said, pulling Dingo into the middle of the seat. "Let's take a ride down the beach, and we can burn one while we take a look at it."

Mordecai squeezed in beside Dingo, who gave him an exuberant canine greeting. He didn't care much for having a tongue bath from a dog but appreciated the comfortable familiarity that accompanied seeing his friend. Down at the beach, they sat in the truck, nose to the water, as winter wind blew sand that hissed against the metal cab. Flip pulled a joint from his cigarette pack, lit it, and handed it to Mordecai.

"This weather just isn't gonna let us get out," Mordecai said, exhaling smoke.

"That's why you gotta be on a steel boat for the winter, dude. Me and Wolf are gonna make money today. You should come with us this winter."

"I can't bail on Tony and Eddie. What'll they do if the weather breaks?"

"It's your funeral, dude. If the weather doesn't break, you're gonna starve, waitin' for it." Flip sucked on the joint and handed it back, but Mordecai waved it off—the euphoria of getting high had become paranoia about his predicament and uncertain future. He rubbed Dingo between the ears.

"Dude, I'll tell you somethin' you can't repeat to *anybody*," Flip said. "Wolf is looking for another guy to head down to the Carolinas with us for the rest of the winter. According to the local scuttlebutt, they're catching dogfish down there in mythological proportions. We get twenty-five cents a pound, and that don't change—no playing fuck-fuck with the dealers. We catch ten thousand pounds, that's twenty-five hundred bucks. Fifteen percent of that is 375 clams—*in your pocket.*"

Mordecai thought about the concept of money in his pocket. It had been a few weeks since he'd known the feeling.

"Wolf is married with five little kids. He ain't gonna allow nothin' to prevent him from providing for his family," Flip said. "So he's developed a reputation for taking crazy risks. Wolf don't wait around for better weather. He's *driven.*" Flip looked at Mordecai and shrugged. "So he's known for coming home with the windows blown out. He's always got fish."

Flip cruised slowly back to the fish pier, and then he left to ready Wolf's boat, the *Desire*, for a day's fishing. Mordecai joined the crowd of guys who were gathered around the hood of Tony's truck.

"There goes Wolfy in that steel boat of his," said Tony. "I remember when he launched that thing. He said, 'You won't see me fishin' around here.' Well, he hasn't gone too far, but he's fishin."

"More than we're doin'," responded Ed.

As they watched the *Desire* chug out of Scituate Harbor, Mordecai thought about Flip's proposal. There were two options: *St. Joseph* or *Desire.* At that moment, one option wasn't going anywhere, but the other was heading through the mouth of the harbor.

Wolfgang Heidde was a hard man and fiercely independent, even among a culture of people who pride themselves on those traits. He was large, with thick, muscled forearms, long brown hair, and a brown beard that made him resemble a grizzly bear. A man of few words and little patience, he was prone to violence and not afraid to fight. He seldom was seen having a good time.

On New Year's Day 1995, Flip and Mordecai were stripping out the mesh from some of Wolfs' old gill nets in a windy beach parking lot. "Stripping nets" was the time-consuming and mundane chore of removing old mesh from a gill net to prepare for new mesh to be hung on the same lines. The nets were three hundred feet long, which required a wide, open space to stretch them out. One guy would work along the float, or lead line, cutting the little knots that hung the mesh to it, while another guy worked right alongside, doing the same to the other line. The salt that saturated the lines would burn in all the sores and cuts on their hands that they didn't know they had.

Today, Flip seemed morose. He and Mordecai had been working alongside each other for over an hour, and Flip hadn't said a thing. It wasn't uncommon for the two to work quietly, comfortable in each other's company and concentrating on work; they didn't need to fill the time with banter. But today, Mordecai could sense that something was wrong. There was a weight pressing on the man next to him. "How are things going with Liz?" Mordecai asked.

"Haven't seen much of her lately." Flip tugged at a stubborn knot with his knife. "She blows me off when I try to talk to her." He tugged harder at the salt-saturated line. "I don't know what the fuck's going on." The knife slipped past the knot and made a shallow gash across the top of his left hand. "Fuck, dull knife. This wouldn't happen if we had new knives."

"Can't we sharpen them?"

"We could, but they lose their serrated edge and never cut as well. The thing to do is get new knives. But Wolf ain't gonna spend money on knives when we can use the old ones." Flip began wrapping plastic tape around his cut. "Wolf just cares about making money."

"So you're telling me he's cheap because he makes money?"

"I'm telling you he's focused. And it's what I need to get to. Forget about Liz and think about getting the nets stripped, rehung, and back in the water—*making money*."

"So what's the deal with Wolf," Mordecai said. "Is he gonna make money or get ya killed."

Flip shrugged. "When he had the *Michelle*, trying to leave the harbor after a northeasterly gale, a wave blew out the windows of the wheelhouse, and knocked Wolf unconscious. When he came to, his deck was awash with sea water and blood from a dozen or so cuts on his face and head." Flip made wave motions with his arms. "Breaking waves crashed through the wheelhouse—the trip was over. But Wolf knew that turning around and trying to return to Scituate Harbor would be suicide."

"Why?"

Scituate is a difficult harbor in a following sea because the mouth shoals up, and waves get bigger and break."

"Really?"

"What the fuck, dude?" Flip looked at him. "How could you live in Scituate and not know that?" Mordecai felt the sting of his greenhorn status.

"Missed it somehow I guess".

"The danger is," Flip continued tugging with his knife at another stubborn knot, "that a boat will pitchpole—go over on its bow and capsize. Wolf's only option," Flip explained, "was to continue heading into the waves coming from the northeast and try the entrance of Cohasset Harbor."

"How was he supposed to drive into the waves with the wheelhouse blown in?"

"Grit his teeth and hang on." Flip returned.

"Really?"

"No. The Coast Guard received his distress call and towed the *Michelle,* into Cohasset Harbor, which is more sheltered by a ledge, which breaks up the incoming surf."

"So Wolf made it in one piece"

"Barely." Flip looked up at Mordecai from the net in his hands. "But he found himself in the spotlight of one who needed to be saved." Flip nodded knowingly. "Wolf was determined to not let that happen again. He would build a better boat."

Mordecai knew of Wolf's reputation, and he knew that Wolf had a steel boat that he and his father had spent considerable time and effort welding together. Mordecai was inspired by Wolf's unbridled ambition and rugged individualism; Wolf didn't sit around waiting for fish to come to him. On the mast of the *Desire* was a riding sail. This was a measure employed to help give the boat stability. On his riding sail, Wolf had stenciled a large dollar sign, so all could see what his motivations were. Mordecai decided that the *Desire* was the boat where the money was going to be.

As the northwest wind brought the increasingly wintry weather of January, Mordecai felt a hunger that pierced him like the cold air. The *St. Joseph* had long breaks between fishing trips and spent days with the nets stowed on the deck, as she gently swung on her mooring lines.

On January third, Mordecai's birthday, he cruised down to the fish pier in the harbor at sunrise to see if they would be getting out that day. Tony and Ed weren't there, so he walked to the coffee shop at the other end of the harbor. As he exited with his coffee, the sun was just creeping over the horizon and illuminated the sky with a pink glow. Then he saw his mother standing in the parking lot. She was holding a cake and waving at him. He hadn't seen her in over six months.

"Hi, Mom," he offered casually, as though he had just seen her yesterday.

She drew a deep breath; Mordecai thought she looked exhausted, but he could tell this was an important moment for her, so he gave her a brief hug.

"We haven't forgotten you on your birthday, Mordecai. I made you a cake, as I've always done."

"Gee, thanks, Ma. You didn't have to."

"I know I didn't have to, Mordecai, but you are still my son, and your father and I still love you."

"Great. Thanks."

She handed him a cellophane-wrapped chocolate cake with white frosting. "Mordecai, you know we love you," She looked at her hands. "We just didn't know what to do with you."

"Yeah, I know, Ma. It's all right. I'm working on a fishing boat now—I guess you knew that, since you found me here."

Her jaw dropped, her expression went from shock to fear, and he realized she had no idea what he had been doing.

"Mrs. O'Brien said she sees you here in the morning on her way to work, so we knew you must be working if you're up early. But a fishing boat? Mordecai, you can't do that."

"Yes, I can. And I have been. Why wouldn't I?"

"Because that's for people who …" She paused a moment before continuing. "Who do that sort of thing."

"Called fishermen," he answered.

She gave him her hardened, "don't fool with me" look that he knew all too well. "Don't be a smart aleck." Her face softened, and he could tell she was concerned. "Isn't that dangerous?"

"Not that I've seen."

"Well, how far do you go out?"

"Not far; just a few miles."

"A few miles! Mordecai, that's still in water that's over your head!"

"Ma. I'm not six anymore." He reached for her hand. "There are always other boats around in case something happens, and besides, we're not gonna sink. The boat is the *St. Joseph,* the patron saint of workers, so we got that, too," he explained. He put his hand on her shoulder. "Look, Ma, I'm gonna be fine."

She took his hand in hers, then kissed his cheek before opening her car door. "Okay, Mordecai. Be safe. You can call us sometime and tell us how you are doing. I wish you would."

"I will, Ma."

He quickly turned toward the fish pier so he wouldn't see her crying, as he knew she would. It was windy as he walked down

Front Street, past the cannon and old ship's anchor in front of the bank, and past Rocco's barber shop. Rocco and Joe were preparing for their day and waved to him when they saw him walk past the window. He continued on toward the Welch Company Gift Shop, and he remembered the charm that store held. He thought of Christmas shopping with his parents and brothers as a little boy—there had been rows of toys and model airplanes on the shelves, beckoning to children. He stopped at the front window and looked through the glass of the now-closed store, as if he were looking for a December day when he was a boy. But there were only the empty rooms, and the face reflected in the glass was no longer a little boy.

Tony was sitting in his truck; Ed was leaning on the hood. Ed noticed what Mordecai was holding. "Whatcha got there, fella?"

"Cake," Mordecai said as he joined them at the truck.

Tony slowly read aloud off the icing on the cake. "Happy Birthday, Mordecai."

"Yeah, it's my birthday, so we can eat it on the boat."

"Not today," Tony said. "It's way too windy." Across the harbor, white caps were breaking beyond the mouth.

"Well, let's have cake now then. You got anything in there to cut this thing with, Tony?"

"I do, actually," said Tony with a grin. He handed Mordecai a brand new Dexter knife, which was used for cutting fish; it was still in its wrapper. Ed held the plate as Mordecai cut the cake into three large pieces. The three men stood on the fish pier, quietly watching the sun come up over the eastern horizon as they enjoyed the cake and coffee. Mordecai was happy to celebrate his birthday in this way with these men. "M-m-m-m. That's some good cake," said Tony.

Ed agreed, and Mordecai thought it was best cake he'd ever had. Fred Dupree, a lobsterman who was a classmate of Tony's at Scituate High, walked by as the three were eating cake and said to Mordecai, "I see they have you fully indoctrinated into their program." The crew of the *St. Joseph* just laughed, not ashamed to be eating cake for breakfast.

Chapter 4
Desire

The next day Flip met Mordecai at the Coffee Corner. Flip looked more enthusiastic than Mordecai had seen him in a while.

"Guess what? Wolf says he'll give you a shot tomorrow as an extra guy."

"No shit. He's offering me the job?"

"It's like a try out. He wants to see how you do hauling monk gear."

"When do we leave?"

"5:00 AM. We're working off of Plymouth at this area called the H buoy. Takes an hour to get there. We're gettin' a good haul of monk and could use a guy just to flake the net, freeing me up to concentrate on picking the fish."

"What if it's windy? Will he still go?"

"Just be there at five. If you're not, we go without ya, and that's it. No second chances."

Mordecai was there at five the next morning, sitting on a piling, when Wolf pulled up in a battered black pickup. Mordecai stood up as Wolf stepped past him in the dark and started down the ladder on the north side of the pier.

"When the main engine starts, you can let go the spring lines," Wolf said, stepping into his boat without looking at Mordecai.

Mordecai looked at the ropes that criss-crossed from the boat to the pier. Down on the boat below, the pilothouse door opened, and the yellow beam of a flashlight cut a swath across the dark steel deck. The metallic clunking of a steel hatch opening rang out somewhere beneath the flashlight's beam, and Mordecai saw Wolf's silhouette as he climbed down into the bowels of the steel boat. Mordecai listened for the sound of Flip's tires as he drove through the harbor village, but there was nothing except the light whisper of wind around the mast and a flutter from the riding sail. "C'mon, Flip," he muttered. "I don't know what the fuck spring lines are." He heard a soft hum as the diesel generator started, and a small exhaust pipe sputtered out a light plume from the overhead. Then deck lights came on, illuminating everything on and around the boat as if it were a movie set. There was a low burp as Wolf tried to crank the main engine over. After two attempts, Mordecai heard the distinct sound of something being sprayed from a can, most likely ether. The big Caterpillar main fired, the exhaust belched, and carbon ash floated down like black snowflakes. Mordecai was staring at the ropes that held the *Desire* when Flip's headlights swept across the misty fish pier. "He told me to let go the spring lines," Mordecai said as Flip approached.

"Why don't ya then?"

"I'm not sure which ones they are."

"Get on the boat, dude. I'll undo 'em and throw 'em to ya."

Mordecai went down the ladder. Flip undid the lines at the top of the pier and dropped the ends down to Mordecai. There was a line on the bow that ran aft up to the pier and one that similarly ran from the stern, crossing each other amidship. "They keep the boat from moving forward or backward. Little different from a mooring, but you'll get the hang after you do it a couple times," Flip called down to him. "Coil those up and stuff 'em under the rail."

As Mordecai finished, Wolf stepped through the hatch and looked at Mordecai, his eyes expressionless. If the face held any expression, it was concealed by the thick beard. "Flip here?"

"Yeah, he's up on the pier, waitin' to let go of the bow and stern."

"Tell him we're set to go," Wolf said, and he went back in the wheelhouse. Mordecai looked up at Flip and said, "Let's roll." Flip tossed the stern line down, then the bow. He hustled down the ladder, stepping onto the rail and then the deck in a fluid motion.

During the hour's steam to reach the gear, Mordecai and Flip burned a joint out on the back deck and watched the glow of dawn light the horizon.

"I've never flaked a net," Mordecai said.

"How did you manage that?" Flip asked.

"I don't know. Ed just does all the flaking. All I ever done is pick."

"All right; it's simple. All you do is stand back here in the net checker," Flip said, jumping into the six-by-eight foot squared-off pen. "You pull the net over the bar," he said, pointing to the PVC pipe that was supported over the table, "and into the net checker by pulling on the float line and standing back here. The lead line will fall away by its own weight, spreading out the mesh in between. Take out any knots in the mesh by tugging on them 'til they come out, and unspin any twists by flipping the lines around until they come to a bridle where the next net starts. Then, untie one side of the bridle and let the twist unspin, and then tie the bridle back."

"Sure. No problem. Sounds easy enough."

"Just try not to screw it up. And if you get confused, don't let *him* know. He's got no patience with greenhorns."

"C'mon. I'm no greenhorn anymore."

"Dude, you haven't even flaked a net."

"Okay, fine. I'll get this done like dinner."

"I hope so."

They arrived at the H buoy—a large, steel navigational aid that floated an hour's steam from Scituate and about halfway across the bay to Provincetown on the tip of Cape Cod. Mordecai saw the bright colored flags from the first of the aluminum high-flyers. The oilskin overalls they had on board were too large for Mordecai, dragging at his heels as he headed out to the stern, anxious but eager to show Flip and Wolf that he was a fisherman. "He was the littlest fisherman." Flip teased. "He was so little his oilskins dragged when walked." Flip gave a stoned sort of chuckle while Mordecai leaned against a checker and took the ribbing with a grin. "Not much to look at, but boy, could he flake a net." Wolf came out on deck dressed only in a thin canvas fishing shirt with orange rubber sleeves and his oilskins, even though the temperature was in the upper twenties. Flip was setting up totes under the picking table, and Mordecai felt sorry for him in his ragged skins—surely he got soaked underneath. Wolf worked the controls at the hauling station amidships on the starboard side and guided the *Desire* to the high-flyer bobbing on the light swell. The steady breeze was constant—it would have made for a rough day on the *St. Joseph*, but the heavier, steel *Desire* handled it, slowly rolling from side to side. Wolf reached out with his handmade gaff, which was the shaft from a hockey stick with a hook on the end, and hooked the aluminum pole of the high-flyer. He grabbed the high-flyer and pulled it into the boat, along with several fathom of line, which he wrapped around the hauler, holding it with his left hand while his right twisted the hauler lever. Hammers clamped down on the line and hauled it aboard. When enough line had been hauled onto the table, Flip passed the high-flyer back to Mordecai, and he brought it back to the rope checker in the stern and began coiling line, as he had watched Ed do on the *St. Joseph* so many times. A loud, metallic clanging signaled that the steel piece of railroad track had come into the steel tray. Flip also passed this back to Mordecai. He placed the steel piece on the coiled lines in the rope checker. Another few fathoms of line came around the hauler, and then the net began dumping on the table in a steady stream. Flip pushed the piles of empty net down the table and said, "Go ahead and start flaking. I'll pick whatever comes up. If we start getting a lot of monk, you can come up and help me when you catch up on the flaking."

Mordecai found that flaking wasn't as easy as Flip made it sound. The lines had to be untwisted, and this worked his back muscles in a way he hadn't felt before. With his arms held up at about shoulder height, he pulled the lead line back with one hand, while the other hand pulled the float line apart—he used a motion similar to doing a breast stroke. The monofilament mesh sprayed a mixture of saltwater and algae slime all over his face, and he could feel it collecting on his lips and eyelashes. The hauler continued to spew a deluge of netting onto the table. Flip worked the table deliberately and methodically, his years of gillnetting showing in his familiarity with working the table. Mordecai saw his body flow in a constant, efficient effort.

This was not at all like the small mesh fishing Mordecai did on the *St. Joseph*, where Tony would stop the hauler, and they would all work at picking the various species from the net. Here, there was monk or nothing, and the fish came around the hauler sporadically. The monk gear had a twelve-inch-square mesh hole that allowed everything through it except the monks—their broad, depressed heads were almost as wide as the fish was long. Monks also had enormous mouths with rows of razor-sharp teeth that angled inward. These fish were, Mordecai soon learned, the only fish to get caught in the twelve-inch-diameter mesh, and there was a trick to picking them out. Flip and Wolf didn't want to waste time on training Mordecai to pick monk, so he would just flake the net. He would hear the wet, splunking sound of a fish going into a tote under the table, then Flip picked another monk, pushed the net down the table, cut the tails off the small monks, and gutted the large monk. A specific process to preparing the large monkfish involved cutting the belly open and removing the liver and placing it into a separate five-gallon bucket. The livers brought a high price in the Korean market. The stomach was left in the belly of the fish, while the rest of the guts were stripped away and thrown overboard. Next, a small hole was made in the stomach and its contents emptied out. The fish was then dunked in a tote of seawater for a rinse and then placed in a tote with other processed fish. Flip moved constantly in this process, wielding his knife like a Spartan warrior in battle.

Mordecai was much less efficient at fighting his way through a twist in the first three hundred feet of net. He untied one of the lines at the bridle and took out the twist, then retied the bridle and continued on until he found another twist. He struggled with the knots on the second bridle, trying to find one he could undo. Flip noticed the pile of mesh building up on the table and jumped back in the stern with his pick, which he inserted into the knot on the float line, prying it apart and quickly undoing the knot. He flipped the lines around, unraveling the twist, and then tied the bridle back in and climbed back over the checkerboard to his station at the picking table. He did all this in a matter of seconds, while Wolf was concentrating on maneuvering the boat to keep the gill nets coming aboard smoothly, without stopping the hauler. Mordecai was relieved to have the twist out, and he now worked hand over hand, pulling the float line back and letting the lead line fall away. It was a much more relaxing way to work, but that relative tranquility was shattered when Wolf turned around and saw the enormous pile of mesh on the table.

“What the fuck! Oh, Jesus Christ. Flip, get back there and fly through that!” Flip jumped back into the net checker without a word, grabbed the float line, and moved through the gear at least twice as fast as Mordecai. “Watch how fast he gets through that,” Wolf growled at Mordecai. “This is how you need to learn to move.”

Mordecai watched Flip as he flew through a twist at a pace that was faster than Mordecai could get through straight gear. A monkfish came around the hauler, wrapped up in mesh, and Wolf shoved it down the table at Mordecai in disgust. The large monk looked like an oversized football with wings and horns; it was all mouth at one end. Mordecai fumbled with the mesh wrapped around it, trying desperately to work it out before Flip caught up with the flaking and had to pick the fish out for him too. Mordecai pulled at the monofilament and flipped the fish over and over, trying to unwind some of the mesh from it, as Flip pulled the last of the net off the table. Mordecai thought he saw an opening in the mesh and reached to pull the mesh down the body of the fish— his hand went into the fish's mouth, up to his wrist. The sharp rows of teeth immediately clamped down, and he felt them pierce first the glove and then his skin. Reflexively, he tried to jerk his hand back, but Flip quickly clamped his hand down on Mordecai's arm. "No!" he shouted, and then, more calmly, said, "Don't try to pull it out." He stuck his thumb and middle finger into the eyes of the fish. "The teeth will break off in your skin, and it sucks to get them out." No more than a second after Flip stuck his fingers in the fish's eyes, the monk opened its mouth, and Mordecai pried his own hand off of its teeth. He pulled off his glove and looked at the rows of cuts on both sides of his hand.

"You gonna be all right?" Wolf sneered. He shook his head in disgust and muttered, "Useless fucking pussy."

"Yeah, I'm fine," Mordecai answered, hoping to sound tough.

"I don't care!" Wolf yelled. "Get back there and flake!"

Mordecai was shocked and angered by Wolf's reaction, but was desperate to perform his job well. More than anything, he didn't want to let down Flip, being well aware it was Flip who had provided another opportunity. He was determined to prove his worth. He jumped in the stern and started flaking as hard and fast as he could. He was doing a fair job of keeping up when Flip reminded him that the knots of monofilament mesh needed to come out. This slowed him down considerably, as he fought with the tangled balls of monofilament until he saw how they tangled and came undone. The sets were much longer than those Mordecai fished with Tony and Ed—more than twice as long. Wolf was fishing four strings of twenty-five nets. That was seventy-five hundred feet of net to flake through, almost a mile and a half per set.

About an hour into the first set, his back aching, Mordecai saw that the high-flyer that marked the end was more than ten nets away—more than half a mile—and he felt like he couldn't finish.

When another twist came over the bar, his achiness and fatigue seemed to double, even as his pace slowed dramatically. The hauler churned out more and more mesh onto the table, and Mordecai watched the high-flyer bobbing at an elusive distance. It felt as if there were knives in the muscles of his back, and he again doubted he would finish the set. But he did, and he greeted the task of pulling the last bridle over the bar with the relief of a marathon runner crossing the finish line.

They still had three sets to go.

Wolf untied the end line from the bridle at the hauler and passed it around the outside of the steel bulkhead, where Flip caught it on the starboard side in the stern and retied it to the bridle at the end of the set. Wolf swung the boat around, and Flip came back to the stern to help set the net out, while Wolf ran the boat north.

"Sorry I'm not keepin' up that good, Flip," Mordecai said.

"Don't worry, man. I know you're trying. Just don't let him get to ya. Keep your head down and mouth shut, and you'll pick it up."

The nets flowed over the spreader bar smoothly, except for the spots where Mordecai hadn't taken the knots out, and Flip warned him that he was leaving too many in. "They constrict the net and affect how it fishes. Watch how hard Wolf freaks out when he doesn't like how the net goes out." They were coming to the end of the set when all of a sudden, Flip said, "Are you all set on your side?"

"Yeah, I guess so," Mordecai responded.

"Holy shit! Look out!" Flip yelled. He pushed Mordecai out of the way just as the steel railroad track came flying out of the checker, ricocheted off the setting bar with a loud clang, and landed in the water as the end line went over the setting bar. Mordecai realized immediately what had happened. Before the end of the set went out, the sternman, who coiled the lines into the checker, was supposed to run the end line around the setting bar and retie it, so that the net went through the setting bar without taking the end line with the anchor and high-flyer with it. Mordecai had obviously forgotten to do this.

"*What the fuck is up with that?*" Wolf yelled from the wheelhouse. Flip picked up the high-flyer and launched it between the posts of the setting bar like a javelin, taking the rest of the end line with it. Wolf stood in the doorway of the wheelhouse, shaking his head and glaring at Mordecai with contempt. Then he went back to the helm, and they steamed the short distance to the next set. The big Caterpillar diesel throttled down as they eased up on the high-flyer that marked the next set. Wolf walked out of the wheelhouse and said, "Try this again, shall we?" He climbed across the table and glared at Mordecai before turning to address the high-flyer that was floating twenty yards from them. Again, Wolf pulled in the high-flyer and passed it to Flip, who passed it to Mordecai. Mordecai coiled the end line to the anchor but this time, he tied the line around the setting bar after placing the anchor in the rope checker. The second set went the same as the first—until they came to some lobster traps that were part of a trawl that had been set over the monk set.

Because the monk gear was selective, Wolf only hauled it about once a week. The *Desire* wasn't making a presence that every boat fishing the area would notice. It was easy to set over a string of nets that was a mile and a half long, as the ends were so far apart that one couldn't be seen from the other. In the area around the H buoy, there were other gillnetters from Plymouth Harbor, as well as lobstermen, their silhouettes flecks on the horizon; they all tried to scratch a paycheck from the same piece of sea bottom. The wire box-like lobster traps didn't fit through the roller, so Wolf had to lean out over the water and try to pull the trap loose from the net. The traps were old and had a lot of sharp edges where the metal wire had corroded. These edges snagged the monofilament, breaking webs and damaging the net. Wolf had pulled out four traps already and was hauling along, still on the first half of the set, when the end of the net came up without a bridle or end lines—just a clean end to mesh, float, and lead lines. Someone had cut the gear.

"MOTHERFUCKER!" Wolf screamed at the sky. He dropped the transmission in forward and steamed full throttle for the other end, almost a mile away. A black cloud of diesel exhaust rose above them as the *Desire* churned the water in their wake.

The problem presented was twofold: first, the net was damaged where it had been cut and would have to be removed from the set, stripped, and rehung. Second, Wolf now had to haul with the tide, and that meant he had to sling the net aboard to keep the tide from sweeping the boat far beyond the net.

They were just cranking up the end lines, and Wolf was passing the high-flyer back to Flip, when a red lobster boat steamed up alongside. The guy running it came out on deck to talk to Wolf, but Wolf glared at him from the hauling station.

"Say, what direction are you running your gear?" the fellow asked.

"It's kinda hard to work when you gotta pull fuckin' pots out of the net, then get cut and dropped," Wolf retorted. "You guys wanna fuck around, my knife is as sharp as anybody else's."

"Hey! I haven't cut and dropped anyone, guy!" the lobsterman snapped. "You came up over me the other day, and I cut my own ground line and tied myself back. I'm just trying to fish around you."

Wolf was quiet for a moment and then said, "All right. I'm running north and south with double flags on my south end and a single flag on the north. You tell your buddies if someone keeps fuckin' with my gear, I'll wipe this fuckin' place out before I go down."

"We've been fishing here for over for over ten years!" the lobsterman snorted. "I'm trying to fish around you, and you act like you're just gonna run roughshod over me?" He went back to his helm, put the boat in gear, "Fuck off!" and throttled up, wake churning as it steamed away.

"Fuck him." Chuck said over his shoulder to his crew. "He's the asshole that did it. We all know it." Mordecai stood at the table wondering to what 'We' meant. If an altercation came to blows, how involved was he supposed to get?

Wolf resumed hauling up the end lines, and the men continued hauling the monk gear aboard. The sun was setting in the January sky as Flip and Mordecai hosed down the boat and scrubbed the checkers. "You think Wolf's tough?" Flip asked. "I remember when we were fishing the other side of the Cape on the *Michelle* a few summers back. There was this boat fishing not far from us called the *Barnacle Bill*. We heard the captain call the Coast Guard on the radio and ask for assistance. We were about to steam over to them and see if they needed help when we heard the Coast Guard dispatcher ask what the nature of the emergency was.

The captain said his crew was in a mutiny, and he had locked himself in the wheelhouse with a gun."

"Are you serious?"

Flip laughed. "Dead serious. The Coast Guard asked the captain of the *Barnacle Bill* if his life was in any immediate danger, and the guy radioed back, 'Well, they're setting the deck on fire right now.' I remember seeing the smoke on the horizon and was relieved that Wolf decided not to get involved."

"How was the crew supposed to get away after they lit the boat on fire?"

"They took off in the life raft and started rowing for home!" laughed Flip.

"That's kind of an outrageous situation, though, isn't it?"

Flip said nothing.

"So the moral of the story is don't fuck with the crew, or they'll burn your boat?"

"No. The moral of the story is, if you think Wolf's bad, imagine how bad the captain of the *Barnacle Bill* must have been for the crew to want to take the life raft home."

Mordecai thought that tough captains were probably just part of the seagoing way of life, with the toughest ones becoming better known. It was Captain Bligh that made *Mutiny on the Bounty* such a legend. Moby Dick probably wouldn't have been the story it was if Ahab been the avuncular Tony Amato.

For that day, they had one thousand pounds of monk. Flip had everything cut and washed and boxed before the hauling was done. At a $1.50 a pound, the boat made $1,500. A little over an hour later, the boat was tied up at her berth on the north side of the pier. A fish buyer from New Bedford had driven up to Scituate to buy the catch, and he paid Wolf cash. Wolf gave Flip three hundred-dollar bills. He turned to Mordecai. "You're a rookie. And I don't like taking rookies. This is a business, and I'm about making money. This boat is going to Maryland in a couple weeks. You want to join us, you better put some time in hauling with us and pick up some skills if you want full share. I'm not paying 15 percent to some greenhorn who can't pick or flake. Here's a hundred and fifty bucks for your pathetic flaking job."

It wasn't the $225 that Mordecai had figured, but he realized that Flip had done twice the work and had twice the skills, so he deserved more. Besides, Mordecai reasoned, a hundred and fifty bucks was a big day's pay, and when he picked up the skills, he would get more.

"I need to haul the gear with Tony and Ed at least once more," Mordecai told Wolf. "Then I'll go with you."

Mordecai was walking down *Front Street*, headed for the sub shop when he ran into Tony. Tony was walking into the package store next door. "Well, it looks like somebody went fishing today." Tony said looking Mordecai up and down. "I'm guessing you went with Wolf and Flip on that big new boat."

"Uh, yeah, well, we haven't been getting out much lately so I thought I'd pick up a days pay."

"I figured. Saw the truck on the pier. You weren't around. The *Desire* was gone, so Ed and I went out and set the gear."

"Oh, so, you didn't need me?"

"We've been doing this our whole lives, what would we need you for?"

"I don't know. I just thought…"

"I thought Wolfy had a shower on that boat so all you pretty boys could shower together." Tony cut in with a straight face. "You smell like shit."

"Huh? A shower,.. What?" Tony couldn't hide his smile when he saw Mordecai getting flustered.

"We're going tomorrow if you can lower your standards enough to come with us."

"Of course. I'll be there." Mordecai felt himself becoming defensive. "I'm not jumping ship, I was just trying to make a buck" Mordecai was thinking of why he needed to justify his actions. Tony just looked at him. "I'll see you in the morning" Mordecai offered. Tony turned and headed for the package store without another word, but Mordecai thought he sensed him laughing.

* * *

"What do you think of the *Desire*?" Mordecai asked Tony the next day.

"The story was that some captain had taken his crew and boat, the *Sea Roamer,* through weather that demolished the boat," Tony said. "She was still afloat but abandoned. Wolf made an offer for the wreck, and from it he created a newer version, the *Desire*. Problem is, in redesigning the vessel, neither Wolf nor his father consulted a marine architect. In its original design, the *Sea Roamer* wasn't a bad offshore boat, but Wolf and his family are inventive and industrious people. Wolf knew what he wanted and believed in his own ability to design what he needed. Having had a wheelhouse blow in on him, it made sense to go with thick Lexan windows married to a heavy steel wheelhouse."

"What's Lexan?" Mordecai asked.

"The extra-strong glass used in hockey rinks. It's heavy. Also, they raised the steel rails another four feet and hey, it all made sense in the yard where the work was being done. The logic was to reinforce the vessel against the sea." Tony waved his hand toward the water. "But when the modified version was launched, it was top-heavy."

"Just about rolled over on a calm day in the harbor," added Ed. "But Wolf's not gonna quit. Even added concrete to the bilge, to give it some ballast."

"Welded a steel I-beam to the keel, didn't they?" Tony said.

"Yeah, I heard that, too," Ed said thoughtfully. "With all that weight they must draw nine feet below the waterline. I don't know if they can get through the mouth of the harbor at low tide."

"I heard Wolf plans to take the *Desire* to Maryland," Mordecai announced.

"And you're thinking of going with him," Tony said. He finished hauling in the end line and placed the high-flyer on the picking table. Ed was in the stern, coiling the lines into the rope checker. "Can you believe it?" Tony said to Ed. "They're chasing the fuckin' things up and down the coast now!" He looked at Mordecai. "You know, Americans just won't eat something called dogfish, but in England, they are the mainstay of the fish and chips market."

"And in Germany, the belly flaps are smoked," added Ed.

"And parts of Asia use the fins to make that shark-fin soup," Tony said. "So the big gold rush is on for this formerly underutilized species." Tony looked at the few that were in a plastic fish tote. "Fill the boat, every day!" Tony shifted his gaze back to Mordecai. "I bet that's what he's hearing. It's a money fish now!"

"One that swims near the bottom while chasing its prey," Ed said from the stern, still coiling rope into the checker. "A perfect target for gill nets."

"I didn't say I was going with 'em," Mordecai insisted, "just that I heard a rumor."

"For years, because there was no market for dogfish, it was all we could do to avoid 'em," Tony said. "They were so abundant that entire days were spent picking and discarding the fuckin' things."

"Getting slammed by the dogs," said Ed. "I remember. Long days of hard work for nothing."

"A face in every window for no money," responded Tony. Neither of them gave Mordecai a chance to get a word in. "Create an export market for dogfish, and these young guys think they're gonna get rich overnight."

"And the price can dive, sometimes less than ten cents a pound when everybody has a full boat," agreed Ed.

"Look," Mordecai interrupted, "I know there isn't the prestige attached to dogfishing like there is with cod, haddock, and all the traditional groundfish. But at twenty-five cents a pound, and potential for ten thousand to fifteen thousand pounds a day, don't you think the chance to make a lot of money is realistic?"

Neither Tony nor Ed answered; they worked in silence, and Mordecai felt not like Jonah but Judas.

Chapter 5 Dope

"We'll make a bundle and get our own boat. Next year, it'll be you and me, splitting the profits fifty-fifty," Flip said one

Saturday morning. He and Mordecai were on their way to the fisherman supply store. Mordecai had decided he would rather have less money and be warm and dry in new boots, skins, and gloves than have a few extra bucks in a cold, wet pocket. Flip said he was going to get by with his mismatched boots and torn, leaky skins. He always seemed willing to endure the discomfort and get the job done. "I'll just fuck up the new stuff," Flip had said. "What's the point?"

"Flip, it's January. Warm and dry is kinda important. Don't ya think?"

"For you, maybe. I'll just tough it out, but I'll give you a ride to the fisherman supply. I gotta pick up some stuff for a buddy who's sick."

"Yeah? What's he sick with?"

"Dope sick."

"What the hell is dope sick?"

"I don't think I could ever explain it in a way that you would understand. It's something that means doin' whatever you gotta do to get through it. And I know I'll do whatever it takes to help him through it, cuz he'd do the same for me."

Mordecai knew that Flip didn't abandon his friends, but he felt better about getting Flip away from friends who were sick from doing dope. Mordecai waited in the truck as Flip ran in to a rundown house with a carton of cigarettes and a gallon of orange juice. The neighborhood was along the tracks of the new commuter rail, and the former residents, who had kept tidy houses and lawns before the tracks were put down, had fled the loud and disturbing clamor of the train. Now, the ramshackle neighborhood was populated by the people who turned up in the weekly police report and headlines. None of the buildings had been painted in years—some were boarded up—and trash lined the street. Two young children in soiled clothes were trying to throw a broken toilet seat like a Frisbee. It landed on the street and clattered to a stop in front of Flip's pickup. Mordecai felt conspicuous. *C'mon, Flip, let's get out of here*, he thought nervously.

As if he'd heard Mordecai, Flip bounded down the steps of the rundown house and strode across the front lawn. "Sorry it took so long," he apologized.

"No worries," Mordecai said, but he was happy to get going.

After Flip dropped him off at his apartment, Mordecai walked over to a small grocery store to pick up a box of macaroni and cheese to have with the cod fillets Ed had skillfully filleted for him. The diet of fresh fish appealed to him now that he had an understanding and appreciation for the history and culture of men who caught them. He exited the store to see his fathers' Buick pull up in front of him. Mordecai froze. He hadn't seen his father since that day he was kicked out. "Mordecai," his father said rolling down the window. "How are you, son?"

"Oh," Mordecai swallowed and fought his trepidation, not knowing how his father would greet him. "I'm okay." His father was quiet a moment as he appraised his son. Mordecai saw his father looking at his old work jeans, the denim frayed and holes worn through from long days at sea rubbing against the canvas lined oilskins.

"You look like you're losing some weight."

"Yeah." Mordecai glanced down at the jeans that he now noticed were loose on him. "I eat a lot of fish now."

"I heard. You're a fisherman. That must be hard work."

"Dad, you wouldn't believe it. There's so much-," Mordecai struggled to find the words. This was something he had thought about; how he would explain to his father the pride he felt in being a fisherman. But he felt it all come at him at once and couldn't put it into a sentence. "ocean." Mordecai's father looked at his son with an expression that told Mordecai he was interested in what his son had to say. "I don't even know how to explain. The ocean; it just goes on-," Mordecai stood before his father looking for the word. "forever." Mordecai's father smiled.

"Missed you on you're birthday", nodding toward the passenger side. "Why don't we take a ride."

Mordecai shrugged, outwardly suppressing what was longing to burst from him. Stories about Tony and Ed, the *St Joseph*, welled in his heart in a wave of emotion. But he swallowed that and got in the passenger side of the Buick, not wanting to start gushing like a little kid. He wanted his father to see that he was a grown man now. As they drove through fading afternoon light,

Mordecai told his father of how he had come to fishing. “So Flip helped you get a job.” Mr Young said. “How is Flip?”

“He’s doing well.” Mordecai responded while remembering the unsettled angst of the experience earlier that day. “He’s got a new truck.” Mr. Young nodded.

“Well that must be some honest work, being a fisherman. Good, honest work. I’m glad to hear you sounding so positive.” They drove to a Sears department store. “I think we should take a look at what they have in here” and Mr. Young parked the Buick.

Leaving the Sears store with a new pair of Levi’s his father had bought for him in a plastic bag, Mordecai felt himself becoming more comfortable in his fathers’ presence. He thought about asking his father for advice. Should he stay put in Scituate on the *St Joseph* for the winter, or go with Wolf and Flip on the *Desire* for an adventure in a new place. Then he realized how that would sound to his father, as if he were quitting again. There was an uneasy silence on the ride back.

“How long do you think you will stay with fishing?” Richard Young asked. Mordecai flinched at the question.

“I don’t see myself quitting anytime soon.” Mr. Young looked thoughtful as he pondered this.

“Must be cold out there.”

“Not that bad. I can take it.”

“Do you think you would want to get your own boat?”

“That’s the plan. I’ve been talking about it with Flip. But we’ve got to save up a down payment first.” The plastic bag from Sears crinkled in his lap. Neither of them said anything for the rest of the ride back to Mordecai’s apartment. As Mordecai exited the car, his father said,

“How do you like where you’re living?”

“It’s all right. Not very big, but I don’t need much.”

“Well it’s a place to start, Mordecai.” His father smiled. “At least you are making your own way as your own man. I’m proud of you for that.”

“Thanks for the jeans, Dad.” Mordecai exited the car with the plastic bag holding the jeans. He thought of another plastic bag he had in the apartment refrigerator. “Hey Dad, wait here for a second.” Mordecai ran up to his apartment and grabbed the bag of fillets. "Here" he said approaching the Buick again. "Bring these to Mom".

Mordecai fished with Tony and Ed the next day and gave official notice that he'd decided to go with Wolf. He felt a mixture of relief and guilt about having somewhere he could go to generate income; he felt bad about leaving Tony and Ed, who were trying to figure out what they were going to do.

"Ed and I aren't trying to support families," Tony told him. "My kids are grown, and Ed, like yourself, is single. We can learn to live as minimalists. Wouldn't hurt either of us to take in our belts a notch or two." He laughed. "I guess you just can't count on loyalty anymore. He looked at Mordecai who just looked at his feet. "Look, you're a young guy, and you're rambunctious; I can see that. But Wolf is maniacally driven. Everyone in the harbor has feared for his life since he started. He's been pushed out there by his family. He's got a successful younger brother, and his family operates like a corporation—the father pushes the kids to excel. It's always been that way for them, and Wolf is under pressure to be successful. If you approach fishing that way, it's a recipe for getting killed. It's a miracle he has survived this long, but his time is gonna come. You know the situation with that boat; it's a disaster. Flip's a good guy, but he has his distractions, too. I know he's your friend, and you guys have known each other a long time, and you like to smoke your pot. But what some of these guys get into can take over their lives."

Mordecai's mouth dropped open in surprise at Tony's acknowledgement that he and Flip got high.

"You think I didn't notice you smelling like cheap cigars in the morning? I know what you two buffoons were doing behind the icehouse. But I'm not talking about that. I see that Flip hangs around with a crowd that you don't want to be part of."

Mordecai had seen heroin mentioned in the news. The newspapers had stories about new Asian suppliers and increased availability and purity. But it wasn't something he thought Tony saw coming into his quaint New England hometown.

"You're gonna do what you want," said Tony. "I know there really isn't any reason to stick around, fishing-wise. But you could get a regular job. And if you like, you could come back fishing with us in May."

"I need money now, Tony," Mordecai insisted. "I don't know how I'm gonna pay the rent."

Tony nodded and extended his hand. "Good luck to you."

Chapter 6
Rollover in Plymouth Harbor

The next morning, Mordecai prepared to head to Ocean City as a sternman on the *Desire*. Before beginning the journey, however, there was work to be done. They steamed to the H buoy to pile the gear aboard for the trip south.

Flip seemed quiet and morose; he'd told Mordecai that things were "going south" in his relationship with his girlfriend. While they hauled, Flip didn't work with his usual energy and effort. In the middle of the second set, Flip said, "I wonder if she needs some space—not cuz she's gotta figure out what she wants but she's already seeing someone else."

"You know how this routine goes, Flip," Mordecai said. "Might as well get yourself ready for the big bombshell that's gonna drop when she tells ya the news for real. So let's just look forward to the trip."

Wolf rolled his eyes and shook his head. "You dumb fuck," he muttered.

Flip stopped working and stared at Mordecai. "What are you saying?" he asked. "Do you know something? What do you mean? Who is she seeing?"

"I don't know; I'm just saying you're probably right."

"Tell me! You know who it is!"

"Flip, I don't know anything."

"Yes, you do! You're withholding information!"

"No, Flip. I'm not. If I knew anything, I'd tell ya, buddy. C'mon, man."

Flip climbed over the checker from the net bin to face Mordecai at the table. Mordecai felt helpless—he didn't know how to help his friend. He could tell that Flip was on the verge of tears and the two faced each other silently. Flip blinked, took off his glove and wiped his eyes as he climbed back over the checkerboard and went back to work, his pace slowed to a near standstill.

Because Flip's pace was slower as he moved through the nets, Wolf hauled them up slower. Wolf wore a look of exasperation but Mordecai knew that Wolf wasn't about to reprimand his star player for having personal issues. But when the next monk came around the hauler, Wolf punched it in the head, beat it senseless, and then threw it on the deck and stomped it a few times. Breathing heavily with his breath billowing in clouds around his head, Wolf turned and glared at Mordecai. They came to the end lines, and Wolf hauled them aboard while Flip coiled them into the rope checker.

"I want to talk to you for a second," Wolf said calmly, beckoning to Mordecai to follow him into the wheelhouse. They both stepped into the wheelhouse; then Wolf turned suddenly, his eyes wild with anger. "What the fuck did you tell him that for?"

"I didn't really think about it. Just helping him get ready for what is probably going to happen. Maybe if he figures it out for himself sooner—"

"That … does not … help us … right now," Wolf said in a measured release of words. "Do you have any idea how much time you just added on to our day?"

"Sorry. I thought I was helping him out."

"News flash! You ain't helping!" he yelled. His large hand swept past Mordecai's head to gesture aft, toward the work deck. Mordecai flinched, bracing himself to be hit. "He's ready for suicide watch, for Christsake! We're never going to get through the gear at this pace. Who's gonna pick up his slack cuz you just took the wind out of his sails? You? Right. Just keep your mouth shut, and let me undo the damage you just caused. I hear you start to say anything stupid like that again, and I'm gonna knock you out before you finish getting it said. Now, go give him a hand."

Mordecai stepped out on deck, relieved to be out from under Wolf's glare, and walked the high-flyer back to Flip, who was coiling line in the stern.

"Wow! Did you see Wolf pummel that monkfish?" Mordecai said with forced cheerfulness. Flip just nodded slightly. "Boy, imagine if that was your head."

Flip regarded him quietly for a second. "I'm sure he would've stopped and felt bad if it was your head," he offered.

"What scares me is he might get a few good stomps in before he feels bad,"

The fish dropped off to less than half of what they had in the previous lift, so there wasn't as much work. Flip picked up the pace again in the middle of the third set, when Wolf started recounting the old days. Mordecai could feel the water that had passed beneath these two. The three fishermen loaded the gear on and headed back for Scituate. When the *Desire* got to the harbor entrance, Flip asked Mordecai if he could handle the unloading, as he had something he had to do.

"Sure, Flip. There are only a few totes. I got it." The *Desire* pulled up to the pier to unload, and Flip climbed the ladder to the top of the pier, where his truck was waiting.

"Where the fuck's he going?" Wolf asked as he strode out on deck.

"I don't know. Maybe he's got to let his dog out."

"Jesus," Wolf muttered. "Trying to keep the crew sane is driving me nuts." He headed up the ladder. "And you're not helping," he said to Mordecai, tossing over his shoulder, "Fuckin' *Jonah.*" As he climbed on to the pier, Mordecai heard him call, "Hey, Flip. Stay in touch. I want to leave in a few days." Wolf lowered the winch sling down. Mordecai wrapped it around four totes of fish, and they were hoisted up to the waiting fish truck. Wolf came back down the ladder and untied from the front of the pier. He put the boat in gear and gave it some throttle to kick out the stern and swing the *Desire* in a wide, graceful arc. The wheel stirred up clouds of muddy bottom sediment that passed just a couple feet beneath the keel at low tide. They throttled halfway around to the north side of the pier, then Wolf backed off the throttle and put the boat in reverse, easing into where the *Desire* berthed. Wolf and Mordecai tied up the boat without a word and disembarked. There were no cash payments, and Wolf never said a word to Mordecai about leaving. Mordecai went home, apprehensive about not being included.

The next day, Flip showed up around ten in the morning at Mordecai's one-room apartment with two cups of coffee—and the news that they would be leaving the next day, as the weather for the next couple of days would be best for steaming south. The boat had to be made ready immediately. Mordecai climbed into the passenger side of Flip's pickup and gave Dingo a rub between the ears. "Those look like some new jeans, never even been washed." Flip noticed. Mordecai looked at the dark blue denim.

"Thought I'd break them in on this trip."

"You're gonna wash 'em before it's over, though. Right?"

"If we find a laundry in Maryland." Flip drove to Wolf's house and pulled into the backyard, where Wolf had a pile of gill nets in grain and feed bags to be brought to the boat. They loaded twenty bags onto Flip's truck, while Wolf replaced a broken window from a ladder that was set against the outside of the house. From inside, Mordecai heard Wolf's wife ask how she was supposed to control the children and handle all the household chores while he was away. His wife, Linda, was a pretty blonde from West Virginia and was known for being rugged herself.

"Look, I'm just trying to do what I can to keep us afloat here," Wolf called through the window. Linda said something in response, but Mordecai couldn't make out what it was. Then Wolf said, "Well I guess you're just going to have to keep him from breaking windows. That means you'll have to tan his backside instead of me." As he climbed down the ladder, Linda's voice came clearly through the open the window.

"But what are we supposed to do about money?"

"For Christsake!" Wolf threw the ladder to the ground with a loud crash. "I gotta get there first!"

Flip and Mordecai got in his truck and headed for the harbor, leaving Wolf and his wife yelling at each other. Flip lowered the bags down to Mordecai on the *Desire*, and then they set off for the grocery store to buy ground coffee, spring water, canned pasta, vegetables, soda, paper towels, and plates and plastic cutlery to have on the boat. They gathered laundry and threw it in the washers. They were walking down *Front Street*, heading for the sandwich shop, when they saw Father McNamara out for his afternoon walk. The father remembered Flip and Mordecai when they had served as altar boys, and he greeted them enthusiastically and then added, "I haven't seen either of you at Mass. Are you going to drop in some time? It's free, you know."

"We usually fish on Sundays, Father," Flip lied.

"I thought fishermen were exempt from going to church, Father," Mordecai said.

"And how so, Mordecai?" Father McNamara asked.

"Because as fishermen, we do our penance every day." Mordecai smiled, thinking the father would find it funny, too, but Father Mac looked at him blankly.

"Actually," said Flip, "we're getting ready to head down to the mid-Atlantic for the rest of the winter."

"Are you? What will you be fishing for?"

"Dogfish and monkfish," answered Flip.

"Let me give you my blessing, boys." The father clamped one of his large hands on Flip's forehead, pushing down Flip's flop of brown hair and completely obscuring his face. He spoke the words of the blessing, and when he finished with Flip, he placed his hand on Mordecai, clamping down on his head before Mordecai could remove his ball cap. Father Mac held firmly to Mordecai's head as he waved the sign of the cross in front of him with his other hand, a spectacle that Flip found quite funny. When the father finished giving his blessing, Flip and Mordecai thanked him and continued on their way.

"I hope some of his blessing got through your ball cap,"

"I hope so, too," Mordecai agreed. "I think we might need it."

The next day was an unseasonably warm day for January. The temperature had reached the low fifties by the time Flip and Mordecai pulled on to the pier. The afternoon sun felt pleasant as they steamed out of the harbor and into the bay, heading south for the Cape Cod Canal. Mordecai watched the cliffs of Scituate become the sands of Marshfield, then the Duxbury and Plymouth beaches, as the afternoon slipped by with the scenery of the seashore. The onset of darkness loomed as they cruised through the Cape Cod Canal. Wolf seemed agitated as he looked at his controls; he said that for some reason, the boat was overheating. "We're going to have to find a place where we can dock and shut down to let her cool," he said.

At the end of the canal was the Massachusetts Maritime Academy. The training vessels lined the west side of the canal. Wolf pulled alongside a tugboat that was docked there. Mordecai hopped off the *Desire* with the bow line and put the loop over the stem on the bow of the tugboat. He used plenty of line, adjusting the amount that wrapped around the bow stem of the *Desire* to use the full length—he'd never be able to hold the *Desire* in the swift current of the canal if the line came up short. But Wolf didn't know that Mordecai had let out so much line, and when he saw Mordecai put the loop on the stem of the tug, he put the *Desire* in neutral. There was about half a second before the swift current fetched up the deep draft boat, and she started hauling ass backward with the tide, taking line for thirty feet until it snapped tight. Looking in through the pilothouse windows, Mordecai saw Wolf stumble into the hatch as the *Desire* stopped short, like a dog that takes off running and forgets it's on a leash. Wolf walked back to the wheel, put the boat in gear, and idled back up alongside the tug. Mordecai hopped on the bow of the *Desire*, quickly undoing the half-hitch on the bow stem, taking in the slack and tying it off again. Temperatures plummeted with the setting sun, and the rope had become stiff and icy, making it hard to work around the stem and tie. Mordecai strained to get it done quickly and was breathing hard from the effort. If he made a mistake here, the *Desire* could get swept out by the current—a real problem, particularly with the engine's overheating. Flip got the stern tied off, and Wolf shut down the Cat while Flip and Mordecai started to set up spring lines.

When they stepped back into the wheelhouse, Wolf was on the phone with his father. "Whatever it is, it never happened with fishing off of Scituate. The farthest we went was the H buoy and back. We haven't steamed this far for a long time, so maybe something is working harder. The transmission is hot, too." Silence for a couple seconds then, "Well, the tide is gonna have to turn to get back through the canal. That's not for almost six hours, and I gotta let it cool. We'll head back after the tide turns."

Mordecai's heart sank. He had hoped that whatever the problem was, it was something Wolf could fix on the spot, and they would again be underway. But it sounded like Wolf was going to need help diagnosing the problem, and this meant the full industrious capacity of the family would be brought to bear on the problem. They had to turn around and go home. Although dejected, Mordecai knew that Wolf must feel ten times worse. He climbed into his bunk, looking emotionally wiped out, uttering, "I think I could fucking cry."

Flip wanted to walk around the campus of Mass Maritime and explore. “I can’t sleep lately,” he said.

Mordecai noticed that his friend’s eyes looked sunken, an appearance that that supported Flip’s claim, and he followed Flip out on deck. “I don’t know if that’s such a good idea, Flip,” he said. “I think they might consider it trespassing, and it might be that we’re not even supposed to be tied up here. If we got caught meandering around up there, that could bring heat down on Wolf, and he’s not having such a great day.”

“Do you what you want, man,” Flip said, “I’d rather explore by myself anyway.” He disappeared into the darkness on the tug.

Mordecai went below and climbed in his bunk, listening to the sound of water slapping the hull and the whirring noise of the wheel free-spinning in the current. He could hear Wolf’s breathing as he slept, and Mordecai soon fell asleep, too. When he woke, it was still dark but the sound of water slapping the hull had shifted, so he figured the tide had changed. He went up into the wheelhouse. Wolf sat in the captain’s chair, looking out the starboard-side window at the water rushing through the canal in the darkness.

“Offshore lobster boat went through here not long ago,” Wolf said calmly. Mordecai looked at the clock on the electronic position finder. It was a little after two in the morning. “If you can find Flip, we’ll head back. But we need to find him before the tide changes again.”

“I’ll find him,” Mordecai answered. “He must be close by.” Mordecai realized that Flip had been gone for over six hours. He wondered where he could even begin to look for him when a figure stood up on the deck of the tug alongside. “That you, Flip?”

“Well, it ain’t big, fucking hairy Sasquatch,” Flip returned with a stoned giggle. He stepped onto the *Desire*, and Mordecai noticed that his eyelids were bloated. *Extra high*, Mordecai thought.

Wolf fired up the Cat. Mordecai let go of the bow line, and Flip let go of the stern lines after Mordecai threw him the spring lines, and they headed back through the dark for Scituate.

The sun already had risen by the time they steamed into Scituate harbor, passing the *St. Joseph* on her way out. Mordecai waved, and Ed waved back. Mordecai wished he was heading out with Tony and Ed, and he imagined what they were saying at that moment: *"Back already? Boy, that was a quick trip. I wonder if they made their fortune."* They undoubtedly had a good laugh at his expense.

The *Desire* was overheating again as they pulled up to the pier. Wolf's father, Bob, was waiting for them, and he climbed down into the engine room to confer with Wolf. Flip and Mordecai unloaded steel sawhorses, cutting torches, and tools from the back of Bob's truck.

Back up on deck, Wolf put on a welding mask and using cutting torch cut two small holes in the steel deck, while Flip passed the steel sawhorses to Mordecai on the boat. Wolf set up the sawhorses over the smoking holes and ran a piece of steel I-beam across them. The I-beam had a hole in the center, to which Wolf hooked a chainfall—a lifting device specifically for heavy items. It worked like a rope and pulley. Bob was in the engine room, directly below setting up the chains to lift the transmission. Mordecai watched the procedure with fascination, although he wondered just what was going on. Other fishermen on the pier came over to watch as well, and everyone seemed to understand exactly what was happening. Mordecai tried not to appear clueless.

Wolf disconnected the loop of chain on the chainfall and ran the two ends of chain through the smoking holes in the steel plate, and told Mordecai to take the heavy floor jack down to Bob in the engine room. Bob stood in about six inches of water, hunched over the transmission, with a droplight suspended from the ceiling. The cramped, musty room was warm from the big Cat, and the odor that permeated the air was one of diesel fuel and oil, along with the rusty scent of salt-water-saturated steel. Bob took the floor jack, placed it under the transmission, and ran the chain under the transmission. Bob unbolted the transmission from the engine and handed Mordecai the large bolts as he did. Wolf had taken up the slack on the chain, so the weight of the transmission was entirely on the chainfall. Bob ran into a snag when the socket wrench would not fit into the space around the last bolt holding the transmission, and a thin wrench would not fit either.

Bob climbed out of the engine room and told Wolf he needed to make a wrench. He took another socket of the same size out of a toolbox and placed it in a vice that was bolted to the bumper of his truck. Taking a metal cutting saw, he sawed the socket in half, reducing its length. Then he took a thin piece of flat metal and welded that to the socket. Mordecai was impressed by Bob's ingenuity and cleverness in fashioning his own tool. He mused that the first fishermen probably exercised similar skills when they made nets from simple twine and made fish hooks out of bone.

The *Desire* had been overheating because rust had corroded the pipes that carried the engine coolant. The boat's cooling system was unorthodox—the pipes that carried coolant ran through the hull, which was cooled by seawater. Wolf's plan now was to do away with that system and install the traditional form of metal pipes that ran outside of and along the hull to carry coolant for the engine. The boat needed to be hauled out of the water so "keel coolers" could be installed. The idea was that the temperature of the seawater would cool the pipes, in turn cooling the coolant itself, which kept the engine at an operating temperature. The only nearby boatyard with a lift that could handle the weight of the *Desire* was Brewer Marine in Plymouth Harbor.

The next day, Mordecai was in one of the bars in the harbor that was frequented by the local fishermen. John Hayes was fishing on the *Wayward,* a boat that just returned from a successful trip. John, like Mordecai, was twenty-one, of a medium build and new to fishing. He had a quick smile framed by a neat goatee and Mordecai had gravitated to his easy going manner around the pier.

"You're from here, so it must be the same old thing to you. But I had never seen the ocean, only heard about it."

"What was it like the first time you saw it?" Mordecai asked.

"I couldn't believe how much of it there was. It just keeps going."

"Yeah, it's big. That's for sure." Mordecai agreed.

"And it has its' own smell," Johns' eyes lit with excitement as he searched words. "like it's a living, breathing thing."

"It is a living, breathing thing." Mordecai liked this. It was fun talking about this new environment with someone who was also new to it. "It's full of life."

"And we can make a living from it!" John laughed. "This where I want to be and what I want to do."

"Me too!" Mordecai and John high-fived. The captain, Tim Caulder, was a smaller guy who looked younger than his years, and was usually more reserved among other fishermen when they congregated on the pier those afternoons while waiting to unload. But Mordecai noticed the Captain was one who quietly observed, noticing everything with the eyes of one who could appraise what he saw quickly. He saw Mordecai talking to his sternman, John, and began buying rounds of draft beer.

"It's good getting to know you guys." Mordecai said as Tim handed him a cold draft. "It's part of the appeal of the lifestyle."

"Funny how cold beer can do that." Tim smiled. "I also like knowing who is interested in making money," Tim sipped his beer. "Who wants to make a trip." Mordecai considered this. He was broke, and these guys could buy rounds for the house. The door to the bar swung open and Tim stared at the figure walking in. "I've never seen him in here." Mordecai turned to see Wolf walk right up to him and Tim. "Wolf, what a surprise." Tim offered as he turned to the bartender. "Let's have a cold one for-,"

"I'm all set, Timmy" Wolf interrupted. "Having a good time?" he directed at Mordecai. Mordecai shrugged. Wolf looked back at Tim. "Tim's always happy to buy beer for a sternman." Tim said nothing and looked away. "Courting help or looking for information?" Wolf asked Tim pointedly. Mordecai was confused.

"Wolf, you need me for something?"

"Plymouth harbor is icing in. We need to get there before the sun goes down and temperature drops. That means we got to leave now." Mordecai's jaw opened slightly. "Don't look surprised, that's how it is in this business. The plan is always subject to change. Put the beer down and let's go." Wolf turned and as abruptly as he arrived, left. Mordecai drained the beer and put the empty mug on the bar.

"So you like Wolf's operation?" Tim asked.

"Wish I could hang around and tell you, but it looks like I gotta go." Mordecai headed for the door.

"I'd like to hear about it some time." Tim called after him. "Sounds like a real hoot."

Mordecai walked into the cold of the outside and the fish pier that lay steps from the warm and comfortable bar. Wolf was pulling the eye of a spring line from a cleat at the edge of the pier. "Having fun with your new friends?" Wolf glared at Mordecai. "Did you tell them anything?"

"Tell them what?"

"What we're doing?" Mordecai was quiet, unsure what to say. "What happens on this boat stays on this boat. You don't tell anyone what we are doing, where we are fishing or what we are catching. Is that clear!?"

"I didn't get the chance to say much of anything."

"It's a good thing I showed up before your drunk mouth gave away the farm. Get those jugs of coolant from the back of my truck, and there's a few nets that can be flaked into the checker on the ride" and Wolf went down the ladder. Mordecai saw that the boat was already running and was relieved to have something he could do on deck rather than take the ride in the wheelhouse with his disgruntled captain.

With the *Desire* overheating, Wolf wanted to get the boat to the marina quickly so they wouldn't have to plow through the ice, thus overworking the engine.

Mordecai took ten one-gallon jugs of coolant out of the bed of the truck and put them on the edge of the pier. Wolf was in the wheelhouse, but Flip was missing. Mordecai began undoing the spring lines, intending to pass the jugs of coolant down as soon as Wolf emerged from the wheelhouse or when Flip showed up. After a few minutes of waiting for the boat to warm enough to steam, Wolf stuck his head out of the hatch and said, "All right, let's go." Mordecai threw off the lines holding them to the pier.

It was almost three o'clock as they headed out of Scituate Harbor, bound for Plymouth, a two-hour steam to the south; Wolf figured they'd get there at sunset. About an hour into the ride, Mordecai was finishing flaking net when two Plymouth boats passed heading north. Mordecai stepped into the wheelhouse, eager to get out of the cold and saw Wolf try hailing them on the radio to ask about ice in the harbor, but neither answered. "Well, even if the harbor's iced in, they must have cleared a path through the channel on their way out," Wolf mused. "Fuck 'em if they don't want to answer us," hanging up the mic, "Assholes."

The opening to Plymouth Harbor was clear, and the *Desire* steamed into a spectacular sunset. Brilliant, fiery light bounced off the dark blue water before them and refracted off the ice-covered rocks along the shore, tingeing them with streaks of bright red. Twilight stars sparkled in a sky about to give way to the inky blackness of night. But as they rounded the point of White Horse Beach, Wolf's fears were realized: the rest of the harbor was completely frozen in. The two boats that had left earlier had plowed through ice—Mordecai could see the trace of their course—but the swift-moving tide had packed frozen blocks of ice back together. And there was another problem: the channel markers, called cans, which served to guide vessels into the harbor, were somewhere under the packed ice. Wolf wasn't familiar with Plymouth Harbor.

"Allright," Wolf said to Mordecai as he headed down the hatch to the engine room, "Pass me those extra jugs of coolant." Mordecai felt a sudden, anxious, fear. His heart pounded as he realized he left the jugs of coolant on the pier.

"Oh no."

"What do you mean, 'Oh no'!" Wolf asked as his glare pierced Mordecai. Mordecai felt speechless but knew he had to answer.

"I left them on the pier."

"You-left-them-on-the-*pier?!*" Wolf's eyes grew even larger. "Lot of fuckin' good they're gonna do us there." Wolf looked like he was going to have a stroke, then paused. Mordecai felt foolish. Slamming the engine room hatch, Wolf muttered "This is what I get for taking a green horn." He headed back into the wheelhouse adding, "Or a Jonah".

Mordecai decided he was more comfortable in the cold on deck.

Wolf had two options: he could try to plow the through the mile and a half of ice to the marina, or he could turn around and go back to Scituate. The boat was already overheating, and there wasn't enough additional coolant. Smelling coolant being burned off, Wolf opened the engine room hatch again and locked it in the upright position. Mordecai saw the answer was clear when the boat did not turn and black smoke surged from the stack. Wolf opted to fight the ice and 'put the coals to it,' pushing the throttle deep into the pocket. The big Caterpillar turbo diesel howled in protest at the additional strain of pushing through ice. Wolf screamed profanities at the boat and punched just about everything in the wheelhouse, Mordecai stayed out on the back deck before he became something that Wolf hit. Steam billowed through the engine-room hatch as the coolant was burned off. They were in danger of destroying the motor. The rhythmic smack of steel against ice added to the cacophony as they plunged headlong through darkness in what was Wolf's best approximation of where the channel was located.

And then the boat churned to a halt. The engine was still full throttle, but the boat was held fast in ice—and it was dangerously overheating. Wolf threw the transmission in reverse trying to back the boat out. But the boat made no motion. Wolf shut her down, leaving just the generator running so there would be heat and power. The night was silent, except for the mellow hum of the generator and the moaning of the wind in the rigging and mast. The sun had withdrawn its warmth, and the night, in its quiet serenity, was cold and indifferent to their predicament. In the distance, Mordecai could see the lights of houses and was reminded that he and Wolf were owed no comfort.

Wolf stuck his head out of the engine-room hatch. "You might as well make yourself comfortable," he told Mordecai. "We're staying for the night."

Mordecai nodded, but remained on deck for a moment longer, hoping to give Wolf some time to cool off. When he went back inside, Wolf was tinkering in the engine room, seeming much more reserved, Steam gently wafted away from the overworked motor, and the humid mixture of coolant and water swirled around Wolf's thick brown beard and hair. In the soft yellow glow of a droplight, Wolf's eyes revealed nothing, and his face, hidden beneath all the hair, was expressionless. As he worked on his machine, he looked as though he were massaging that part of himself that was strained. Wolf only showed one emotion: anger. Now, however, he seemed to be able to soothe himself by tinkering with the machine he had nearly destroyed. As Mordecai peered through the hatch, the scene reminded him of a boxer in a dingy dressing room after a bout or a gladiator after battle, and Mordecai tried to determine who had won. Wolf looked up from his machine and regarded Mordecai silently; then he rose and went forward to the ladder. When Mordecai went topside, he found that Wolf had gone to the sleeping berth in the bow and was in his bunk.

In the wheelhouse, Mordecai warmed a can of Beefaroni in the oven, then climbed into the captain's chair and turned on the television. He thought of asking Wolf if he was hungry but decided it was better to let him sleep.

An hour passed, then two. Mordecai had dozed off, in the captain's chair when suddenly the boat lurched to port. Mordecai was startled awake, but his surprise quickly turned to sheer terror when he realized that the boat was going over on her side. "Wolf!" he called, panicking. "We're going over!"

Wolf came up into the wheelhouse and replied calmly, "I know, Mordecai." The boat was listing at almost a ninety-degree angle. "We're aground, meathead." The ice had been holding the boat upright, but when the tide ran out, the boat had plunged through the ice that had been holding her until she came to lay on her side in about four feet of water. The beach was less than a quarter-mile away, but between the beach and boat was the channel; they were on a mud flat. To make matters worse, the ice was not strong enough to support a man's weight, so walking out was not an option. The pull of the swift-moving tidal current would suck anyone who tried to wade off the boat to certain death under the ice.

Mordecai stumbled on the bulkhead that was now where the deck should have been. Wolf perched in the wheelhouse with one foot on the now nearly vertical deck, and one on the port side bulkhead. He reached for the boat phone. Mordecai looked to Wolf for instruction as he tried not to trip over the assortment of gear that became wedged in the corner between deck and wall. Wolf dialed and there was an uncomfortable silence. "Yeah, Dad." Wolf said into the phone. There was another quiet moment. "We're aground off White Horse Beach." Wolf's voice lowered to near whisper. "I don't know. I don't know this harbor and the cans are under the ice." Mordecai sensed Wolf's embarrassment, and a feeling of sympathy for the man he had felt he needed to impress suddenly came over him. "No, I tried that, she won't back out." Mordecai thought about going out on the back deck to give Wolf a private moment with his father. "I'm an asshole? Dad, I can't see where the channel is." The port side rail was under two feet of freezing water forcing Mordecai to join Wolf in this moment of defeat. "Yeah, well, anybody could pull us off but the Coast Guard is going to need to break up the ice first so they can get to us." Wolf listened to the voice on the phone. "If you could call the Coast Guard on the phone; that would save me from having everyone with a vhf radio hearing about what an asshole I am." Without another word Wolf hung up the phone. Mordecai shifted his stance which was almost as uncomfortable and awkward as the silence. "Don't step on the wheelhouse windows." Wolf snapped. "You'll pop them out and we'll have water in here." Wolf rubbed his temples while Mordecai tried to pick up the pile of boots, skins, gloves and raincoats that littered where he was standing. "Oh what's the use!" Wolf declared. "Just leave that shit." Dropping the items in his hands, the two stood in uneasy silence. Several minutes passed while Mordecai desperately tried to think of something he could say to alleviate the tension. Suddenly, a voice blared from the vhf radio. "*Desire. Desire*. This is United States Coast Guard, Boston. Come back on channel 16." Wolf reached for the radio and turned down the volume, rolling his eyes as he sullenly picked up the mic.

"Yeah, this is *Desire* on channel 16."

"What's your situation, Captain." Wolf's head slumped.

"Yeah,. Uh., We're aground off White Horse Beach, in Plymouth Harbor."

"Roger that Captain. Are your lives in any immediate danger?"

"No, no. It's nothing like that. We just need to be pulled off this bar."

"Roger that Captain. How many people do you have on board?"

"It's myself and a sternman"

"Captain, that's yourself and a crewmember?"

"Roger that."

"Captain do you have heat and power at this time?"

"Oh, yeah. We're fine." Trying to sound cheerful, "Just need a tow if you could get a cutter over to us." There was a moment where Mordecai heard hope in Wolf's voice for a discreet end to this debacle. Several quiet minutes passed. Mordecai heard a thrumming sound and opened the wheelhouse door to peer out. He looked up in time to see lights streak a short distance above the stricken vessel. A thunderous roar bellowed as the flying machine passed over. The lights in the sky flew a short distance away. Mordecai watched the lights turn in the sky half a mile away and re-approached the *Desire* to hover about 50 feet above the ice alongside the boat. Mordecai saw the distinct orange and white color pattern of a Coast Guard, Jayhawk helicopter. A brilliant white light shone down from the Jayhawk and illuminated the scene. Excited, Mordecai yelled over the deafening roar, "Wolf! It's a helicopter!" Mordecai saw Wolf's posture slump again.

"I didn't think it was the Hale Bop Mother Ship, Mordecai." Wolf, head in his hands muttered, "Fuckin' *Jonah*" The radio crackled again.

"*Desire, Desire.* This is Coast Guard helicopter pilot. Come back on 16"

"Oh Jesus fucking Christ" Wolf moaned, "So much for discreet." He reached for the mic.

"This is *Desire* on channel 16."

"Captain, what are your intentions at this time?"

"Well, we got the generator running, got heat, power. I guess we'll just sit here till the tide comes in. Can't do much till then."

"Roger that Captain." There was a silence from the radio. Then, "Captain there is no way of telling whether the boat will right or fill with water when the tide comes in. We advise you and your crewman put your survival suits on and be evacuated."

"I'm staying with the boat." Wolf returned. Mordecai however, had dug out a survival suit from the pile of items against the bulkhead. He was busy putting it on when looking at him, Wolf said into the mic, "But it looks like my guy wants to come off."

"Could you repeat that Captain?"

"We have one man being evacuated."

"Roger that Captain. We're lowering a basket…." Mordecai didn't hear the rest having stepped through the wheelhouse door. Mordecai tried to balance outside without falling in the water. The powerful sound of the helicopter's rotor blades reverberated off the frozen seascape, and the gusts it created kicked up particles of ice that stung Mordecai's face. Mordecai quickly learned that his survival suit, or immersion suit, was like an oversized wetsuit that covered him from head to toe in rubber. He struggled with the thick rubber of the cumbersome suit. Mordecai knew Wolf was arguing to stay with the boat, so he headed out to the back deck, where he would be visible to the pilot.

But the helicopter didn't move. Wolf stuck his head out the wheelhouse door. "If you want a ride home, you got to stuff those loose net tarps in the fish hold. The pilot said they might be sucked up into the blades when they hover over the boat." And quickly shut the wheelhouse door. Mordecai stuffed the tarps into the fish hold, The restrictive rubber of the survival suit resisting efforts. *Considering how our luck is going*, he thought sourly, *that would be a fitting end to this fiasco. "Hey, Wolf, you get to stay with the boat now 'cause our ride home just crashed through the ice in a ball of flames. Does this make me the Jonah?"* When the deck was clear, the helicopter lowered a basket onto the ice a few feet from Mordecai. Mordecai decided this meant he had to go to the basket, and began to climb over the rail.

"No, you idiot!" Wolf yelled from the wheelhouse door. "The spinning rotors give off a static charge that needs to be grounded. They'll bring the basket to you." and shut the wheelhouse door again. The helicopter hovered the basket over to the rail and Mordecai climbed in. On the first attempt to lift him up, the cable that supported the basket caught on the mast. The crewman who was working the winch on the helicopter lowered the basket down again, then suddenly,hauled it back. Looking up, Mordecai saw that Wolf, wearing his survival suit, was guiding the cable by the mast. *Apparently, he's decided to join me for the ride home.*

The noise inside the helicopter was loud with the door open. Mordecai was winched into the helicopter and a Coast Guardsman helped him out of the basket and into a seat as the basket was lowered back down. The Coast Guardsman yelled into Mordecai's ear, "Are you all right?" Mordecai nodded. "Are you the Captain?" Mordecai shook his head. The winch hauled the basket back into the helicopter and Wolf climbed out of it refusing help from the assisting Coast Guardsman. Wolf sat down next to Mordecai as the Guardsman working the winch shut the door. The roar of the engine diminished with the door shut and Mordecai looked at the two Guardsmen. Wolf sat with his head propped in his hands.

"So." Mordecai offered. "You guys do this all the time?"

"Shut up" Wolf said without moving. "Don't talk."

The Coast Guardsmen dropped them off at Plymouth Airport, and Bob came to pick them up; it was a long, quiet ride back to Scituate.

When Mordecai arrived back at the bar for his truck, he decided to grab a quick beer. He approached a group of fishermen who were watching TV, and in the middle of them, looking higher than a lab rat, was Flip. "And here he is!" announced Flip.

"Man, you won't believe the night I just had," Mordecai said. His comment was met with uproarious laughter from the group.

"You were just on the eleven o'clock news," laughed Flip. The Coast Guard had filmed the entire rescue. Now everyone wanted to hear the story, and beers piled up on the bar.

Chapter 7
Haul Out

Wolf and Mordecai drove to the Plymouth town pier the next day to consider options for getting the boat back. A swarm of reporters pressed Wolf for details about the now overly dramatized rescue. The *Desire* had righted herself on the incoming tide and sat stuck in the mud. Because of the scrutiny of the press, Mordecai figured Wolf must feel like the sober guy who slips on the sidewalk and lands flat on his back, right in front of a bar on a busy street, where everyone was watching.

Another Scituate fisherman, Danny Zephyr, whose operation was more like a floating party, offered to meet Wolf at the Plymouth town pier to help pull the *Desire* off the mud flat. The Coast Guard had dispatched an ice-breaker, and the outgoing tide carried the chunks of ice out of the harbor. Danny had no problem steaming right up to the pier, and Wolf and Mordecai climbed aboard Danny's *Hillary Rose*.

Music blared, and Danny's coked-out cronies and a couple of girls sat amid a collection of beer bottles. At a table in the wheelhouse, Mordecai saw a guy cutting lines of cocaine on a mirror; others passed a joint. In the middle of it all, with a euphoric grin on his face, was Flip. "Hey, dude, you looked kinda cute on TV in that big red Gumby suit." He laughed as he handed Mordecai the joint.

Mordecai smiled as he considered the way that these guys went through life—as if it was a video game handled with a buzz on. Helping out Wolf seemed to just add some amusement to the afternoon of partying. Mordecai accepted a beer that was offered to him but politely declined the offer to do a few lines of cocaine. He laughed when he saw Danny's riding sail—it was stenciled with a giant Jolly Roger—and even Wolf managed to crack a smile and joke about his predicament as they steamed over to his stuck-in-the-mud boat.

"Looks like you ran out of water." Danny offered.

"Must have forgotten to pay the bill." Wolf returned

Danny pulled right up alongside the *Desire*, and Wolf and Mordecai climbed aboard her. "I see Flip getting a tow line ready. Get up on the bow and catch it when he throws it too you." It was all business as Wolf immediately transformed back to the ogre. "Hurry up!" Flip threw Mordecai a towline from the stern of the *Hillary Rose* and Mordecai put the loop end on the bow stem. Flip tied off the other end to a cleat on the steel A frame on the stern of Danny's dragger. The *Hillary Rose* idled forward until the slack in the line became taut. "Get off the bow, you idiot!" Wolf yelled. "That line snaps it'll cut you in half!" So Mordecai felt disappointed as he scurried over the overhead and dropped down onto the back deck of the *Desire.* He wanted to be helpful, and returned to feeling foolish. The *Hillary Rose* sent a dark cloud of diesel smoke into the air as Mordecai heard its Detroit diesel engine wailing from the stack. Wolf also buried his throttle deep in the pocket. But neither boat made any progress forward. Mordecai walked into the wheelhouse pensive, knowing Wolf would be stressing, but he wanted to see the action going on in front of the boat. Salt water popped out of the stretching tow line as the two boats ran full throttle. The *Desire* sat like an anchor, refusing to budge. Danny weaved his boat back and forth, trying to wrestle the *Desire* from the mud. "Danny's not afraid to put the coals to it." Wolf announced. "Lot of guys would be afraid to do that for somebody else." Wolf looked at Mordecai and Mordecai could see he was impressed. "Afraid they'd blow the motor." Wolf turned back to the wheel. "Not Danny. He's a real fisherman".

Still, the two boats made no progress forward. Wolf shook his head and looked at the temperature gauge on the instrument panel. "C'mon, c'mon you pig", Wolf growled. Mordecai had no idea what they would do if this didn't work. Wolf flipped open a tide chart on the dash. "It's still a couple minutes before high tide. We might still get a little more water in here to work with us." The engines of the two boats continued emitting a deafening racket, and again steam came from the engine room of the *Desire.* Danny continued working the wheel of his 55 Bruno dragger, weaving back in forth before Wolf and Mordecai. Danny wasn't afraid to risk his motor; Wolf was leaving his in the pocket too. Mordecai was certain a blown motor on either of the two boats would be the end of this effort. Then he realized the expense a blown motor would be to Wolf; in time lost fishing and the cost of rebuilding. Mordecai stumbled backward and slammed into the wheelhouse door as the *Desire* gave a sudden lurch. The two boats powered forward. Mordecai saw Wolf pull himself up from the floor of the wheelhouse and quickly reach for his throttle. Danny had already backed off his throttle as Wolf reached for his. The *Desire* was hurtling towards the stern of the *Hillary Rose* and the tow line was slackening and passing beneath the *Desire*. "Fuck!" Wolf exclaimed as he cut the wheel in a frantic effort to avoid smashing into his rescuer. Mordecai looked out the windows of the wheelhouse to see Flip race out on the back deck of Danny's boat. "Get that loop off the bow stem!" Wolf yelled. "We get that in the wheel we're screwed." The wheel cut hard to port, the *Desire* passed just a few feet from the stern of the *Hillary Rose* as Mordecai made his way to the bow. He pulled the loop from the bow stem and tossed it to Flip on the stern of the *Hillary Rose.* Mordecai saw Flip get soaked as he rapidly worked the line from the water hand over hand, the wet rope dousing his jeans as he pulled.

Freed from the mud, the *Desire* made her way to her original destination of Brewer Marine as the *Hillary Rose* curled away in a turn towards the mouth of the harbor. When the *Desire* pulled into a slip at the marina, reporters swarmed onto the pier. Wolf hit a switch that shut off the bilge pumps. "There's gonna be fuel in the bilge that leaked out of the tanks while this thing was lying on its side. Don't need fuel all over the harbor in front of these media seagulls." Wolf looked at Mordecai. "Then we'd really be fucked. The fines are huge." Wolf looked up at the camera lights on the pier. "We'll make like we're leaving then come back." Under the glare of camera lights and reporters, Wolf showed no urge to return to the boat. "Captain, were you afraid for your life?" The questions came as reporters pressed around the two men trying to make their way to a pick up truck where Wolfs' father waited. Wolf managed what Mordecai felt was his best approximation of a smile.

"No, it was just a simple accident. Probably happens all the time." Wolf offered as he pushed through. Climbing into the center of the pick ups' bench seat, Mordecai said, "No one asked me if I was scared."

"That's because nobody cares Mordecai." Wolf snapped as he slammed the truck door shut.

"What are we doing?" Wolfs' father stated more than asked.

"Lets' just go home." Wolf answered in a defeated tone.

The next day, there was a fire in New Bedford, and the *Desire* was old news as it was raised out of the water by a large crane and set on blocks and stanchions in a parking lot.

Mordecai soon realized that there was a long list of things to do when a boat was hauled out, aside from the major repairs or additions. Zinc blocks needed to be changed; the bottom needed to be scraped and painted; rope, mesh, and other items need to be cleared from the wheel; and there was also a general inspection of the hull. It was while Mordecai was painting the hull that he noticed a man looking up at the *Desire*. He was thin and gaunt, and the lines in his face made it seem like cracked leather. He was wearing an old plaid wool shirt, and on his head was a faded and frayed ball cap. He stood staring up at the boat without saying a word. After a somewhat awkward moment of silence, Mordecai asked if he was looking for Wolf. The stranger eyed Mordecai slowly, although he seemed to look right through him. He took a pack of cigarettes out of his shirt pocket, lit one and held it between fingers that shook slightly. He looked at Mordecai. "You work on this boat?" he asked. His look sent a chill down Mordecai's spine, and Mordecai was suddenly and inexplicably afraid to admit that he did. All he could manage was a nod. Again there was a silence. After a moment, the stranger said, "Last time I ever went to sea was on this boat. That was December, 1981, and it was the *Sea Roamer*, captained by Arthur Davey. I was part of a three-man crew fishing some sixty miles east of Cape Cod." He paused and licked his lips as though his mouth had become dry. Mordecai waited for the man to continue. He felt something dreadful held him in an icy grip. "The weather forecast had been wrong," the stranger said, "calling for two separate low-pressure fronts, twelve to eighteen hours apart, but they both came together and settled right on top of us. The seas grew, wind blowin' around seventy. At first, we decided to ride it out but then realized that heading home was our best option." He drew a breath and exhaled slowly. “The other sternman and I got the fish put away in the hold, and then we got in our bunks for the ride home. Then there was this sudden, tremendous crack, and sea water just poured over us. Topside, we found most of the wheelhouse torn away, and the captain knocked unconscious, with several bad gashes on his head and most of his right ear torn off.” He looked hard at Mordecai. “You hearing what I’m saying? A rogue wave smashed through the wheelhouse, flooded the boat, and knocked out all the navigational instrumentation, the radio, and the steering station.” He put his hands on his hips as he stared at the boat. “We tried unsuccessfully to revive the captain—amid all that blood, seawater, broken glass, and wreckage. We thought he was dead. Then, as we discussed our options, the motor sputtered and quit.” The stranger took a long haul on the cigarette. “Without power, we figured we’d get ‘side to’ in that sea and get swamped, so we prepared to abandon ship. We were soaking wet and trying’ to get the survival suits on ourselves and Arty—that’s what we called the captain—and trying to deploy the life raft. We threw the rest of the food and flares into the life raft, not knowing how long we would be in it. The emergency position indicator radio beacon had been torn away when the wave hit, and the radio was gone. There was no way to communicate with anyone. The life raft was tethered to the floating wreck by a long nylon cord, but getting the captain’s limp body into the raft was just about impossible. We were getting slammed by better than twenty-five-foot seas.” He made an up-and-down motion with his arms. “The slightest slip, and we could’ve lost Arty. So we decided to wait to abandon ship. But then the nylon cord that tethered the raft broke free, and the raft, the flares, and the rest of the food were gone in an instant. There was no choice but to keep the wreck afloat. We grabbed a five-gallon bucket and bailed out the flooded engine room. One of us scooped water and passed it to the other, who dumped it overboard.” He flailed his arms again, showing how he’d worked. “The work was tiring, but it kept us warm.” He paused and looked at the boat with haunted eyes. “After a long night, we got her emptied out. In the early morning light, we started trying to hot-wire the dead motor—the ignition had been torn away with the wheelhouse. We weren’t having much luck, but then, suddenly, Arty came to and started directing what to put where—and then he lost consciousness again.

We couldn't believe it when the big Caterpillar rumbled to life. We felt like we'd been sent a blessing, but still, there was no way to tell which direction we were heading. Clouds completely obscured the sun. We put a Stillson wrench on the rudder post and steered her by holding on to the wrench and directing the rudder. We assumed the wind was out of the northeast, so we began heading in the direction we believed to be west. But the wind had actually shifted to the northwest, so we actually were heading in the wrong direction. On the fourth day, we were spotted by a Coast Guard Albatross search plane. The Coast Guardsmen dropped a bright orange package to us with a radio, flares, and some yellow dye, along with a note advising us of our position and directing us toward a rendezvous with a Coast Guard cutter. The note also asked if we required a medevac. I lit a red flare to signal that we did. Later, a Coast Guard helicopter delivered more supplies and a pump, and then lifted Captain Davey to safety. When the helicopter left, we could see the lights of the cutter way off in the distance, but we still weren't out of the woods." He laughed nervously, as if even now he couldn't believe it. Tears formed in his eyes. "I spotted a red glow under the dashboard and smelled smoke—it was an electrical fire. We were so close to rescue, yet now the boat was burning." He wiped his forehead with his shirtsleeve and squinted up into the bright sunlight. "We shut the engine down and sprayed the burning wires with fire extinguishers. I never thought that engine would start again. But, miraculously, it did and we continued. Two more long hours later, we were taken aboard the cutter, and the wreck began the tow home."

Mordecai stared at the tray of red paint and pushed the roller brush in the paint until little swells formed. When he turned to ask the stranger what happened after that, the man was gone.

"Hey, you done with that yet, or are you gonna milk it all day?" Wolf yelled as he came down the ladder.

"Hey, Wolf, you won't believe the story I just heard. One of the guys from the *Sea Roamer* was just here."

"Dude, I didn't see anyone," said Flip from topside.

"He was just here!"

"Yeah, maybe he was the Jonah on that trip, and you two can compare notes sometime—after you finish painting the hull! Now get your ass going!" Wolf stormed away.

Most sane people would walk away while they still could, Mordecai thought. But then he scolded himself. *A quitter would. That's why they're called quitters. They won't know the glory or the money.* Then he reversed his own position again. *But why do I need to be his whipping boy to make money?* Answering himself once more, he thought, *Oh, did he hurt your feelings? You pussy. Maybe you're just scared. Maybe you're not tough enough for this, like Flip.*

"Don't let him get to ya, man," said Flip from topside. "There's nothin' to go back to in Scituate, and Wolf's gonna' make us rich. You'll be happy when we start making money."

"Yeah, I guess. I just got a little freaked out by that guy's story."

"What guy?"

Chapter 8
Steam South

The boat had been "splashed" back into the water, outfitted with keel coolers, new zincs, bottom paint, and myriad odds and ends. The only element missing was Flip. The weather was perfect for the journey south—light southwest winds; unseasonably warm; sunny skies. The *Desire* rolled lazily back and forth on a gentle swell as it headed through the bay for the Cape Cod Canal. Mordecai stood on the aft deck alone, watching the shoreline slip by. He was feeling adventurous but that feeling was tempered by a small pang of anxiety. They were underway. He basked in the rays of the winter sun's light a few minutes longer, thinking about a day when Flip had taken him out mossing in his skiff—just two boys out on a boat. He let that day grow in his memory, loving the way the sun reflected off the water; how they were working, like grown men.

But that memory was of a time when moss was still harvested by hand. By the early 1990s, foreign producers farmed the moss at a price with which the local mossing business in Scituate couldn't compete, and life was a lot different for both Flip and Mordecai. Now, he was on his own, and Flip had let him down. Like time and tide, Wolf waited for no man, and when Flip hadn't shown up at the pier, Wolf decided to take Chavez Jarvis, a recovering crack addict who had lost all his teeth to the habit. Chavez meant well—he had some experience with gill netting and was enthusiastic about the trip—but something about him irritated Mordecai. He couldn't move quickly around the boat, as he had bad hips, which he said was a war injury from Vietnam. Chavez talked constantly and told tall tales. If he were to be believed, he'd been everywhere and done everything, although money flowed around Chavez the way the tide flowed over a bank. Still, Chavez was just a bump in its path. It didn't matter how much he made; he was always broke and homeless and sleeping in the back of cars or on fishing boats. More important—at least to Mordecai's mind—he wasn't Flip. Mordecai had looked forward to an adventure with Flip, but Flip had chosen something else.

When he went topside to the helm, Mordecai found Wolf sitting in the big captain's chair, which actually was a car seat taken from a Cadillac. Chavez was talking.

"I got a Chevy truck."

"Really." Wolf returned in a flat tone. Mordecai could see Wolf needing a well-received break from Chavez's stories. Were it not for Chavez, the wheelhouse would have been quiet and dark, except for the green glow that emanated from the radar screen and the hum from the Cat. Wolf's eyes showed the weight of the last week.

"Yup. Monster truck, with a four-fity-four. You should've seen the pussy jumping in that thing when I was lighting up all four tires on Hollywood Boulevard."

"Where's the truck now?" Mordecai had to ask. Wolf looked at Mordecai with a fatigued and irritated glare, his eyes saying, *Why would you care? He's full of shit, don't encourage him, I need a break.*

They were in Buzzard's Bay, east of the historic fishing port of New Bedford and bound for the next waypoint on the course, Block Island. "You gonna take the watch?" asked Wolf as he got up from the comfortable chair. "Wake me up if we have to go around anything."

"I can handle it," Mordecai replied.

"Just don't hit nothing," said Wolf.

"I drove an oil-tanker on the west coast." Chavez began.

"I can't talk now, Chavez." Mordecai made like he was busy watching the radar though there was nothing on the screen. "I got to pay attention here."

"Well just come get me if you get confused. I've forgotten more about seafaring than most will ever know."

"Ok, Chavez. I'll remember that. But I've got it under control for now." Chavez went forward to his bunk and Mordecai breathed a sigh of relief.

Sliding into the captain's chair and surveying his instrumentation, Mordecai felt like Neptune, the god of the sea. For the moment, he was master of his destiny, and he guided the vessel toward the bounty that awaited. In actuality, he wasn't guiding anything. The autopilot navigational computer ran the boat along the coordinates that Wolf had preset. Mordecai's job was simply to watch the radar for ships that might be running in their path. It seemed as easy as watching television.

The first hour was uneventful— just darkness, a gentle roll, and the constant thrumming of Caterpillar diesel power vibrating through everything. The few blips on the radar screen were of distant fishing boats scattered across the ocean. Through the wheelhouse windows, Mordecai could see their lights pitched against the inky blackness, like the stars in the night sky, and he could relate their position to the screen. The chatter of other fishermen on the radio kept him company—the overnighters brooding over regulations, light banter, and periodic laughter. It was typical of late-night fishing. It seemed to Mordecai that there must have been at least six different boats taking part in the conversation, and the guys seemed to know each other pretty well.

Far off in the distance, Mordecai could see the running lights of what was a considerably large blip on the very edge of the radar screen. Five miles away and churning northward at 15 to 20 knots was a 5,000-horsepower tugboat, pushing a three-hundred–foot barge. The object was moving toward the *Desire*, but Mordecai ignored Wolf's request to wake him up and instead, he turned the boat east himself to give the other vessel a little more room. What he did not realize, however, was that in a shipping lane, traffic stays to the right, just like cars on the road. Mordecai watched with growing uneasiness as the blip on the radar headed right at him.

At three miles' distance from the rapidly oncoming vessel, he turned more to the east, and when the vessel was two miles from him, he turned even more. Nothing he did took the much smaller *Desire* from the path of this beast—a tanker—which surely would slam through the *Desire*'s steel hull, crushing it like a beer can as she rolled beneath the larger vessel and entombing the crew as she plunged to the bottom. He tried to relax and figure out how to evade its path, the bow of which now loomed one mile away and which still was lined up dead center for a collision.

Mordecai turned more to the east, stymied that they could still be on a collision course. Half a mile became a quarter and then, the blips on the radar were married together in a deadly embrace. The two vessels were so close now that the radar could not distinguish between the two. The monstrous bow of the steel behemoth loomed in the darkness to starboard. Peering anxiously through the wheelhouse windows, Mordecai could see the white froth of the sea kicked up across its bow and enormous anchors just below the bow rail. The giant was right on top of the *Desire*—and then Wolf bolted into the wheelhouse. He saw the giant bow that was about to crush them, and he pushed Mordecai aside and grabbed the controls, burying the throttle deep in the pocket. The big Caterpillar diesel whined as the turbo charger fed extra horsepower to the churning propeller. A bright searchlight from the tanker illuminated everything in the wheelhouse.

"What the fuck!" Wolf at Mordecai. "You cut right across their bow!"

Mordecai's heart raced in terror. He could only mumble, "Are we gonna make it?"

Wolf sighed heavily and gritted his teeth. "I don't know." The big Cat growled as it pushed the *Desire* along at a greater clip. They were so close now that the searchlight from the giant bow above them could not angle down onto the smaller boat, and the wake from the bow pushed the *Desire* aside. Steel screeched and sparks flew as the hulls of the two vessels scraped each other. When the *Desire* had scraped her way three-quarters of the way down the hull of the tanker, the vessels separated. As the tanker passed, the searchlight came back around to bear on the *Desire*, and again the wheelhouse was bathed in brilliant light. Mordecai inhaled deeply and then slowly expelled his breath. They were alive and unhurt, but Wolf was livid. "I guess I can't even try to get any sleep, huh?" Wolf exclaimed. He went down below to check the inside of the hull for damage. Along the starboard rail and along the length of the boat was the glisten of freshly exposed steel.

"All you had to do is ask me." Chavez exclaimed waving his hands. Mordecai was caught between hating himself for becoming the biggest fool on the boat and thanking God that he was alive. Mordecai quietly thanked God that he was alive. He stepped out onto the deck and sucked the cold night air deep into his lungs. In the distance, the lights of Block Island twinkled in the darkness. In a moment of weakness, Mordecai wished for the sanctity of dry land.

Chapter 9
Atlantic City

We may find it, out on the streets, tonight, baby
Or we may walk, until the morning light, maybe.

—Bruce Springsteen, "Incident on 57th Street"

Mordecai didn't think he'd be allowed to take another watch for the rest of the trip, but splitting the watches between two guys meant less downtime in between, so the next day found him back in the captain's chair as they cruised off the coast of New York and New Jersey. Large container ships littered the radar screen, with the traffic of commerce between New York's busy harbor and the rest of the world, but none was as threatening as the night before. The day slipped by uneventfully, and Mordecai spent long stretches of time alone, when not on watch, sitting on the pile of nets in the stern. Chavez chattered at Wolf until finally, Wolf got away from him by going to the engine room, where it was too loud for conversation. Then Chavez joined Mordecai on the net pile in the stern.

"I hope you can keep up. I want to make some money." Chavez said.

"Me too." Mordecai answered. He endured the litany of one-sided stories, as much to take some of the load off Wolf, on whose guidance they all depended, as to provide some compassion for Chavez.

"I was on the off-shore boats during the big Pollack runs of the eighties." Chavez volunteered. Mordecai just nodded and sensed a desperate loneliness in Chavez. "I'd pick, cut, gut and gill thirty thousand every day."

"Wow." Mordecai returned with an empty expression. "You must have made a lot of money."

"Fucking right I did."

"What did you do with it all?" Mordecai looked at Chavez wondering what the answer could be. Chavez looked at Mordecai and for a rare moment, was speechless. It was cold and damp on the stern. Mordecai wore his oilskins over layers of wool, but Chavez wore only jeans and a sweatshirt.

"Fuckin' cold out here." Chavez said pulling his hood over his head and returned to the heated wheelhouse.

That night, Wolf woke Mordecai to take another watch around eleven o'clock.

"I've set the autopilot for Atlantic City. We're gonna need fuel when we get there. I want you to wake me up when we get five miles outside the harbor." He emphasized each word of "wake me up" with a jab of his index finger into Mordecai's chest.

Mordecai nestled in for the watch to Atlantic City. The autopilot showed there were three hours remaining to the waypoint. The fog ahead was thick, but the radar screen clear. Far off in the distance, Mordecai could see the lights of Atlantic City reflecting off the night sky.

They arrived at the harbor entrance at two a.m., enshrouded in a blanket of fog so thick that even the bow was invisible. The searchlight couldn't penetrate more than a few feet, which left Wolf to navigate by the charts, Loran position indicator, and radar. The only evidence that there might be a city was the light in the sky above. Standing on the overhead as a lookout, Mordecai peered into the fog that hung like cotton gauze, trying to make out anything. Wolf was stressed out over being in a strange harbor and not being able to see. Mordecai knew that running aground in Plymouth was still fresh in Wolf's mind. Suddenly, light pierced the fog as a fishing boat, lit by dozens of deck lights, steamed slowly by and then was again swallowed by fog. As the *Desire* continued ahead slowly, the fog seemed to lift slightly, and Mordecai could make out the outline of a dock directly ahead. He pounded on the overhead and twisted the searchlight so it shone on the dock, illuminating where they could tie up. Wolf pulled alongside the dock with a maneuver as smooth as silk. Mordecai and Chavez tied her up and all three disembarked to explore this new harbor—and the city of roulette wheels and blackjack tables.

"I bet ya five hundred bucks I'll run into some broads I know here" Chavez volunteered. Wolf and Mordecai exchanged looks.

"I understand this place is open all night. Maybe we can get something to eat," Mordecai said as they made their way along a deserted slip intended for summer pleasure-boaters. The fog had lifted enough that Mordecai could see that they had tied up right across a street from an enormous casino. Looking back toward the marina, however, the boat was completely obscured.

"Just don't get lost if we split up. I want to fuel and get outta here at sunrise." Wolf warned. "And don't get drunk!" he added, the afterthought making Mordecai wish Flip had been there to explore this place with him.

Walking through a casino in his fishing boots, beneath the flashy lights and mirrors, Mordecai felt out of place. Still, the human condition in Atlantic City was amusing at best but mostly depressing. The few people who were in the casino seemed like hangers-on at a party that had ended. Vacuum cleaners hummed busily, adding to the cacophony of bells and whistles from slot machines. Mordecai watched the roulette wheel for a while and had a couple free cocktails that were served at the tables. Despite the outward elegance of the casino, he decided that the patrons looked like bored, working-class folk who probably were hoping for that one big hit that would save them from their dull existence. It suddenly occurred to Mordecai that fishing made him no different than the folks around him. He had come to that casino in a gamble—although for a modest amount of money—but at stake was his life. He wanted out of that casino.

Once he walked outside, he realized that he had no idea where he was. The fog had lifted to reveal a damp January night in Atlantic City. Bright neon signs spilling showers of light announced the Taj Mahal or the Sands Casino. He wandered down the street, walking nowhere in particular but in no hurry to return to the confines of the boat.

The city was quiet, except for the occasional sound of a car splashing along the wet streets, and the neighborhoods looked more than a little uninviting. He made his way along a darkened street and heard the echo of surf pounding on a beach in the distance. The glow he'd obtained from the alcohol he had consumed earlier was wearing off. He turned down a dark alleyway, heading toward the sound of surf. In the alley, he saw a guy wearing fishing boots who was handing money to someone shadowed in a doorway. The person in the doorway was in silhouette, but Mordecai could see that the guy in the boots stuffed something in his pocket and started down the street. Mordecai thought about following him, thinking he was probably headed for where the fishing boats were in the harbor, but he soon decided that he didn't like the looks of the direction where the guy was headed. Instead, he followed the sound of surf and, with a sense of relief, found the beach.

The sun crept up and lit the horizon with a pink glow as Mordecai walked on the beach. Waves struck lightly at the sand with a gentle hiss, and great dunes hunched like massive sleeping dogs, guarding the city against the sea.

The placid morning turned as Mordecai thought of Wolf and how livid he would be if his crew wasn't there for fueling the boat. *He just wants us back in shackles for the rest of the journey so we don't discover we value our freedom over our jobs*, Mordecai thought morosely.

In the early light of dawn, Mordecai saw the casino he'd visited and thought the boat was moored behind it. He decided to walk through the building, rather than walk around it—his legs were tired from slogging through beach sand—and he found the inside of the casino as brilliantly lit as ever. He went up and down escalators, trying to find an exit, but he kept going from room to room with more machines, tables, and bars. Exhaustion set in as he realized that this place was designed to keep people in, and he felt as lost as he could have. It was then he heard a sound from behind him, like the rattle of loose change in a cup. Chavez limped along with a plastic cup full of quarters, collected from a night at the slot machines.

"Hey, Mordy, where ya been? Ya make any money? I'm on a roll." He delivered his toothless smile.

Mordecai was surprised by the realization that he was actually happy to see Chavez. The man's constant jabbering had been annoying for most of the time on the boat, but now Mordecai felt like he had found a long-lost brother. "Naw, I've just been exploring. Hey, Chavez, you heading back to the boat?"

"Yeah, I guess so."

"I'll go with you," Mordecai said casually.

Chavez wasn't lost at all and the sun was climbing above the horizon and the murky cloud cover as Mordecai followed him, hobbling out of the casino and over to the marina dock where the boat was moored. Chavez's cup of change jingled every step of the way.

Wolf stood in the wheelhouse, going over some charts. "Well, well, if it isn't my wayward sternmen. I bet you two had a good night."

"It was okay," Mordecai mumbled, "although I'd have preferred a shower."

"There's a bathhouse over there," said Wolf, motioning out the wheelhouse window.

Mordecai grabbed a towel from his duffel bag and bolted out across the wooden docks to the bathhouse. A security guard was checking the doors and examining the locks—the place clearly wasn't open. But Mordecai approached him and said, "Say, do you think you could let me in there just long enough to get a hot shower?"

The guard looked at Mordecai's boots. "You're a fisherman, huh? We just had a crew of you guys in lock-up. I'm not authorized to let you in here. And judging by that last crew that came through, it doesn't look like we need any more of your type." He locked the door and then said smugly, as one who preferred to be alone with his laughter, "Give it up, kid. I know your type, and I know you're not looking to get clean here."

Chapter 10
Ocean City

Mordecai was confused by the security guard's reaction, and he wondered if Flip had run into a problem similar to the one the guard had described. Had something happened on shore that had led to his not being on the boat? Mordecai was familiar with the lesson of Huck Finn, that the water was sanctuary and shore was where trouble arises. The boat was running by the time Mordecai returned, and Wolf and Chavez were ready to get fuel. He stuffed his towel back in the duffel bag and went topside to untie the stern lines, as Chavez let go of the bow lines. The *Desire* steamed over to the fuel dock, where they topped off their tanks and then threw off their lines for the final leg of the journey.

The dense fog that had enshrouded the town on the previous night made for a drizzly, gray day. Mordecai watched the shoreline slip past as they steamed toward the mouth of the harbor for the open sea. The casinos and hotels along the beach, like the regurgitation of society, sat guarded by the massive dunes and just beyond the purging element of sea.

"I guess the city does sleep," Mordecai said. "Looks pretty quiet right now."

"Working people sleep," said Chavez. "The hucksters are just waiting for the festival to start again"

"Festival?"

"The festival of losers seeking what they don't have," Chavez retorted. Mordecai wondered if anyone in the city noticed the early morning light on the beaches or the harmony of the shore birds that combed the sand and surf in a timeless foraging effort.

"Maybe the people are asleep to the beauty of the natural order, like time and tide," Mordecai thought out loud. Wolf and Chavez looked at him as if they had just sniffed a sewer.

"Great," Chavez sneered. "We got a fuckin' philosopher on board."

"That place needs a tidal-wave enema," Wolf said, turning to look back at Atlantic City. Then his jaw dropped, and Mordecai looked back to see two smaller boats, with blue lights flashing, racing toward them from the inner harbor. As the *Desire* steamed slowly along, the smaller boats rapidly closed the distance between them.

"What the hell did you guys get into last night?" Wolf asked. "Are they looking for one or both of you?" Chavez and Mordecai swore they'd been on their best behavior the night before. "Well, they don't look like they're comin' out for a romantic view of time and tide!" exclaimed Wolf. The maritime authorities made no attempt to hail *Desire* on the radio and instead, sat grim-faced at the helm of their police boats. Wolf grabbed the radio and hailed them. "Fishing vessel *Desire* calling the boat off my stern on channel sixteen."

"This is the Atlantic City harbormaster. How can I help you, Captain?"

"Yeah … uh … are you coming after me?"

"We're just going to the mouth of the harbor with you, Captain."

"That's pretty weird." Wolf said hanging up the radio mike. "They just came out to give us a farewell escort? We don't need a fuckin' parade." At the mouth of the harbor, the escorts peeled away and headed back in the other direction. Mordecai thought it seemed like someone wanted to make sure they left.

The next eight hours passed uneventfully. The seas were calm as they steamed south along the Jersey coast, past the tip of Cape May and the Delaware Bay, to the southern end of the Delmarva Peninsula, the geographic term for the eastern shore counties of Maryland, the state of Delaware, and two counties of Virginia, which extend down the Atlantic seaboard. The three men spent most of the day alternating watches and going through gear, checking knots on end lines, and splicing in new line where needed. Wolf and Mordecai said little, but Chavez wasn't quiet for long. "I fished the big boats when I got back from 'Nam, but left cuz I was making so much money touring with the Rolling Stones." Chavez was standing in the open hatch to the wheelhouse. It was his watch, Mordecai and Wolf were working on gear. "Being a Hell's Angel, I had the gang's commitment to the band." Mick wanted me to write songs with him, but I was busy partying with Keith. He's more my kinda' guy. Know what I mean?"

"How's it looking up there, Chavez?" Mordecai asked looking for a break. "Radar clear?"

"Relax Mordecai." Chavez flashed his gums. "We ain't gonna hit no tugs on my watch." Mordecai wished for earplugs. He wondered how Wolf took it so well and then saw the wads of paper towel stuffed in his ears.

It was late afternoon when the *Desire* entered the harbor of her destination. Ocean City Harbor was far different from Scituate, where the fishing fleet intermingled with the pleasure boaters. The western harbor was entirely commercial and industrialized fishing. Two-hundred–foot steel sea clam boats unloaded their catch at bustling docks that thrived with the hum of heavy industry. Large trucks backed into loading bays, as giant cranes hoisted steel cages full of clams off the boats. Blue-white flashes of welders' torches contrasted sharply with the grayness of the afternoon, as the roar of diesel engines emanated from all sides. They slipped past this scene, moving toward the back of the harbor where they hoped to find a place to tie up. Mordecai felt like a speck of dust entering a giant whirling machine.

Toward the back of the harbor was a wooden building with a deck over the water and illuminated signs of beer logos. Atop the roof, a sign read "Harborside Bar and Grill." Just beyond the Harborside were a series of tie-up slips, packed with smaller fishing boats. The boats had hailing ports painted on the sterns of fishing towns on the East Coast. An empty slip in front of a closed fuel dock provided a berth, so the men tied up the *Desire* and went over to the Harborside. This seaside watering hole was everything a fisherman's bar should be—simple wooden floors covered with peanut shells, a jukebox, and a pool table toward the back of the bar, where Massachusetts accents and Southern drawls mixed together in the crowd of men wearing fishing boots. This was clearly the first stop for many after a long day of fishing. Mordecai ordered two beers, one for Chavez and one for himself. Standing next to Mordecai and Chavez was a guy about Mordecai's age. His long blond hair was pulled back in a ponytail, and he wore a T-shirt that read "Chatham: a quaint little drinking village with a serious fishing problem." He held a beer in one hand and a shot in the other. He turned to face Mordecai. "Say, bud, where you out of? Haven't seen you around before." He downed the shot and took a long pull of beer.

"I'm Mordecai. This is Chavez. We're on the *Desire* out of Scituate, Mass."

"Hey, I'm Tiger, with the *Decisive* out of Chatham." He extended his hand, and Mordecai and Chavez each shook hands with him. "We're practically neighbors back home. You know any of the boys from Cape Cod?" Mordecai and Chavez knew no one and Tiger introduced them to the guys on his boat and to some of the other boat crews, and these newfound friends were happy to buy beers for them—and they kept them coming.

The story for most of the guys was similar. They came from coastal communities and had signed on with boats that followed the dogfish up and down the coast, from Portsmouth, New Hampshire, to Wanchese, North Carolina. The boats they worked on were between thirty-five feet and fifty feet and served as both workplace and home for many. Some of the guys had hotel rooms, while others secured beachfront condos at off-season rates. Those who lived on the boats had the advantage of being able to quickly depart if they heard that fish were being caught to the north or the south. Some guys chased the fish this way; others waited, banking on the fish migrating south to the Carolinas for the winter and then back to the Northeast for the spring—they figured if they missed the fall run to the south, they could just stay put and catch the fish on their way north. Many took their chances, going as far south as Wanchese and negotiating the treacherous inlet, a graveyard of many ships and sailors. The enticement of Wanchese was that more fish could be caught there because, according to popular theory, that was where the fish schooled for the migration north.

The lifestyle of the rogue boat and tramp gillnetter had dawned on the mid-Atlantic fishing communities with the advent of the dogfish market. It was not long after the boats started targeting dogfish that they began following the fish up and down the coast. Ironically, the Southern fish folk didn't mind the influx of the Yankee fishermen—or if they did, they didn't show it. Fishermen in harbors like Ocean City didn't even know there was a market for dogfish until Northern fish processors approached

Southern fish dealers about unloading, packing, and trucking dogfish to their processing plants in Boston and New Bedford.

Mordecai learned that when the Northern boats first started showing up to target dogfish in the early nineties, the Southern boys got a good laugh. “Dogfish!” they’d scoffed. “What the hell you gonna do with those?” But when they saw the whirlwind of cash these yankee fishermen became, it wasn’t long before many of the Southern boats joined the effort. There were gillnetters in Ocean City, but they had never seen a net lifter—a winch powered by a hydraulic motor that hauled the net up from the sea floor. A series of hammers attached to a horizontally spinning cylinder clamped down on the lines of the gill nets, then released the net on to the picking table, where the sternmen picked out the fish. The Southern version of the gillnetter consisted of a big drum reel on the stern of the boat that the net wound around. Fish were shaken out of the net and picked out before the net wound around the drum. Before long, many of these boats were converting over to net-lifters.

The next day, Mordecai awoke on the boat to howling winds. From the sound of it, they wouldn’t be going out to set. And another day with all the nets on the boat meant another day without money. Mordecai’s head was throbbing with a hangover. The previous night had gone on until two in the morning. Now, Mordecai crawled out of his bunk, stepping carefully so he wouldn’t disturb Chavez, and climbed through the gangway to the wheelhouse. As he poured water into the coffeemaker, he noticed that a man in sunglasses was standing on the dock, looking at the *Desire*. Mordecai decided to introduce himself, so he stepped out into the sunlight, and waved at the stranger. “Hi, I’m Mordecai,” he said, offering his hand. The stranger looked at Mordecai’s outstretched hand without accepting it. “You boys all from Scituate?”

“Uh … yeah,” Mordecai said, shoving his hand in his pocket.

“You got Teddy Davis with you?” he asked. Teddy was a Scituate gillnetter who had a knack for always being in the middle of controversy.

“No, it’s me and two other guys.”

"Then I guess I won't be needing this." The stranger pulled a pistol out of his jacket pocket and stuffed it in the back of his pants. "That bastard fucked with my boat last year in New Jersey. I been wonderin' if he was gonna show up with the fleet this year."

Mordecai shifted his weight from one foot to the other. He decided that talking about Teddy wasn't a good idea and he wasn't sure he even wanted to admit to this stranger that he knew him. The smell of freshly brewed coffee wafted from the wheelhouse. "Would you like a cup of coffee?" Mordecai offered. The stranger accepted and before long the talk turned to fishing.

Later that morning, a friend of Wolf's, Fred Good, stopped by to see if they wanted to go with him to take a look at the inlet. Mordecai recognized Fred as someone he'd seen Wolf talking to at the Harborside the night before. They drove down the narrow road, past marine supply stores, cottages, and trailers, until the road joined Highway 50, which took them over the bridge to Ocean City. They came to a large rotary that led to four-lane, one-way strips that were designed for large-volume traffic of summertime vacationers. Little cyclones of windswept sand danced on the empty street through a heavily developed area of high-rise apartments, hotels, and restaurants, which sat lifeless, waiting for the summer crowds. They drove south down the strip until the pavement ended in the lot of an amusement park. Here, the beach stopped, and the inlet flowed past a breakwater. Several hundred yards away, across the inlet from where they parked, were the dunes of Assateague Island. There were a few other pickups already there, and Mordecai recognized a few men from the Harborside. Fred had said they would "take a look at it," meaning they would determine if the weather did or did not permit fishing; this was a frequent winter ritual. Ostensibly, the purpose was to determine how dangerous the inlet looked, but it usually became a morning of chewing the fat with other fishermen over coffee. Some fishermen called the beach flypaper because more often than not, no one went fishing when they "took a look at it." It was the third week of January, and Fred told them there had been many of these mornings.

"Weather just hasn't let us out, so we sit here, parked by the beach, with coffee and conversation. It's easier than fishin' but we ain't makin' money here." Fred went on to educate his friends about the inlet, and Mordecai soon learned that the inlet to Ocean City harbor was not always as it appeared. A powerful storm in 1933 formed the new inlet, and engineers used this to make it a permanent waterway, providing a convenient gateway to Atlantic fisheries. It also put Ocean City on the map. But although the entrance was marked by red and green cans, vessels that followed the markers came to the edge of treacherous shoals. With the regularly shifting sands, the inlet changed with the tide, and getting through could be a harrowing experience, particularly when an outgoing tide clashed against an incoming sea. Wind-pushed waves against the tidal current created what was referred to as the "washing machine effect." This morning, dry land looked like the safest place from which to observe this battle of wind and tide. Mordecai decided that leaving in the predawn darkness to negotiate the inlet could be the scariest part of the trip.

Fred warned them, "You want to turn north before the last can and run parallel to the beach for about a quarter-mile before turning east." Mordecai could see waves break where Fred had pointed, across the shoals on the edge of the harbor.

Later that morning, Wolf put them to work on the *Desire,* preparing the ground lines that would anchor the high-flyers to the sets. From what he learned from Fred, they'd be fishing in deeper water than Wolf had expected, and so he instructed Chavez and Mordecai to bring extra lines out of the hold and to make sure each set had enough line on it. Otherwise the high-flyer would be pulled under. Wolf handled most of the mechanical chores, like checking the engine oil, generator oil, and transmission fluid. Mordecai counted out fathoms of line with Chavez and secured the anchors for each set. It was crucial to the safety of the crew that the high-flyers be properly set up in a fashion that would allow them to go off smoothly, without catching on anything on the deck. The sternman had to stand next to the lines to throw the anchor for the end of that set. The anchor system for each set consisted of a Danforth anchor, which was the same type used by most small boats for anchoring, as well as a sixty-pound section of railroad track, about two and a half feet long. The end of the net had several fathoms of ground line between the net and the Danforth, several more fathoms of line to the piece of railroad track, and about forty fathoms to the high-flyer. This elaborate system of anchoring the net was necessary because of the sandy bottom of the mid-Atlantic. The Danforth operated by digging into the bottom when tension was applied to it. The heavy piece of railroad track prevented the high-flyer on the surface from floating up the Danforth anchor and carrying it into the net, which would create mayhem.

As they prepared the gear for setting, Mordecai tried to foresee every possible scenario where something could go wrong, like the wrong net end, or bridle, tied to the wrong ground line and taking the wrong anchor with it. The tangled lines could easily result in a trip to the bottom with the anchor for the unsuspecting stern man setting the gear. They prepared four sets of fifteen gill nets to be set—enough end lines and anchors for a crewman to become confused with the order.

The three men spent the rest of the day coiling lines out of boxes into neat piles in the stern, counting fathoms of line to make sure they were long enough, and positioning the anchors so they were arranged in a row, hanging on the rail in the stern in the order they were meant to go off. Despite all this preparation to make things go smoothly, Mordecai knew there would still be plenty of opportunity for the unexpected to happen. Chavez hadn't stopped jabbering all day; Mordecai hoped the man had put as much effort to his end of the lines as he had to his endless chattering. According to Chavez, he'd been everywhere and done everything, drank all the beers, had all the girls, and caught at least two of every fish that ever swam. *He's driving me nuts*, Mordecai thought.

Wolf was silent except when grumbling about something that might not be going the way he wanted. He was becoming more and more miserable and increasingly quiet, which Mordecai attributed to the pressure to catch fish and the fact that they had no money. They heard from other fishermen that the weather had not been very fishable this year and getting out was difficult. If an individual boat misjudged the weather, set the gear, and then was not able to get out and haul it the next day, the nets would load up with crabs that devoured whatever fish were in the net and creating the necessity of extricating them, which was a hellish procedure. Crabbed-up gear meant days of working for nothing while they got the gear fishable again. As they worked, they heard someone on the radio tell another boat that he was on his second day of picking through crabbed-up gear, and it would likely be another day of labor at least before the nets were ready to fish again. Hearing this, Wolf's eyes opened wide, and he stormed up to the wheelhouse and snapped off the volume switch for the radio. Still, the weather forecast for the next day was for winds from the northwest at ten to twenty miles per hour and diminishing. It looked like they might get out.

Chapter 11
Setting

Mordecai woke to the rumble of the big Caterpillar diesel coming to life. He and Chavez climbed from their bunks and went topside to throw off the lines. Wolf was already in the wheelhouse, going over his instrumentation and keeping a close eye on the big Cat as it warmed. At 4:00 AM, the harbor was bustling with activity. Boat crews gathered on the docks, and some boats were already underway, with powerful lights cutting through the cold of predawn darkness. Mordecai carefully made his way through the dark up to the bow on the slippery steel deck, moist from the mid-Atlantic air. He heard the sounds of preparing for a harvest—pickup trucks pulling up to boats, guys talking and laughing, diesels running. There was a tingling excitement, a positive charge on the polarity of uncertainty that electrified the air, signifying the anticipation of the catch. Although the *Desire's* nets had not yet been set, and so today would not bring a catch for them, it was the act of getting the nets in the water so that the next day might yield a catch that brought a sense of giddiness to Mordecai. He felt the energy radiating from everyone around him who participated in the ritual, a brotherhood of hunters about to forage a hostile sea in the middle of winter. *This was why I'm here*, he thought. *This is what makes fishermen professional gamblers, willing to ante up their lives against whatever fortune the ocean might—or might not—yield.* He felt alive.

Wolf rapped on the Lexan glass of the wheelhouse and signaled to throw off the bow line. Chavez let go the stern, and boat and crew were underway. Mordecai stood on the deck as they joined the procession of boats leaving the harbor. The inlet to Ocean City Harbor was calm, and they headed north before the can and ran along the beach. Wolf then turned southeast and set the autopilot for the waypoint forty miles offshore. It would take the *Desire* four hours to get there, putting their estimated time of arrival at around eight o'clock. Mordecai climbed back in his bunk for more sleep before his turn at watch came up. About an hour later, Wolf gave a rough shake of Mordecai's shoulder.

"Follow me to the wheel," Wolf ordered. "Looks like everybody's a little faster than us. Radar is clear; everyone else is up ahead. Wake up Chavez in an hour and a half."

The wind was blowing enough to make the boat roll and pitch, and Mordecai quickly realized how different this was from fishing in a bay, where Cape Ann and Cape Cod offered some protection. Here in the open ocean, winds kicked up bigger seas than he ever would have seen in Massachusetts Bay. Mordecai listened to two fishermen talking on the radio discussing the loss of a friend back home.

The pink glow on the eastern horizon—the direction in which they were headed—became the blazing ball of a rising morning sun. When the brilliant orange sphere rose half above the water, a voice on the radio cut through the ongoing conversations of fishermen keeping each other company. "Boys, would you look at that sunrise. This is beautiful."

These guys must have seen hundreds of sunrises in their fishing careers, Mordecai thought. Still, the radio went silent as the crews of more than a dozen boats silently watched the sun rise above a shimmering sea. For two of those fishermen, Mordecai was sure, that sunrise was the memory of a friend.

When his watch was up, Mordecai went below to wake Chavez, who was snoring contentedly in his bunk. Chavez snorted, kicked off his blankets, went topside, and took a leak over the side of the boat, Then he came in, burped, grabbed a bag of chips, and settled in the chair for his watch. He started to tell Mordecai about the latest girl he'd met—"With tits bigger than those of the girl on the cover of this porn mag"—but Mordecai went below, and with the drone of the big diesel emanating from deep in the bowels of the boat, Mordecai climbed back in his bunk and fell into a blissful sleep.

He was awakened by the sound of the engine throttling down. They had reached their destination and would be setting out the nets. Topside, Mordecai pulled on his oilskins as Wolf swung the boat around in several wide turns, surveying the sea bottom on the fish finder. The fish-finder sonar showed patches of red above the solid red that represented the bottom. Mordecai went out back to make one last check over the lines to see that everything was set up properly and not tipped over. The coils of rope end lines were stacked, filling the rope checkers in the stern, where Chavez and Mordecai stood when setting. The sea was choppy, with bigger swells than they had fished in at home. With the heaving sea, it was a bit of a trick just to stand in the rope checkers.

"How does it look on your side, Chavez? Are they gonna go off all right?" Mordecai asked, looking around and noticing that land was nowhere in sight.

"Did I ever tell ya about when I was the sound guy for rock 'n' roll bands?" Chavez said. "That was a complicated feat of engineering. This ain't nothin'. I'm an expert."

"I believe you, Chavez. I just want everything to go smooth."

Wolf made one last turn over the spot. He pointed the bow north and gave Mordecai the signal to let the high-flyer go. Mordecai tossed the high-flyer as the *Desire* bobbed up and down on eight-foot swells. The end lines ran over the stern and into the sea until they came to the first anchor. As the boat ran up a swell, the lines picked up speed and slowed as the boat came down on a swell. Mordecai looked at Chavez to see if he was ready and then tossed the heavy piece of steel railroad track over the side. There was only a couple of seconds to grab the next Danforth anchor before the ten fathoms of line between the two anchors went over and became taut. Mordecai knew if he wasn't quick enough, the second anchor would be pulled over, uncontrolled, as the boat moved forward—and that could possibly hook him and drag him over, too. He tossed the Danforth anchor smoothly, and the nets soon after began to flow over the setting bar and into the sea.

"There they go, Chavez," Mordecai said. "Let's see if we can get some fish." The first set went off with no problems, as did the second.

When they came to the third set of nets, Wolf noticed another gillnetter approaching from the south. Sticking his head out of the wheelhouse door, he bellowed, "Hurry up with that next set! I want to get on this piece of bottom before that asshole does. There's fish here!"

Chavez and Mordecai hustled to tie on the bright orange poly-balls and high-flyers for the set, and Mordecai heaved the high-flyer overboard and let it take out some line. "Throw the anchor! Throw the fucking anchor!" Wolf yelled from the wheelhouse. Mordecai pushed the heavy piece of steel over and tossed the Danforth. Wolf gunned the throttle to cover the bottom quickly and claim it as his own. Setting out at full throttle, the anchor bit into the sea floor, and the nets flew off the boat. This was, Mordecai soon realized, a perfect example of how trying to save a minute could cost an hour—if not someone's life. At the end of the set, something went wrong. The net came to the end lines on Chavez's side, snagged, and were going off in a big snarl. With his bad hips, Chavez wasn't able to jump out of the way to avoid getting wrapped up in the lines. He pulled at the clump of line as it was dragged over the stern and fumbled with the line wrapping around him.

"Wolf! Stop the boat!" Mordecai yelled as he jumped over the checkers to help Chavez. When the line got tight, the strength of one man was not enough to hold back the forward-moving boat. Wolf had to throw the boat in reverse and "back her down" to take the tension off without backing into the net and getting it caught in the propeller.

The line going around Chavez had the anchor pinned up tight against his back in a ball of tangled line, which got tighter as Mordecai leaped into the checker. Mordecai knew that Chavez wore a knife on his belt for cutting the line, but the line that was tightly wrapped around his waist prevented Mordecai from grabbing it, and his own knife was gone. Thick smoke belched into the blue sky as Wolf gave the boat throttle in reverse.

"Oh, Jesus! Oh, Jesus Christ!" Chavez yelled as he tried to fight the snarl. The line had pinned his arms to his body. Chavez was panicking for Good reason. The heavy *Desire* didn't stop easily and still had some forward momentum, even in reverse.

"Hang on, Chavez. I got ya! I got ya!" Mordecai told him as he tried to pull at the tightly wound line.

"Fuck, it's crushing me!" Chavez screamed as the line stretched tighter and tighter. If the boat didn't start to come back in the next couple of seconds, Chavez would pop over the stern and go straight to the bottom with the anchor. Smoke continued to plume into the sky as the big Cat growled in reverse. Mordecai grabbed Chavez, trying to hold him in the boat until it could back down enough to take some tension off that line. Mordecai held on to Chavez until it seemed he would snap overboard as if he were on a giant elastic band. Mordecai looked forward to where the knives were kept, but to grab one and cut the line, he would have to jump forward. And to do that, he would have to let go of Chavez, who then would surely go flying off the boat with the anchor. But if he didn't let go of Chavez, Mordecai would go over with him.

"Don't let go off me, Mordecai1 Don't let fucking go of me! I'll go right to the bottom!" Chavez looked at Mordecai with an expression of absolute horror. His eyes were the only part of his body that he could move, and they were pleading, terrified. Mordecai hung on with him, watching the line get straighter. Creaking tension from the line squeezed water from the threads, and Chavez groaned from the strain. Mordecai squeezed his grip, but he was sure Chavez was going over—and then the boat slowly began to come back and ease the tension on the line. A second later, the line was loose enough to pull Chavez free. As he stepped out of the lines, the *Desire* idled along in forward, and Mordecai untangled the lines as they went over. Mordecai tossed the anchor for the last set; a pale and visibly shaken Chavez readied the last high-flyer.

"You all right, Chavez?" Mordecai asked, trying not to sound irritated—or worse, scared—that he had gotten caught, although he knew that it wasn't his intention or his fault.

"Yeah, Mordy, I think you'll have to put up with me for another day."

With the last set in the water, Wolf pointed the bow west, and the boat headed for the harbor. When Chavez and Mordecai stepped into the wheelhouse, Wolf turned on them with a hostile glare. "Is the circus over now?" he asked.

"It was an accident, Wolf," Mordecai countered. "We should just be happy that Chavez didn't go over."

"It's your fuckin' fault, too, asshole!" Wolf exploded. "Don't tell me I should just be fuckin' happy. If you can't do the job, I'll get someone else." For now, the boat was home, so Wolf had a captive audience, and he knew it—Mordecai and Chavez had no money and nowhere to go. Mordecai slipped out of his oilskins and went below to the sanctuary of his bunk. Chavez looked out the window, not saying a word for the first time since they left Scituate. Mordecai knew getting "set over" was one of the risks of gillnetting, and everybody who gillnetted knew someone who had gotten set out with a net or anchor line. They all accepted the risks of the job. Wolf's reaction made Mordecai realize that they were all trying to make their way in a new place, and Wolf was just as scared—probably even more because it was his operation, and success or failure rested squarely on his shoulders. *I might be walking on eggshells with Wolf,* Mordecai thought as he lay in his bunk, *but making the best of it and helping Wolf get things done efficiently means I'll go home with some money*. That would be his end of a down payment on a boat; that was the best outcome he could hope for.

Wolf took the watch himself for the entire ride home and didn't speak to anyone. The boat and crew arrived at the dock, and the men tied up without a word. Wolf went below to his engine room, but Chavez and Mordecai headed over to the Harborside Bar, where several other boat crews had gathered. The beers were flowing, and Chavez was an explosion of sound as he told everyone about his valiant effort to free his shipmate from the anchor lines and how he single-handedly saved the day. Mordecai spotted an empty space at the bar and walked over to order a beer. A pretty blonde bartender handed him a frosty bottle of Bud, and Mordecai took a long pull off it. He turned around when he felt someone tap his shoulder—it was Wolf's friend, Fred Good.

"Wolf's not gonna have a few beers with the boys again?" Eddie asked, twisting a cube of chalk on his pool stick. Mordecai nodded toward Chavez, who now was making animated motions with his arms as he spoke to other bar patrons, and told Fred about the incident with Chavez and the lines.

"What about Wolf?" Fred asked. "Did he freak out?"

"You know, I've heard about clinically depressed people, but it's like Wolf's clinically pissed off."

Fred nodded agreement. "I fished with Wolfy, too, you know, out of Block Island two years ago. When things don't go the way Wolf wants, he needs someone to blame—doesn't matter if it's not your fault."

"Why? What happened on Block Island?"

"I been fishing my whole life, and you know what he says to me when I suggested a different way of doin' something? He says, 'Oh, yeah, smart ass? What do you got? You're nothing!'"

Fred took a pull off his beer and wiped his mouth with the back of his hand. "So I says, 'First of all, I can sleep at night. And I don't hate my job, and I don't hate myself.' He had nothin' to say about that. Then I helped him load the gear on and quit when we got in."

"You still talk to him, though," Mordecai observed.

"Yeah, I talk to him. There are no real friends in fishing'; just guys you can get along with in the bar. We're all after the same fish, so to a point, we work together cuz one boat can't catch 'em all. But watch what happens when your boat is the only one gettin' fish. Everybody sets on the same little spot, trying to catch the same fish before the other guy does, and everybody gets their nets tangled with everybody else's, instead of finding their own spot. Then nobody catches anything but a big cluster-fuck of nets. Then they're not friends; they're just another group of assholes fuckin' you up." Without another word, Fred walked over to the pool table to rejoin the game.

Mordecai decided to decompress by taking a walk over the bridge to the amusement park, look for a Laundromat, check out the boardwalk, chill out on the beach, and explore the shoreline for the rest of the afternoon. He walked past Chavez on his way out and tapped him on the shoulder. "Hey, Chavez, I'll see you back at the boat."

"And that's the guy I saved!" Chavez exclaimed to the small crowd at the bar.

Chapter 12
Commuting

Ocean City was a ten-mile–long peninsula situated between the Atlantic and Isle of Wight and Assawoman bays. In 1869, Isaac Coffin built the first beachfront cottage to cater to vacationers, who came by stagecoach and ferry to fish and experience the rugged beauty of the Atlantic shore. By 1881, a rail line connected Ocean City to a new era of development. A relationship between the vacationing members of the leisure class and a destination had begun. With the end of the Second World War, Ocean City experienced a development boom that made it a favorite and affordable ocean playground for the East Coast's working class.

The boardwalk at Ocean City was a strip of dive bars, tattoo parlors, souvenir shops, and hotels, making up the business end of this elbow of sand. The amusement park was a ghost town of bright pink-, yellow-, and green-painted buildings that housed shops, restaurants, and bars that catered to the throngs of people that mob the beach in summer. Today, the weather was sunny and mild, and the smell of pub food enticed couples to come out for a stroll, as well as bringing out the hungry, pan-handling souls who capitalized on the weather for a handout. A small man in an Elvis suit mumbled to himself and walked in little circles. He began following Mordecai, walking in a hurried shuffle, and calling out, "You! Look at you! You fool! You're nothing!"

Mordecai turned to look at him. "You might be right," he answered.

"Look who follows you. You follow the fools, too!"

Maybe, Mordecai thought. *Maybe*.

Mordecai walked on, thinking of Elijah from *Moby Dick* and his prophecy of doom for the crew of the *Pequod* just before they sailed. Then he admonished himself for getting spooked by a half-wit who thought he was Elvis.

Mordecai continued down the boardwalk until it ended at the large parking lot for the amusement park next to the inlet. The rides and attractions were boarded up and tarped over. He walked through the park until he came to the waters of the inlet and looked out to sea. *Ok. We made it here and the nets are set. It's all about what you are going to give up to us, now.*

Mordecai returned to the boat to find it empty—the duffel bags were missing. He learned from the bartender at the Harborside that Wolf had gotten them a room at a local hotel. A somewhat drunken Fred Good was leaving the bar for the same hotel and gave Mordecai a ride. The Francis Scott Key Hotel had the stately charm of a Southern plantation. Large willows lined the long driveway, and from the front it hardly looked like a hotel, but around back were the rooms that were home to a couple dozen different nomadic boat crews. The back parking lot was full of pickup trucks, each adorned with high-flyers, poly-balls, and plastic fish totes. Mordecai found the room with Wolf and Chavez, who were lounging on the only two beds. With three guys and two beds, they decided to alternate who would sleep on the floor. It was just one room but there was a kitchen area and a bathroom with a hot-water shower—a luxurious change from the boat. That night they took showers and watched TV. Wolf made macaroni and cheese with Scrapple, a cheap pork product that he'd found in the nearby supermarket. Wolf also mentioned there was a Laundromat next to the supermarket. After Mordecai and Chavez finished up cleaning the dishes, they met Tiger in the parking lot to smoke a joint, and the three of them could smell meatloaf baking in one of the nearby rooms.

"That's from Billy's room," Tiger informed them. "Too bad you guys already ate. Billy does meatloaf about once a week—you don't want to miss it. He slices it and bakes bacon and cheese in the middle. That's right where I'm going when we finish this," he said, handing Chavez the joint. Mordecai went back up to the room, threw some laundry in a trash bag and headed out for the Laundromat. As he walked across the parking lot of the supermarket, he thought about the day he left home for Flips' place taking just what he could carry. In the Laundromat, he stuffed the contents of the trash bag into one of the washing machines, looking at the new blue jeans that now had a few days wear on them. He wondered if he should call his parents and tell them where he was, what he was doing.

For most boat crews, the night before a potential fishing day meant a good meal and an early night. Food expenses usually came off the top of the check, just like fuel expenses. Mordecai was eager to start making money so that he could share the ritual of good meals before fishing. He was hopeful that his ambition would be realized when they hauled the next day.

At 4:00 AM the men of the *Desire* once again joined the procession of boats leaving the harbor. An hour into the ride, Wolf woke Mordecai up for the watch. As he climbed out of his bunk and sleepily pulled on his boots, he could feel the boat heaving on giant swells.

"So we get the shit kicked out of us every day I guess," Wolf muttered as he climbed to his bunk.

The boat lurched from side to side as it bobbed up and down on the swells, and despite all his time on the water, Mordecai fought the urge to vomit as he sat in the captain's chair. Seasickness was part of the job; he knew some people never got over it, and now he wondered if he was one of them. In his bunk or working on deck, Mordecai usually was able to suppress it, but riding in the wheelhouse got to him, especially first thing in the morning. He was glad that he'd had nothing to drink the night before—seasickness was much worse with a hangover.

It began with nausea, and every heave of the boat was worse than the last. Then came the urge to go "number two." The toilet was a five-gallon plastic bucket with a little water in it. Mordecai believed if the bucket spilled in the wheelhouse, Wolf would wipe the carpet with the spiller's face, so he stepped out on the deck with the bucket. The cold winter air made him think twice about planting exposed butt cheeks on a wet plastic rim. *But Mother Nature isn't gonna wait*, he thought. Mordecai found the driest spot on deck that offered something to hold on to so he didn't slide across the deck while sitting on the bucket. As challenging as it was, it brought some relief to the experience of seasickness. And as he sat on the bucket, he watched the white-crested waves crash over the stern. The view was spectacular and for a brief moment, he forgot about being sick as his body relieved itself. But with that done, the nausea set in again, and the rest of the ride was torture for him. Mordecai tried to hold on long enough to dump the bucket overboard and run back inside to check the radar. With the bobbing motion of the boat, however, he was having a hard time just getting his pants back up. He was finally able to dump the bucket, get back in the wheelhouse, and check the radar. Then he turned and ran to get back to the open deck before he vomited on the carpet. He heaved onto the deck, and realized he'd need to take the whole ride out in the elements. The best chance to straighten himself out was to stand on the open deck, breathe the fresh air, and keep his eyes on the horizon.

Periodically, though, he had to check the radar. On one of these checks, he noticed three blips behind the *Desire* to the west. Not long after, all three overtook the *Desire*, which was rolling side to side at seven knots. From the deck, he watched the three fiberglass gillnetters—forty-two-foot Brunos—doing at least twice the *Desire*'s speed and hammering through the swells without the rolling and rocking. Their design allowed them to plow through a heavy sea, rather than being tossed about on top. Their diesels sounded like the roar of hot rods as they passed. Mordecai thought the boats looked much more comfortable. He thought about the grass being greener on the other side, but he doubted that any grass could be as "green" as he was at that moment.

Mordecai finished his watch and woke Chavez. Then he put on his oilskins and settled down on deck.

Chapter 13
Hauling

When they reached the gear, Wolf popped out of his bunk with his eyes as wide as saucers. He looked stressed as the three men readied to haul. He saw Mordecai on deck with his oilskins on.

"What? Are you fuckin' sick?" he asked. Mordecai just nodded, and Wolf glared at him. Mordecai couldn't help being seasick, but Wolf's anger betrayed something much more unnerving—it was the fear of not surviving, whether physically or financially.

Steering from amidships, Wolf lined up the boat to grab the high-flyer marking the sets. He pulled the high-flyer aboard and ran the line through the hauler so that they were hauling the first set. Chavez coiled the line in the stern as Mordecai stood at the table, eager to start handling fish. The anticipation of the catch built as the mesh from the first net was wound aboard. First it was a couple crabs, then a skate, and then, a couple dogfish! Mordecai was encouraged but knew that they were going to need a lot more to make this venture profitable. More empty mesh was dumped on the table from the hauler. There were a couple more dogfish, then a few mackerel, which Mordecai threw over the side—he knew that mackerel didn't keep well in a gill net and quickly became crab bait. Chavez was flaking, and Mordecai discarded a few more mackerel and the crabs that had been working on them.

The bright morning sun reflected off the water, and above them flew a cloud of birds, the type that escorted fishing boats. Concentrating on his work, Mordecai threw more mackerel overboard and then noticed white birds diving out of the sky. The mackerel would get a few feet below the surface before the birds, circling from a height of about twenty feet, dove straight down for the fish. They made hardly a splash; with their wings folded, they pierced the surface of the water like an arrow. He later learned the birds were gannets, and they hurtled out of the sky like dive bombers. All he could hear around him was the zip, zip, zip of the birds, just a few feet from where he stood. It was the first time he'd seen gannets and thought it a spectacular scene.

"Hey, Jonah!" A mackerel hit him on the side of the head in an explosion of saltwater and fish scales. "When you're done looking at the birds, we got some work to do." Mordecai proceeded to pick fish as fast as he could, but there weren't many fish—a few dogfish that weren't really adding up, skates, crabs, and the mackerel that went back overboard. Wolf kept the nets on and called Fred Good on the radio. They hauled all the gear and had about twenty-five hundred pounds of dogfish—that would bring about $630 after the cost of the fuel. Mordecai's and Chavez's shares of that would be about $90. *Not bad for a day's pay*, Mordecai thought. Then he reconsidered. *But not real Good when you break it down over a twelve-hour day and throw in getting sick on the commute. We're gonna have to find the fish to make the money we came for.*

Chapter 14
Flip's Arrival

During the first week of February, Mordecai stood on the deck of the Harborside and watched a gill-net boat offload dogfish against a sunset that reflected off the water of the harbor. The end of a conveyor belt was lowered down to the boat, and the fish rode on the shallow grade from deck to the dock. At the top, the fish rolled off the belt into a vat packed with ice that would be trucked north. Mordecai was noting how many fish they'd caught when he saw the *Wayward* steam down the channel for the back harbor. The *Wayward* was from Scituate, and Mordecai hadn't seen Tim, Mark and John, since the afternoon drinking beer in the harbor bar before the fateful Plymouth excursion. John had started fishing on the *Wayward* in the same week that Mordecai had started fishing on the *St. Joseph after* moving to Scituate from Missouri with his mother and stepfather. It was an unexpected move for him—John was heartbroken after his fiancée in Missouri broke their engagement, so he decided to join his parents in Massachusetts. When he saw the ocean for the first time, he was enchanted by the majestic and infinite expanse of sea and knew this would be a place where he could find himself again. He went down to the pier one day and introduced himself to the first fisherman he saw; that fisherman was Tim, captain and owner of the *Wayward*, and the next day John went fishing. A new life began for him then, and that same week, he met Flip and Mordecai.

As the *Wayward* slowly chugged passed the Harborside, Mordecai saw John standing on deck and gave him a yell, holding his beer high. John grinned broadly and waved at Mordecai. Behind the *Wayward* was a much smaller boat, weaving as it followed. The name painted on the bow was *Dogpound.* Mordecai couldn't see who was on it, so he finished his beer and went down to the back dock to welcome the boys from the *Wayward*.

"Well, I'll be damned," John said as he stepped off the boat. "Look who's the first person I see in Maryland." He grabbed Mordecai's hand, and his smile said he was happy to be where he belonged.

"How was the trip?" Mordecai asked. John shook his head. "Never a dull moment." Pulling up next to the *Wayward*, was the *Dogpound*, with Flip at the helm. He grinned and said, "What's happenin', bro?" Mordecai was surprised to see Flip and even more surprised to see who was with him—it was the guy Mordecai had seen standing in the shadowed doorway on the night he was lost in Atlantic City. The guy looked at Mordecai with sunken eyes and stepped past him without a word. Flip's white shepherd, Dingo, jumped off the *Dogpound* to join the men all standing on the dock. Chavez broke beers out of a case he'd lugged down to the dock, and they all toasted a successful journey. After downing the beers, they climbed in the back of a pickup for the ride to the hotel. John and two others in the crew, Tim and Mark, decided to share a room; Flip decided to grab a shower and then go back to the boat. "What about your sternman?" Mordecai asked. "Doesn't he want a shower?"

"He knows the area. He'll take care of himself," Flip said. On the ride to the hotel, Flip told Mordecai that a fish broker had bought the *Dogpound* and convinced Flip to take it to Ocean City and run it for him. "I'm sick of workin' to make someone else rich. I'm fishing for myself now. I split the profits with the owner, but I am the captain of my own destiny, brother!"

"Where did you get that dead guy?" Mordecai asked.

"That's Tommy. He was looking for a site in Atlantic City, so I hired him for down here."

After the *Wayward* crew cleaned up, Mordecai returned with them to the Harborside for burgers and chowder. Over dinner, John told the story of their trip down.

"Flip had the offer to run the *Dogpound*," he explained, "and he asked Tim if he could follow us down the coast. He planned to leave earlier because the *Dogpound* runs a little slower than the *Wayward.* We took care of some odds and ends, getting ready for the trip, and left Scituate Harbor a couple hours later. We were steaming south through a foggy afternoon, and Tim was watching the radar. He saw a blip moving erratically across the screen. Now, Tim is familiar with the radar blips of lobster boats that dart from trawl to trawl, but what was unusual was that the *Dogpound* came steaming out of the fog from dead ahead, going the opposite way. Our boats barely avoided colliding. I guess Flip realized that he almost ran into the *Wayward*, and he turned the *Dogpound* around to follow. Then, south, along the Massachusetts Bay coast, our course took us to the canal entrance at Manomet in Plymouth. By this time, the afternoon had become night, and both boats exited the Cape Cod Canal and steamed across Buzzard's Bay. We put into Block Island shortly after three in the morning so we could get refueled when the fuel dock opened at seven." John lit a smoke.

"But when the fuel dock opened, and the *Wayward* topped off her tanks, there was no sign of Flip. Tim waited another hour, and then an older fellow, maybe in his sixties or seventies, came walking down the docks with Flip in tow. Flip was walking in a sort of defeated shuffle—and he was soaking wet. Then the older man called out toward the *Wayward*, 'Is this fella one of yours?'

And Timmy answered we'd been waiting for him. 'Well, he's your responsibility now,' returned the gentleman. 'I went out for breakfast early and when I came back to my sailboat, this fella was curled up in my bunk, soaking wet and fast asleep. Says he doesn't know how he got there or how he got soaked.'

"So Tim and I thanked the man for returning Flip and for not calling the police—we told him that Flip was really a good guy and meant no harm. The guy suggested that we should 'supervise him a little better in the future' if he was drinking heavily enough to wind up on the wrong boat. The man left, and Flip jumped onto the *Dogpound* without offering an explanation. He went below and fired up the boat, and came topside with dry clothes on, and started to let go the lines."

Tim had been nodding along with John's words as John told the story. Now, Tim interjected, "I was bewildered. I asked Flip if he wasn't going to top off with fuel, but he just said that he had plenty and let the lines go. I figured he knew what hc was doing so both our boats left the harbor and again took up our journey, headed south.

Several hours later, the *Dogpound* ran out of fuel a couple miles outside of the New York Harbor entrance. It was like a gauntlet for us to run through with all the large freighters entering and exiting the harbor. That was tricky enough, but now, I also had the responsibility of pulling Flip out of harm's way. I knew that it'd be a miracle if the *Dogpound* were not crushed. I managed to turn the *Wayward* around and get a towline on the *Dogpound.* We somehow dodged the ships that charged in and out of New York Harbor, and we towed the *Dogpound* to safety. I let Flip refuel with diesel we had on board in five-gallon containers. After that, we continued on toward Atlantic City and arrived in the afternoon. Flip headed off into the city by himself, while our crew cooked dinner on a portable grill and settled in for a night on the boat."

Mark, the third member of the crew, had been listening quietly but now he picked up the story. "The next morning, we woke to find Flip and this new guy, Tommy, awkwardly crossing the deck of the *Wayward* to get to the *Dogpound* that was tied up alongside. Tommy was barely able to open his eyes, and when Flip slurred an introduction, he couldn't really get a sentence together. John asked if he was gonna be okay, and Flip answered, 'Hell, yeah, dude. I was made for this,' but he stumbled as he said it. Hours later, Flip was still incoherent, and we had to wait for him to straighten out enough to remember how to start the boat."

Mordecai listened to the story, trying not to be overly concerned about Flip. "He's devastated over the breakup with his girlfriend," he said. "Maybe this kind of grief just has to run its course."

"Yeah, but I wonder what the story is on this crewman he picked up," John said. "It's easy to find a bar where there's a guy with no attachments who needs work. I just hope Flip isn't gravitating toward a bad element again. I want to see things work out for him down here."

Mordecai stared at the floor. "I'm trying to believe that Flip will get his shit together," he murmured. He had been happy to see Flip arrive, but this news that the crew of the *Wayward* had shared with him seemed to point Flip in an entirely different direction.

Chapter 15
Assateague

I came in from the wilderness, a creature void of form,
"Come in," she said, "I'll give you shelter from the storm."
—Bob Dylan, "Shelter from the Storm"

Four o'clock the next morning brought heavy southwest winds. Wolf, Chavez, and Mordecai stood on the beach at the inlet, "taking a look at it." They were the only boat crew to even bother checking. Southwest was a deceiving wind direction. It usually brought warm air and looked calm from shore. But out where the fish were, there was no "lee of land"—no shelter; there was just wind and water. "The only lee out there is homely and ugly," Chavez muttered. Mordecai watched the waves curl on the beach at the harbor entrance. The weather was not in their favor; it would be a crazy risk. He hoped they would just get back in the truck and go for breakfast like the other crews. No other boats went this day, and so if they were to go, they'd be alone out there. Wolf stood on the beach in front of the pickup's headlights, staring at the horizon in the pre-dawn darkness. His fists were clenched. Mordecai was scared shitless that he'd decide to go. Then, without a word, Wolf walked back to the battered old Ford pickup he'd been loaned from a fish dealer, jumped in, and drove away, leaving Chavez and Mordecai standing on the beach.

"Aw, that fuckin' asshole," muttered Chavez. Mordecai didn't mind the two and a half mile walk—he actually preferred it to the awkward silence of the ride in the truck, but walking was harder for Chavez, with his bad hips. But he knew what hurt Chavez more than the walk was the lack of respect. Wolf seemed to need to rail against something—it didn't take much to set him off into one of his explosive tirades—and because the weather was not something that could be punched, kicked, or smashed, that left the people around him. Avoiding him altogether was the best way to salvage a day off.

"C'mon, Chavez," Mordecai said encouragingly. "We're probably better off going down to the breakfast shop and seeing what some of the other boys are doing."

"Yeah, I'm comin'," sighed Chavez as he limped along the beach in the chill gray dawn.

The "breakfast shop" was a spot not far from the hotel that actually was a gas station/general store/diner. Mordecai and Chavez walked along the dark beach, down the empty streets of Ocean City, and across the bridge to the rural countryside of West Ocean City to the breakfast shop. At 5:00 AM, it was full of fishermen. Some sternmen were feeding their hangovers with plates of scrambled eggs and pancakes on one side of the café, while captains congregated with coffee and discussed the worries of captains—where the fish were, when would they get out to haul, and if the gear would still be there. Sternmen had a stories about girls they met in harbor towns or girlfriends at home, but the embellished nature of fish tales seemed to apply to women as well. On the mornings they didn't fish, they rehashed slightly different versions of old stories. The café buzzed with the familiar chatter of men from the sea on land.

Like a motley family, they generally hung around together on days off because they were all each other had. Although they were not, by habit, inclined to think about beer in the morning, a day off and the proximity to saltwater invoked an urge to resist societal norms and indulge in a rebelliousness. Even for a bunch of guys who worked on the ocean, being near it was a call to bend the rules. It was usually only a matter of time before beer began to flow, much like water through the inlet on a moon tide.

Sitting among the sternmen was Flip. Wolf, who hunkered with the captains, wouldn't even look at Mordecai and Chavez as they walked in. Mordecai heard Wolf tell another captain that a sternman "will always be just a sternman. Treat 'em good, and they become prima donnas. You gotta treat 'em like a mushroom—keep 'em in the dark and feed 'em shit."

"Hey, dude," said Flip as Mordecai and Chavez approached a table of sternmen. Chavez moaned a sigh of relief as he lowered himself onto the bench seat of a crowded table. "Out for a morning stroll?" Flip asked with a smirk.

"Yes, you fuckin' asshole," Mordecai responded. "Your asshole ex-boss left us on the beach." The table of guys laughed. Mordecai grinned, accepting that a staple of American humor would always be the misfortune of others. Nowhere did this seem truer than in the hard-scrabble existence of commercial fishing. The hike for Chavez and him had made them the morning vaudeville act. As long as no one was seriously hurt, no one saw anything wrong with a good laugh at someone else's expense. Mordecai knew that being able to roll with the punches was all part of their stoic approach to survival.

"If you can handle some more walking," Flip suggested, "some of the boys are heading to Assateague Island to see the wild horses. We'll take a truck, though. You two look tired."

Mordecai wanted to see the thirty-seven–mile strip of barrier island that he'd heard the locals talk about. It sounded like a mystical sort of place with a lot of history. The remote nature of the island had made it a renowned spot as a hideout—in the seventeenth century it was used by pirates, like Blackbeard; and in more recent times, by prohibition-era rum-runners.

After shoveling down some bacon, eggs, and pancakes, Mordecai, Chavez, and Flip climbed in the back of a pickup with Tiger and some of the boys, and they headed out to Assateague.

On the way out, Mordecai could tell there was something wrong with Flip. Outwardly, he tried to be his typical jovial self, but Mordecai noticed he didn't look good. Huddled in the back of the truck, he had the same yellow complexion and sunken eyes that Mordecai had seen on Flip's new sternman, Tommy.

"You cold, Flip?" Mordecai asked.

"Naw. I'm Good," Flip said dismissively. It was a cool, breezy ride in the back of the truck, but they were dressed as if they were about to head out on the Atlantic, so the temperature was tolerable. Flip, however, just kept shivering. Mordecai wanted to believe that his friend would be okay when they got out of the truck, but he couldn't dismiss the way Flip looked when he thought no one was watching—Flip looked like a frightened animal.

The sand dunes and beach grass of Assateague reminded Mordecai of home, though the beach was much more expansive, and wild ponies meandered across the sand dunes. They parked by a large sign that recounted the history of Assateague Island. Everyone climbed from the truck and started walking on the beach, but Mordecai stayed behind to read the sign. He learned that in 1649, the British vessel *Virginia Merchant* sailed for Jamestown but was struck by a storm. The ship anchored off Assateague, and a party of men dispatched to explore the island. For an unknown reason, the ship left the men behind and was unable to retrieve them. Ten died of exposure. In order to survive, the remaining members of the party were forced to cannibalize six of the dead. Eventually, they were rescued by Native Americans, who provided food and shelter and then escorted them to Jamestown.

The ponies that Mordecai and the others had come to see were descended from various shipwrecked horses that had swum ashore, as well as domesticated stock grazed on the island by seventeenth-century farmers, who sought to elude mainland taxes and fencing requirements. Although originally domesticated, the ponies were now wild, getting most of their food from marsh and dune grass and fresh water from brackish ponds. The sign explained that in the late 1970s, an attempt was made to improve the breeding stock of the herd by introducing forty western mustangs, but most of them died in the first year.

The northernmost tip of Assateague Island was also the southern edge of the inlet to Ocean City Harbor. In the distance, the northern side, where the amusement park was located, was a cacophony of bright lights, carnival rides, buildings, and development, while the Assateague side, with its sand dunes, beach grass, and ponies, was an example of nature in balance, unfettered by man.

"I think I like it better on this side of the inlet," mused Flip. They were walking along the beach, watching the ponies, who took little notice of the merry band of guys on a day off.

"Funny thing about mankind—how progress is measured along the blade of a bulldozer," Mordecai offered. "I guess the road to civilization is paved."

"Civilization!" snorted Flip. "And all the bullshit that goes with it." He stopped walking and pointed at the silhouette of a lone pony, outlined against the shore. "That's what I wish I could be."

Most of the ponies along the beach were in groups of two to twelve animals, but this solitary animal was grazing by itself.

"Flip, that's a dumb fuckin' horse," offered Tiger as he handed Flip a burning joint.

"A dumb fuckin' animal that's perfectly good with where it's at," Flip responded. "Don't need to think about it, even." He took the joint and held it to his lips but didn't take a hit; he just watched the animal. "He's just good where he is."

Tiger looked at Mordecai quizzically, then shrugged his shoulders and casually walked away over a small sand dune. Mordecai stood on the beach next to Flip and watched the pony move slowly among the clumps of dune grass. "I wish I could stay here," Flip whispered, almost to himself.

"We're gonna work on getting our own boat first, right?" Mordecai encouraged him. "Then we'll have our own place and could even live on it if we had to." Mordecai waited for Flip to respond. When he didn't, Mordecai added, "I mean, it might get a little rugged livin' out here."

A hard look came across Flip's face, and Mordecai could see that it was deeper than just cynicism; it was the look of a soul who was being defeated. Flip started walking again, and Mordecai just let him go, not knowing how to fill the silence. He watched as Flip disappeared over a sand dune, and at that moment, Mordecai realized that although he and Flip were on the same beach, they were in very different places. The southwest breeze that would have been hellish offshore brought unseasonably warm air, and Mordecai felt content to just walk along the beach in the comfortable jeans his father had bought him. Flip, however, was running from something that he clearly could not get away from.

Following the direction the others had taken, Mordecai sauntered over a sand dune and saw them gathered around the only man-made object on Assateague Island—the ribs and planks of a boat. By the looks of it, it was an old schooner. The timbers were exposed by decades of winds that had shifted the sand, as though these fishermen were meant to find her. They climbed about the timbers like a bunch of kids playing on a jungle gym. The wreck was several hundred yards from the reach of the cascading surf, but shorelines change over the years. Mordecai wondered if the vessel had been searching for shelter in an inlet or was driven ashore. Either way, it had foundered on the shore of Assateague.

Mordecai watched and listened to the others as they explored and examined the wreck.

"Check it out!"

"This is so cool. Look at the size of those fuckin' timbers!"

"Yeah, it looks like they just squared off an oak tree to make 'em."

"I wonder what happened with this thing—how it wound up here."

"Maybe there was cannons on it!"

"Maybe it was a pirate ship that went aground. That's why no one knows about it, cuz they all got away."

"How do you know they got away?"

"I said 'maybe.'"

Mordecai walked closer to the wreck. "It might have been a pirate ship. They used to hide in the bays along here." He examined the exposed length of the vessel. "And it might have been just a ship that was driven ashore in a storm. I wonder if men died here."

And there it was—as real as the timber jutting out from sand; a fact of seafaring life as true today as when man first took to the sea. In the predicament of a storm, the question arises of whether to ride out the storm at sea or seek shelter in a harbor. Seeking shelter could mean getting smashed on the shore. The Ocean City inlet, with its disparity of two shores, was where these men, not much older than boys, exchanged one environment for another. Mordecai thought of Huckleberry Finn and what he learned—that sanctuary was on the water. If that were true, then sanctuary was, at best, uncertain. Twists of fate turned like the weather, and they were tempting fate on an unforgiving sea, adapting and living for a time on the wild blue. The wreck was irrefutable evidence that they might, for a time, adapt like the ponies—but they were never far from the fate of the mustangs. Mordecai looked at the ship's ribs protruding sharply from the sand and saw them cast against gray sky like arched headstones.

There was a wild commotion on the other side of a sand dune that sounded like an animal in protest. They just started off in the direction of the sound when one of the larger ponies came bolting over the dune. On its back was Flip, holding on to its neck, with his legs flapping behind him. The pony was determined to lose this unwanted passenger and furiously galloped past them. Mordecai thought idly that Flip was probably about the same size as a Pony Express rider would have been. He looked like he was holding on for a few seconds, but he couldn't keep his legs on the animal. He lost his grip, fell off, and planted his face into a sand dune. The crowd of sternmen ran over, laughing wildly. Flip picked himself up and tried to brush the sand from his nose and eyes with his hands. The pony stopped a short distance away to resume its grazing, this time keeping an eye on Flip.

"I just wanted to ride him, dude," he said. "The thing freaked out on me." They all laughed, clapping Flip on the back and congratulating him for his brief tenure as a cowboy. Unhurriedly, the band of guys made their way back to the pickup, where they found Chavez stretched out in the back, snoring, with a beer perched on his stomach.

The band of fishermen cruised along the beach after letting some air out of the tires so the truck could get traction in the sand. The guy with the pickup was a stocky kid from Chatham named Andy who had driven to Maryland so that his boat and crew could have a vehicle. It had become everyone's vehicle of choice, and today, three guys were up in the cab and seven in the bed. Andy had beefed up the truck with large tires and off-road suspension. The throaty growl of dual exhaust bellowed from beneath the tailgate. Andy hit the gas and let the truck pitch sideways, the tires throwing sand in arcs behind the rolling party. The boys whooped and laughed as the truck bounced along the beach. Being wild came naturally for them—the nectar of their existence. Mordecai wanted and needed that feeling of being wild to fully acknowledge his being on his own time—and just *being*. He was getting drunk on freedom.

The truck bounced off the sand on to pavement, and the ride smoothed out as the truck headed back down the road for West Ocean City. Andy pulled over at a mini-golf course with a go-kart track, and the fun continued with a round of both. Mordecai remembered something he had read: "We as a society are defined by how we spend our leisure time." The thought antagonized him as he putted and raced. He was having fun outwardly, but inwardly, he realized it was all slipping away. He thought of Tony's prediction that fishing as a livelihood was coming to an end. Like youth, his way of life would not go on forever. In recognizing the fun of it all, he also came to the realization that there would be a day when he would be too old to fish. He watched Flip wander away from the crowd of sternmen playing mini-golf and head for a men's room behind a building. Amid the frivolity of playing mini-golf and racing go-karts, he wondered where all of them were headed.

Chapter 16
Greed

The next day the sea gently rolled with light winds from the west. Mordecai's watch showcased another spectacular sunrise, and again he slept soundly while Wolf took the first watch and Chavez took the last. After Mordecai turned the watch over to Chavez, he woke to a bright, sunny day, with light clouds streaking the blue sky high in the stratosphere. He was out on deck with his gear on, taking in the beauty of it all. For Mordecai, leaving the wheelhouse to step out on deck was a transformative experience. Inside the boat, there was a claustrophobic feel—cramped, musty, tight quarters shared with two other guys. On deck, it was just the opposite. The wide open expanse of sea and sky unfolded in all directions. He watched a gannet circle the boat, high above the mast. Its circle drew tighter and then, folding its wings and diving, it pierced the water and re-emerged with a baitfish in its mouth. In that moment, Mordecai felt an immense satisfaction watching the bird and sky. He thought it was ironic that he should feel so free, despite the fact he was more confined than he would have been on land. The boat was the capsule of sustenance—it kept them relatively dry and sheltered from the sea, while providing purpose. On the boat, the men fulfilled a role in the natural order, harvesting fish. Out on deck, with the birds that followed to feed on what they discarded, they were a link in the food chain. Mordecai realized then that he wasn't there for the money. Money was something he needed, an inconvenience that could be addressed through this interaction with the sea. He looked up at the dollar sign on the riding sail that fluttered impotently in the light breeze. If it was just about the money, then it would be valueless for him; he would be in the same boat as Wolf. In that moment, he saw that his freedom came from not needing to be on the sea but from wanting it so much that it defined him. He laughed at the irony of this realization as Chavez stepped out on deck, and Wolf stuck his head out of wheelhouse. "What the fuck are you laughin' at, you weird motherfucka?" Wolf spat out.

"Nothin', Wolf. Just happy to be here," Mordecai said cheerfully. Wolf went back in the wheelhouse, shaking his head, but Chavez regarded Mordecai as though he was wondering what kind of drugs Mordecai hadn't shared with him. Mordecai just smiled and kept his thoughts to himself.

As they set out the gear, Wolf noted the fish finder sonar showed impressive marks just above the seafloor—probably schools of dogfish—and he decided to set out the gear and immediately start hauling back, once the last set was out. These short soak sets were feasible when there were a lot of fish around. Once the last high-flyer had been set out, marking the end of the last set, he swung the *Desire* around to retrieve the high-flyer that marked the first set. Wolf came out on deck, wearing his gear. Steering the boat from amidships, he lined up the *Desire* to come up on the aluminum pole that floated at a forty-five degree angle in the light wind, Bright orange flags fluttered from just beneath the triangular tip. The fluorescent flags reflected against the blue of the sea, as did the pink poly-balls. The yellow line pierced the depths until it was swallowed by the blue-green, and Mordecai coiled the line back into the rope checker, where it had been just an hour before. The line coming around the hauler yielded an anchor, then five fathoms of line, the Danforth, and more line. Then it began dumping a steady stream of pink mesh onto the table that was loaded with clumps of lively dogfish. Chavez and Mordecai pulled them around the hauler by hand—there were so many that they prevented the hauler from getting a grip on the lines. The table was loading up fast, as Chavez pushed piles of fish tangled in net to Mordecai, who was fully preoccupied with just getting the fish around the hauler. Wolf turned from his hauling station long enough to push the pile of fish and net down the table. Mordecai felt his blood pulsing in his arms, shoulders, and back. Soon, the pile on the table reached as high as his chest. He started picking fish, firing them into the checkers as fast as he could. He had enough time under his belt that he had developed the skills to work the fish out of the net quickly with one deft motion. He felt the heat of his working muscles as sweat soaked his clothes. He was thankful that he had spent the money for the more expensive thermal underwear that wicked away the sweat and allowed him to stay dry. As long as the fish were coming up, he had to keep going. He was reminded by the fatigue building in his arms and back that he should pace himself. Wolf looked like a junkie, getting a taste of what he craved, but he was shy of exuberance. The radio was alive with the chatter of fishermen tipping each other off to the presence of fish.

"Hey why don't you boys try a string down this way?" one said. "Cuz we got what we can handle right here," another responded. The fish were everywhere. Everyone was making money.

While they worked, the sonic booms of navy jets emanated from the depths of blue sky. They were too high to be seen, but the sound of their staccato blast felt like gods battling in the atmosphere. Their presence punctuated most of the afternoon and seemed to make Wolf jumpy. He'd glare at the other boats, specks on the horizon, and snarl at his crew to move faster, even though they were working at full effort. "Let's fucking go! What am I paying you for?" Mordecai thought about that and wondered when they were going to see a paycheck. His shoulders, arms, and back burned from wrestling so many fish from the net. They were literally up to their waists in writhing fish that stabbed them with their horns in their death dance. Mordecai and Chavez had to pay attention to where they threw the fish on the pile—if the boat became overweighted on one side, it could potentially capsize.

Wolf yelled at Chavez for throwing fish on one side of the boat, and then blasted him for loading up the other. There was no way around Wolf's temperament. What should have brought satisfaction instead made him consumed with getting even more.

Mordecai knew that they had better than ten thousand pounds on, and he noticed the boat was sitting well below its waterline, with the deck at sea level. If any more weight was on her, the scuppers would be underwater and wouldn't allow her to clear her decks if waves came over the rail. The ability of a boat to clear her decks of water helped determine the seaworthiness of the vessel. If the deck was forced down to water level, there was nothing to stop the sea from pouring in. They were coming to the end of the last set of nets, but fish were still coming fast. "Wolf, the scuppers are going under," Mordecai said.

Wolf turned and glared. "Just keep picking fish, asshole! If you knew anything, you'd know that we can't sink. The deck's watertight. We can steam with it under water. Plug the scuppers with fish if you're so scared."

Mordecai did just that and noticed that there was so much fish on the deck that they could be packed tight against the scuppers and keep all but a trickle of water from coming through.

After hauling the last set, the boat was even lower in the water, and the deck was laden with fish, rail to rail, and heaped as high in the middle as Mordecai was tall. The sun was setting as the *Desire* began the four-hour steam home. Mordecai and Chavez were exhausted but happy. Even Wolf's demeanor seemed to have a sense of a job well done, although he didn't say it. His heavy beard would have concealed a smile, but his eyes had lost their hard edge as he looked over the pile. But there was still the chore of unloading all this weight of fish when they got in.

The three men slept and alternated one-hour watches, with the boat gently rolling side to side in its hypnotic imitation of a giant, aquatic cradle. Everyone got sleep on the ride home, and Mordecai was grateful for the dry blankets and sleeping bag of his bunk.

The *Desire* reached the inlet of Ocean City Harbor a little before nine o'clock that night and steamed around the tip of Assateague to the harbor. The dock was crammed with full boats, all waiting to unload and all low in the water. Peering through the darkness, Mordecai noticed that the *Dogpound* was not among them. The *Desire* came alongside the last boat in line and tied off to her to wait their turn to unload. Two hours later, the boat and crew pulled up to the unloading dock, and a conveyor was lowered down to the deck. Stiffly, Mordecai and Chavez began throwing fish onto the canvas belt that carried them up to a vat on the pier. Muscles that had stiffened up on the ride home protested the exertion, but the two sternmen worked through it. Wolf was up on the pier, watching the unloading operation and seeing that his fish were not mixed with those from another boat. At the late hour and in the dark, it would not have been difficult for an unscrupulous fish broker to "misplace" a vat of fish, and an exhausted crew wouldn't notice. An hour later, Mordecai hosed the blood from the deck. The numbers came down: 13,700 pounds. The crew of the *Desire* finally made some money. Mordecai took solace in knowing he was no Jonah. He had worked hard and felt instrumental in accomplishing what they had come for. The crew of the *Desire* had shown themselves—and everybody else—that they were fishermen. Now, Mordecai wanted to have a beer with his fellow fishermen and exult in the glory. After tying up the boat in her berth, Chavez and Mordecai headed to the Harborside. Most of the other boat crews were there, tired but happy. Looking off the deck, Mordecai saw lights coming down the channel at the harbor entrance, weaving as they approached. It was a small boat, low in the water, and Mordecai was relieved to see Flip at the helm. The *Dogpound* listed heavily and careened off the pilings as it pulled up to the dock. The exhausted dock workers once again lowered the end of the conveyor, and Flip and his sternman began unloading fish. Mordecai turned away from watching them, preferring to watch the pretty blonde bartender move delicately behind the bar in her faded jeans. The intensity of the day washed out of him as the first beer went down. He was ready to order another and mentally undress the girl behind the bar, when a scream from the unloading dock, followed by a splash, rolled through the harbor.

Mordecai bolted around to see a dock worker tumble on the ground in pain, holding his hand. The portside rail of the *Dogpound* was smashed, and the tip of the conveyor stuck out of the water. The bar emptied as fishermen rushed to help. Flip, clearly wasted, didn't seem to acknowledge what had happened. He had finished unloading and pulled away from the pier before the dock hands could pull up the conveyor. The base of the conveyor caught the rail as the boat pulled away, and the conveyor was pulled off the dock and into the harbor. When the unfortunate dock hand had seen this happening and tried to hold the conveyor back, his finger was cut off as the machine went over. Putting the boat in gear, Flip steamed full throttle across the harbor to his berth. The fishermen gathered around the dock, watching as their boats rocked and banged against each other in the large wake.

"Son of a bitch!"

"Who is this fuckin' asshole?"

"Somebody should drop a dime—that guy's a menace."

"I think the *Dogpound* needs to be impounded."

Flip had definitely rubbed some people the wrong way. Mordecai wished he could explain his behavior and tell these guys that it really wasn't like Flip. But the cold hard fact of the matter was that it *was* Flip—and really messed up.

A crowd of fishermen headed to have a talk with Flip, who had tied up on the other side of the harbor. It would take a few minutes for everybody to walk around, so Mordecai ran ahead but on reaching the *Dogpound*, he found neither Flip nor his sternman. It was clear they'd left in a hurry; the boat had not even been hosed down and was slick with blood and gurry. The crowd of fishermen gathered around the small boat and viewed the grisly scene with disgust. All knew that it was not good publicity for fishermen if boats were left looking like the inside of a slaughterhouse, even in the off-season.

There was nothing Mordecai could do. He had started walking home to the hotel when Tim from the *Wayward* pulled up in a pickup truck loaded with groceries. Tim offered a ride, and Mordecai hopped in. When he told Tim about the incident with Flip at the dock, Tim rolled his eyes. "Jesus, I just passed him and that freak-show heading the other way over the bridge. Looked like they were thumbin' their way into town. The fish show up, we finally have a chance at making some money, and he's gonna party instead of getting some rest? We'll all need our strength if the fishin' keeps up like today."

Mordecai would have thought about the prospects for tomorrow, but his mood had soured when he realized that Flip must have found a supplier in Ocean City. At the hotel, he headed up to his room for a few hours' sleep before another early morning on the sea. Outside, the wind moaned faintly from the northeast.

Just before 4:00 AM, the three men climbed in the back of a pickup for the short ride to the boats. The wind had not come any harder, but it was still out of the northeast, raw and biting. Trucks at the inlet shone their lights over sand to the water. The water of the inlet churned like a washing machine. Because the wind had been so steady, a bit of a sea had come up, and Mordecai knew the ride would suck.

And it did. It wasn't quite rough enough to justify not going out when the boat was making money. So after four hours of gut-churning tossing and heaving, the crew of the *Desire* hauled. Again, the nets were loaded, and they piled on the fish. The wind blew the crest of the growing seas into a cold, driven spray that stung their exposed faces. The swell lifted the boat, and the crest sheared off to crash into the deck—and the men on it. Fatigue from the day before still rode heavily on their working backs. The motions to extract fish, more reserved and calculated to conserve energy. The fish however, were on their first day of being caught in a gillnet and resisted with convulsive thrashing. The men fought through and set back the first string of nets. The second went the same as the first and it was noon when they set it back. At the end of the third set they had more fish than the entire trip the day before, and there was still a full set to go. That meant they had to load on the weight of fish in the fourth set and the net itself. With the boat already low in the water and the seas running around fifteen feet, the crew knew the wind would not need to come much harder to make this a scary situation.

"Wolf, are we really gonna haul the last one?" Mordecai asked. "This is starting to look a little crazy."

Wolf turned like he was confronting someone who had challenged him to fight. "You want to start swimmin' right now, motherfucka? 'Cause you're on this boat to work, not think." He turned back to the wheel.

Mordecai had been concerned, but now, he was afraid. He looked over at Chavez as if there was something he could say, but both knew that there wasn't. As they began hauling the last set, they quickly realized that there were more fish than in any of the others. Exhaustion rode heavily on aching backs, arms, and shoulders. Mordecai's forearms burned from the exertion, and warm blood coursed through them from the effort of fighting his way through the last set. The pile of dogfish mounded several feet above the rail. The most lively of the fish, freshly picked from the mesh, rolled off the pile and back in the ocean. At first, Mordecai felt the desperation of losing money, but that soon gave way to an inner voice that said, *Be happy with what you have*, and at that moment, they had a boat that was full of fish. *If we survive the ride home, it will be a profitable trip*, Mordecai thought.

The last high-flyer was hauled aboard, and Wolf brought the boat around slowly. Heavy and low in the water, it labored awkwardly. It seemed an act of God that more of the waves weren't coming over the rail. Wolf ran the boat north as they set out and Mordecai became relieved as every fathom of net flowed over the side, and heavy lead line no longer weighed down the boat. They came to the end, and Chavez threw the heavy anchors, letting them take the line and then the high-flyer, leaving just the weight of fish. The *Desire* was still low in the water.

Mordecai was exhausted, and the boat was rolling hard enough that he decided getting something to eat was too much work. *I must be too tired to be seasick*, he thought as he crawled into his bunk. Although the added weight of the fish helped take the snap out of the rolling, when the boat rolled to one side, Mordecai feared it wouldn't right itself. He looked across the berthing space and saw Chavez lying in the opposite bunk, eyes wide, staring at the overhead. Mordecai lay on his back in the bunk as motion pitched him from side to side. As he gradually became confident that the boat wasn't going to roll over and that he wasn't going to land on the deck, he let himself go to sleep. He dreamed he was rolling a rock up a mountain, his shoulder wedged tightly against stone, as he struggled against gravity. Step after step, his feet clawed for traction, fighting to keep the massive weight of the stone from rolling back over him. Suddenly, the resistance ceased, and the rock rolled away. He could only watch as it rolled down

dropped onto pavement. Knees buckled as the crew crashed to the deck. The steel I-beam that had been welded to the keel had dropped into a sand bar where the channel used to be. Wolf shoved the throttle in the pocket. The big Cat growled and exhaust belched into the dark sky. Between the swells, the boat was aground and at almost a forty-five–degree angle as another swell approached. The next wave crashed across the pile of fish, and the boat lurched to port. Fish tumbled over the rail and into the sea as the swell first crashed over and then—suddenly and violently—lifted and pushed boat and crew farther into the inlet. The deckload of dogfish became heavily unbalanced to the port side. The throttle was still in the pocket, and the boat was propelled forward at a fearsome speed. The *Desire* was picked up and then surfed down the front of a giant wave. Chavez struggled to get his boots on in the wheelhouse, and Wolf screamed at him to get on deck. Mordecai was looking at where the life rings were hanging on the bulkhead when there was another tremendous impact. He slammed down hard against the wheelhouse door and crumpled to his knees. He tried to pull himself up, realizing that the *Desire*, with the excessive weight of her design and the deck load of fish, had plowed into the sandbar again. He knew it then: they would be pounded to pieces unless she was made light. The next wave hit, side-swiping the pile of fish and sweeping more overboard to port, but a great mass of the semi-buoyant pile flowed toward Mordecai and crushed him against the wheelhouse door. The saltwater avalanche of fish, their sharp horns protruding from their dorsal fins, punctured his skin in a dozen places, and the searing heat of the wounds radiated through his arms, legs, and torso. With a straining effort, he pulled himself out of the pile, but there was no way to open the wheelhouse door. Wolf and Chavez were trapped inside, and he was alone out on deck, with the waves crashing down. He started throwing the fish over as the *Desire* lay on her side. The boat lurched as every wave hit. Water ran inside his oilskins as he labored furiously to get the weight off the deck. The boat was getting pummeled and threatened to roll over completely with the crash of every wave. Panic-stricken, Wolf and Chavez hollered for Mordecai to move the fish from the door so it could open. He was trying to do this, but every wave pushed more fish against the wheelhouse and the door. Mordecai made some headway, but then the next wave would bury the door in more fish—and there was no other way out of the wheelhouse. The boat moved a few feet over the sand bar with every crashing wave. Mordecai was throwing fish away from the door and over the side as hard as he could, oblivious to the fatigue incurred by the effort to bring them aboard. The pointed spines of the fish continued to puncture, slice, and tear his hands as he desperately grabbed and fired fish overboard. The fish defied his effort, as though the insane paradox of his action could not involve them. As fish, they had fulfilled their role in the rational world when they were caught by the fishermen. Finally, Mordecai got enough weight off the door for Wolf and Chavez to force it open. Chavez tumbled out on the deck and started throwing fish overboard. They were trying to stand on a forty-five–degree angle that lurched with every wave. Panicked, they worked like madmen, throwing their harvest away to save their lives. After another tremendous crash, Mordecai felt weightless. Dark green surrounded him as he cart wheeled. His arms instinctively wrapped around his head to protect it from the impact of hitting against the steel bulkhead. But it didn't come. The sound of water and the rush of cold filled his ears. He was underwater and didn't know which way was up. It seemed that a long time passed, and Mordecai tried to yell. A bubble came out of his mouth and headed toward his feet. He was upside down. He twisted and followed the direction of the bubble until he was on the foaming surface. The *Desire* was twenty yards away and floating right-side up. With most of the deckload of fish gone, she was driven across and off the other side of the sand bar to the deeper water. The frothing, washing-machine effect of the inlet churned the water. Mordecai's boots were filled with water, and he felt himself going down. He couldn't swim toward the boat, and even if Wolf knew where he was, there was no telling if he would be able to get the boat over to him. With every wave that washed over his head, Mordecai thought it would be his last view of the world above water. Here, at the point where they exchanged two worlds between two very different shores, Mordecai felt his mortality. A wave washed over him, and for a moment, he was under. He kicked off his boots Then he broke above the surface, and he was looking at the amusement park. An insane clown laughed at him from the haunted house, its eyes wide open with delight. Again, he slipped beneath the surface. He fought his way back up and gulped the air, desperately trying to breathe. Clawing the water in a vain attempt to reach the lights of the park, he went under again. Sound was muted, and cold invaded every inch of his body. Again, he came to the surface, and the insane clown was drinking with the little man in the Elvis suit from the boardwalk—Mordecai's Elijah—and they were toasting his ambition. Mordecai couldn't see the *Desire*; he didn't even know if Wolf and Chavez had noticed he was gone. As he came to the surface again, something grabbed the hood of his raincoat and pulled him upward. Large hands grabbed his arms and pulled him up onto a bright white deck. He had seen these men before, these men who were looking down at him. A tall one with a mustache went forward, and Mordecai felt the familiar sensation of a boat going into gear. An excited voice exclaimed, "They made it! They're off the bar!" The two fishermen looked at Mordecai sitting on the deck, crumpled and wet.

"I'll call 'em."

From the wheelhouse Mordecai heard the calm voice of the tall one. "*Desire, Desire*, this is fishing vessel *Sacajawea*. Come back on channel 88." There was silence for a moment, then Wolf's voice came over the radio. "Yeah, this is *Desire.*"

"We've got your man, Captain. He's a little wet, but he looks all right."

"Yeah … well … I'll tell you what. You can keep him."

The wind-powered waves had created a sandbar across the mouth of the inlet. This was the reality of finding the way home—it was not a given that it would be the same as when the fishermen left. The *Desire*, with the excessive weight of her design, encountered this predicament as she drew twice as much water as the Brunos.

Following the *Desire*, lighter now that she was less the load of fish, the Bruno cruised down the harbor. After tying up alongside the dock, Mordecai heard Wolf yelling about the asshole who threw his day's pay overboard, distracting himself from the larger terror they had just experienced. Wolf never asked about the condition of the man who'd gone overboard.

“You know,” said the tall fisherman to Mordecai, “you might want to consider working on another boat.” His tone was quiet and measured.

“Thanks for pulling my sorry ass out of the drink,” Mordecai said. “I wish we could have met under different circumstances.” Mordecai was now wearing a pair of dry jeans that were about eight inches too long for him and a similarly oversized flannel shirt that the mate had procured from somewhere on the boat. The flannel was warm and dry, with the light scent of someone’s aftershave; it reminded Mordecai of wearing his father’s shirts as a kid. As he climbed from the boat, the clothes gently hugged his damp skin. “Could I get you fellas’ a beer after I help you unload?” Mordecai asked. The men politely declined the offer and said he should just get warm; they could handle the unloading themselves. Mordecai thanked them for the dry clothes and said he would return them in the next day or so. He wasn’t prepared to deal with Wolf immediately, so he went over to the Harborside.

Everyone wanted to hear the story, and Mordecai must have told it a half-dozen times. With every telling, the crowd laughed and clinked together a fresh round of beers. Eventually, Mordecai tired of the story and looked for Flip in the crowd. “Hey, does anybody know if the *Dogpound* went today?”

“Nope, sat on the mooring all day today,” said an old-timer with a beet-red nose. Undoubtedly, the old-timer had not budged from his mooring at the bar all day. Mordecai guessed he was someone who could afford to spend his time alternating between the soap opera on the bar’s TV and the theater of the absurd that was the surrounding fishing culture. “Saw him today though,” he said. “Looks like he’s pallin’ around with that guy that got fired off *Ladyslipper.* They were lookin’ pretty messed up this morning. Had his sternman with him, too. Whatever those boys are up to, it’s no good. I can tell you that.”

“Say isn’t that fella a buddy of yours?” someone asked Mordecai.

Mordecai remained quiet, yet angry at himself for being ashamed that Flip was his buddy. He stared at the floor.

"I tell you what," another fisherman said. "There been some stuff missing from boats 'round here, and I'm willin to bet it's those boys."

"I've never known Flip to steal," Mordecai said meekly. "He's acting strange, but I've never known him to be dishonest."

"If it is him, he's gonna have a lot bigger problem than getting messed up on shit if these boys come down on him," said one of the locals. "We like you Yankee boys just fine, but nobody likes anybody comin' here to steal." It wasn't said in a hostile way; Mordecai knew they just wanted to get the message across that theft would not be tolerated.

Mordecai knew he needed to talk to Flip. Having a good name among these people was key. Once someone got a bad reputation, he was done. Mordecai was getting along with the folks at the Harborside, and the owners had even let him open a line of credit. He didn't want Flip's antics to cost them both. Maybe getting a site on another boat, sooner rather than later, was a good idea.

Chapter 17
Independence

At the hotel that night, Wolf said nothing, as though the entire incident had never happened. Mordecai was thankful for that, because the job was home. He realized that, like Chavez, it was all he had, so in the dark of early morning, Chavez and Mordecai accepted the hand they were dealt and headed for the boat with Wolf. The weather was rough, but Wolf wanted to load the gear on because the weather was supposed to take a turn for the worst the next day. It was one of those days when nobody wanted to fish, but if the gear wasn't hauled, they would be screwed—it would take days to clean mackerel and crabs out of the nets. *As much as it sucks*, Mordecai thought, *it's better than the next option.*

Flip showed up at the boat as they were leaving at 4:00 AM, looking more like the guy Mordecai remembered and less like the creature he had been morphing into. His hair was pulled back out of his eyes, and Mordecai could see the smiling, happy guy that everybody liked.

"Can you use an extra hand?" Flip asked Mordecai. "My gear's already aboard the *Dogpound.*"

Mordecai and Chavez agreed it would be Good to have Flip aboard, although with an extra man, it would mean taking a 10 percent share instead of fifteen. On a day like this, however, they were more concerned with getting the gear loaded on as quickly as possible than with taking a lesser share. On the steam, when Wolf went down below to his bunk, Flip burned a joint he had in a cigarette pack. Afterward, Chavez and Mordecai hit their bunks when Flip volunteered to take a watch. When they arrived at the gear, even Wolf was smiling and joking as the crew put on skins and boots. Mordecai could tell that he was happy to have his old friend along, too. Flip brought an array of skills to the operation that sped things along considerably. His sternman experience came through as he worked at picking and flaking with the deftness and coordination of an athlete. Although he looked happy, he seemed to have trouble keeping his eyes open. Mordecai pondered this situation. They *had* burned a joint during the steam out, and Flip took the whole watch all the way to the gear. When Mordecai woke and went topside, he still felt high but not as high as Flip looked. The fish dropped off to about half of the previous day's lost catch, so it was no problem loading the fish and the gear on. With the extra hand, the hauling went fast, and the men didn't have to take the time to set the nets back. It was before noon when they loaded the last set of gear on, and Wolf pointed the bow west. They steamed in, unloaded the fish, tied her up, and headed over to the Harborside for the first after-fishing beer. It was late afternoon when they walked in, and it was the usual crowd. The air smelled like a room full of guys who had fished all day. Mordecai was leaning on the bar next to Flip when he noticed two girls. Mordecai wanted to meet a girl and knew the best thing for Flip's broken heart was another girl—he'd been so down lately, Mordecai wanted to believe that having a new girlfriend would fix him.

"All right, Flip, there are a couple hotties over by the pool table, and you and me are gonna bust a move on 'em."

"No, dude, you can, but you're solo on this one. I got some shit I gotta take care of." He polished off the rest of his beer, put the empty bottle on the bar, counted the roll of cash Wolf had given him, and headed for the door. "Warm 'em up for me. I'll be back later."

"What? You're leaving your wingman in a target-rich environment? What the hell could be so important?"

"I got captain shit to take care of, like making sure the *Dogpound*'s still floatin'."

Mordecai knew that a captain needed to stay on top of things, like making sure that batteries stayed charged and the pumps kept working, so he let Flip go. On his own now, Mordecai moved over toward the girls.

Flip never came back to the bar, but Mordecai got drunk with the girls. He tried using the "Why don't you come see my boat?" trick, but they didn't go for it. They just left him with a considerable tab, but Tiger helped him out with it. "Oh, what the hell," Tiger said. "I was talking to them too."

"Damn," said Mordecai. "Thought I was getting somewhere with the blonde."

"Yeah, you were getting your wallet lightened up with her."

It was late when Mordecai said good night to his friends, and by the time he reached the hotel, the lights were off. The wind howled outside, and he was sure there would be no fishing the next day. The wind slammed the storm door shut behind him, and he noticed Wolf stir in his bed. Mordecai rummaged through the fridge, looking for something to eat.

"Mordecai, quit making so much noise and go to sleep," Wolf muttered.

"Fuck you, I'm hungry," Mordecai slurred. He heard the bed springs creak but paid no attention to it. "And another thing, you piece of—" Before he could finish spitting out his epithet, Wolf was standing next to him … and then Mordecai saw a flash of stars.

He woke up in the dark on the parking lot outside the hotel room. He managed to get into the hotel laundry room that night through a window, and he spent the night there, lying wrapped up in blankets on a shelf. The next morning, he had a vague memory of getting through the window and dropping to the floor. He had no idea what time it was when he awoke, but bright sunlight assaulted his eyes as he let himself out. His head was throbbing as he meandered down the street toward the breakfast shop. The wind howled out of the northwest, and this meant that no boats would go fishing. Mordecai was glad because now he wanted out of Wolf's program. Today, everyone would be around, and he could find another site. He walked across the parking lot of the gas station/diner just as Wolf, Chavez, Flip, and a couple other guys climbed into a pickup. Mordecai walked up to the truck a little sheepishly, but Wolf just stared out the passenger-side window, refusing to look at him. The other guys suppressed smiles.

"Nice shiner, dude," said Flip. Mordecai caught a reflection of himself in the truck's mirror and realized he looked like a bum who'd crawled out of the gutter. "I'm starving," he said. "I'm gonna get some chow. I'll talk to you later."

"Like that?" Flip asked incredulously. "All right, dude." Flip was laughing as the truck backed out of the parking lot. "Good luck." Mordecai walked into the diner and had a seat at the counter. He wished for a large pair of sunglasses when he saw the waitress looking at his shiner from a distance. She didn't seem eager to serve this patron who looked like he may be trouble.

After breakfast, Mordecai walked the mile and a half to the pier where the boat was tied up. The boat wasn't locked, so he went in and grabbed his stuff. His oilskin pants and raincoat were there, but his boots weren't. After looking for them in exasperation for a few minutes, he realized that they were on his feet; he had slept in them. He carried his stuff down the pier and threw it on the *Wayward.* Along the docks, fishermen were gathered at some of the slips; some were drinking coffee; some were working. Strewn about everywhere was the flotsam and jetsam of commercialized, industrial fishing: coils of rope, four-by-four–foot plastic vats used for trucking fish, bright orange poly-balls, the colorful flags of high-flyers, and piles of net. One crew was trying to untangle a large ball of net that Mordecai figured had been wrapped up by the tide—three guys had the net spread out on the dock, and a small crowd of fishermen seemed entertained by their efforts. As the ball of nets came undone, a light cheer resounded along the docks as the net was pulled back aboard.

Although there were several different groups on the pier, Wolf was not among them. Mordecai walked back to the hotel, hoping Wolf wasn't there—he wanted to grab his duffel bag without confrontation. Mordecai feared that Wolf was likely to have a fit when he realized Mordecai was leaving him short-handed. The mid-Atlantic areas were warming up to temperatures consistently in the lower fifties during the day, but the late March wind still had a bite. Mordecai turned his collar up as he walked to the hotel.

Chavez was in the room by himself, lying on the bed watching a modern western. "How you feelin' today?" he asked without taking his eyes off the screen.

"I'm grabbin' my stuff, Chavez. I'm done with this circus."

Chavez didn't say anything for a moment; then he motioned toward the nightstand. "Wolf cut us checks this morning, but they're from the local bank at home. I don't know who would cash 'em down here." He looked at Mordecai for the first time. "You oughta throw a brontosaurus steak over that."

Mordecai snatched the check off the nightstand. His eyes widened as he looked at it. *Five hundred bucks? We've been down here a solid month for five hundred bucks?* And drawing the check on a bank from home was Wolf's ploy to prevent his sternmen from seeking their independence.

"The other news," said Chavez, taking a drag on his cigarette and exhaling with smoke through his toothless gaps, "is that we're taking the boat home today and flounder-fishing the bay this spring."

Mordecai saw this was all part of Wolf's plan for keeping his crew in indentured servitude. This meant that Mordecai could search for another site—without money or a place to stay—or steam home and get the five hundred bucks. And because Wolf was leaving today, Mordecai had to make up his mind quickly. "Not me, Chavez. I'm getting another site. What about you ?"

Chavez just stared at the screen. Jon Bon Jovi was belting out the soundtrack of *The Young Guns* as the credits rolled. "You got another site?" he asked, now looking at Mordecai.

"Not yet, but someone's gotta need help down here."

"You got any money?"

Mordecai shoved his hands into the empty pockets of his jeans and looked at the floor. "Not really."

"What ya gonna do?"

"I dunno. Start looking, I guess."

Chavez rolled on the bed and stubbed out his cigarette in an ashtray. "I'll take the steam home with him, I s'pose." He reached into his pocket and pulled out a twenty. "Here—take this. I won't need it on the boat."

Mordecai accepted the bill and looked at it a moment. He didn't know where Chavez got the money, and Mordecai doubted he had another twenty. "Thanks, Chavez." Mordecai folded the bill carefully in half, looking at it while searching for the right words. "I don't know what to say."

Chavez waved it off. "I'll see ya back home when you get there. You can take care of me then."

"All right, I'll do that. It might be a while, though," Mordecai said.

"We'll see," Chavez called after him. He started another Marlboro as the door shut.

Mordecai was walking along the road with his duffel bag slung over his shoulder when a pickup pulled up next to him. It was Flip, with his dog, Dingo, on the passenger seat.

"Where you goin'?" Flip slurred. He tried to look at Mordecai, but his eyes were half closed. The truck reeked of beer, and there were empties everywhere in the cab. Mordecai told him what he could remember of the night before, and Flip laughed. "Yeah, I heard about that. Wish I could have seen it. Must have been funny as hell."

"Well, it wasn't that funny for me at the time, but I just grabbed my stuff. I quit, but Wolf don't know it yet. He's leaving today. I got no job and a useless check for five hundred bucks."

"I think I can help you with the check, dude. Throw your stuff in back. We'll drop it off at the *Dogpound*, and get that check cashed."

Mordecai tossed his bag in the bed and squeezed Dingo over on the seat between him and Flip. They cruised over to the *Dogpound*, and Mordecai threw his bag down below. He noticed that the boat had been scrubbed down and for the most part, everything looked in order. *Flip must have some semblance of control*, Mordecai thought, *although he looks real unsteady and is having a hard time keeping his eyes open.*

They drove over the bridge to the Strip, which was the beating heart of Ocean City during summer, and pulled into the parking lot of a small building with a fading sign that read "Pawn Shop." Flip seemed to know the guy behind the counter. He explained the situation with the check while the guy looked at Mordecai.

"Let me see it," said the guy behind the counter. He got on the phone and read some numbers off the check to someone on the other end, then walked back to the counter and said, "This is an out-of-state check, and normally I wouldn't cash it, but because I know Flip, I'll do it for 10 percent."

Mordecai figured that $450 was better than nothing, so he thanked the guy, and he and Flip headed out.

"So where you wanna go now?" Flip asked.

"Back to the harbor, to look for a job."

It was little after noon when Flip dropped him off at the Harborside. "Hey, dude," Flip said, "can I borrow fifty bucks? I'm a little short."

"Yeah, sure, Flip." Mordecai peeled off a fifty. "I'm going to get a burger and see if I can catch any scuttlebutt on who needs help. You wanna come?"

"Naw, got stuff to take care of. I'll see you later."

"All right. Drive safe." Mordecai climbed out of the truck and watched Flip pull away down the sand-lined road. Mordecai hadn't asked Flip for a job—he figured that as a captain, if Flip had to borrow a few bucks, things must not be going too well. Out of a $500 check, Mordecai was already down to four hundred. Still, that was more than he'd had when he woke up.

In the Harborside, Mordecai saw Tiger throwing darts with a few other guys. Tiger gave him a high-five and asked how it was going.

"I need to find a new site and a new place to stay," Mordecai answered.

"Have a beer, and we'll go talk to a buddy of mine," Tiger said. "I think he's looking for someone." Mordecai had a burger and waited for Tiger to finish playing darts. Chavez shuffled in and took a seat a couple stools down. Without looking at Mordecai, he said, "Wolf's looking for ya."

"Did you tell him I quit?"

"He noticed your stuff was gone and asked me what you were doin'. I said I didn't know. I'm just here to tell you that he's ready to leave. He's looking for you, and he's bullshit."

"Maybe I should get the fuck out of here before he finds me," Mordecai said. As he rose to pay his tab, the door to the Harborside swung open and in strode Wolf. He walked right over to Mordecai, who now felt the burger hitting his stomach, even as his heart pounded in his throat.

"So what's it gonna be?" Wolf asked pointedly, folding his muscled arms across his chest.

"I'm stayin', Wolf. I like it here. I'm gonna stay."

Wolf said nothing as he eyed Mordecai with contempt. "You better think long and hard about stayin', cuz if you do and I ever see you again in Scituate, I'll fuckin' kill ya."

Mordecai backed away from him as Wolf continued eyeing him with a hostile glare. Then he dropped his big forearms to his side and muttered, "Come on, Chavez." He turned and left, slamming the door behind him in anger. Chavez slumped on his stool with a sigh, then stood and limped toward the door. Mordecai called to him, "Hey, Chavez, you did real good. It was good fishing with you." Chavez turned and paused with his hand on the doorknob. With a resigned look, he said, "Good luck," and then he was gone.

About an hour later, having forgotten about Tiger, Mordecai stepped out into the afternoon sunshine and walked over to the docks. He stared for a moment at the empty slip where the *Desire* was no longer berthed and realized that he was on his own. He was headed toward the *Wayward* when he saw Tiger helping a guy who was working on a truck. Mordecai walked over, figuring he would ask Tiger about that friend of his who might need help.

"Hey, I was just talking about you," Tiger said. He introduced Mordecai to the guy who was working on the truck. "This is Mark Simms, also from Chatham." The fellow who pulled his head out from under the hood was the guy who had pulled Mordecai out of the water a few days earlier.

"Oh, hey, I still gotta return your clothes," Mordecai said. "Are you looking for help?"

"I might need a guy," Mark said as he went back under the hood. "What I don't need is trouble. And that Scituate buddy of yours with the *Dogpound* looks like he's plenty of it." Mordecai looked downward at his feet. "That boat you were on—the *Desire*. They're gone?" Mark asked while turning a screw on the carb.

"Yeah, left this afternoon. Goin' home."

"Why didn't you go with them?"

Mordecai thought for a minute. He didn't want to start bad-mouthing Wolf, and he wasn't sure about the real reason he wanted to stay in Ocean City. "I guess it's because I see the potential for this place to make money."

Mark looked at Mordecai for a second, then went back to tuning the carb. "That's the right attitude, and I want someone who wants to make money." He put down the screwdriver and wiped his hands on a rag. "I'm going tomorrow. We'll try you out and see how you do. But I don't want that guy from the *Dogpound* or any of his stew-bum friends comin' around my boat. I'll give you a chance, but if you bring trouble, I'll show you trouble like you've never seen." He said it so calmly that it wasn't personal or even offensive, but Mordecai knew that he meant it—and he looked like he could back it up.

"I understand," Mordecai said. "What time tomorrow?"

"Five o'clock in the morning. If you're not here, I go without you, and that's it."

"All right, then, five it is. I'll see you then."

Mordecai decided to take a stroll over to the boardwalk to help work off the lingering hangover. First, he stopped at a gas station convenience store and picked up a bottle of spring water. *Some water and a walk, dinner, and tomorrow's a new day.* Mordecai was feeling upbeat about his prospects as he headed for the bridge.

The remnants of the hangover were disappearing as the rejuvenating spring water and fresh air washed through him. He cruised along the boardwalk, enjoying the light exertion of the walk. He spotted Dingo sitting just outside the door of a bar, so he walked over and gave her a rub between her ears. She sat and waited calmly, as though familiar with this routine. Mordecai ventured inside, wondering what Flip was up to. It was dark inside, and as his eyes adjusted, he saw half-dead–looking patrons regard him with suspicion. He didn't see Flip; the crowd looked like mostly bikers—lots of black leather vests and jackets, with stacked-heel motorcycle boots. Some were burly, tough guys with neck tattoos who didn't look happy to see someone they didn't know. The other half of the crowd looked like they'd been in Auschwitz. Moving along the wall toward the back of the bar, Mordecai slipped past a woman who had the same dopey, eyes–half-closed look that he had seen on Flip. She looked like she might have been very pretty oncc, but now her skin was pasty yellow, with deep crow's feet around her eyes. *She's a bone rack*, Mordecai thought. He moved past her, saying, "Excuse me," and she stopped talking to glare at him.

"You lost?" she asked. Mordecai shook his head and kept moving toward the back to find Flip. In the hallway that led to the men's room, Flip was arguing with a guy that looked like a nerdy bookworm gone bad. The argument grew aggressive, and the nerd shoved Flip and told him to get the fuck out. The crowd immediately shifted to back up the nerd, and Mordecai knew that Flip was going to get his ass kicked.

"Whoa, whoa, wait!" Mordecai yelled coming forward and grabbing Flip. "We're leaving!"

"And a lot quicker than you came, fuck-face!" said the guy who'd shoved Flip. Two large, biker types grabbed Mordecai and Flip and propelled them through the room toward the door. Both were tossed out and landed in a heap on the boardwalk, which Dingo observed with patient interest.

"What the fuck do you think you're doin'?" Flip demanded, picking himself up. Mordecai turned around to see who might have followed them out and was relieved that no one had; then he realized Flip was talking to him.

"What do you mean? I was just seein' what you were doin', and it looked like that crowd was gonna open up a can of whoop-ass on you."

"Maybe I don't need you helpin' me out, asshole!"

"This is the thanks I get for stickin' up for a buddy?"

"Maybe you should just mind your own business and quit stickin' your nose where it don't belong. You could get it busted that way. C'mon, Dingo." And with that, Flip staggered off down the boardwalk. Dingo dutifully followed, then stopped and looked back at Mordecai for a moment.

Mordecai stood on the boardwalk in shock. He couldn't believe Flip's reaction. He turned and headed the other way, toward the amusement park, though he knew there was really nothing down there for him. He knew Flip was there, trying to score smack. For Flip, the only moment of reprieve would come when he was high. *None of this is my problem or business*, Mordecai tried to tell himself, but watching Flip self-destruct was getting tough. Mordecai was at a complete loss of what to do. *Tomorrow will be a new start for me*, Mordecai thought. He wanted the same for Flip. He just didn't know how to help him. He hoped that Flip would see that a guy could start over with a new outlook, another chance. Maybe Flip could put behind him whatever heartbreak drove him to grovel before the degenerates as he just had.

As Mordecai neared the amusement park, the rumble of a diesel engine reached his ears. A gill-net boat was racing out of the inlet and steaming north along the beach, It was almost five o'clock in the afternoon, and Mordecai wondered where the hell they were going.

Mordecai walked back across the bridge and through the streets of West Ocean City—past the glittering hotels, dive bars and tattoo parlors, and eventually the working-class reality of trailer parks, coin-operated laundry, small homes, and T-shirt print shops. It was this side of the bridge that allowed the other to exist. It was the draw of the resort side that created livelihoods for the people of the west side, but without people to work the hotels, wait the tables, and print the T-shirts, there would be no Ocean City. Mordecai moved through this relationship between east and west like an island. He thought about his situation, how he was there because that was where the migration pattern of a fish had brought him. Migratory fish are habitual tourists, and so must be the fishermen who follow. The biggest irony was that his following something that followed the dictates of nature had brought him to Ocean City. Maybe Flip's dalliance with drugs was just a part of what had happened to sailors for centuries. Maybe it was natural for a fisherman to have a weakness. Maybe it *was* the lesson of Huck Finn. Maybe the water was sanctuary, or maybe the *wild* was the haven, if horses could learn to live in the wild and not only survive but *thrive*. Mordecai thought about Flip's romantic ideal of life among the Assateague ponies and wondered if maybe Flip was on to something.

The walk had made him hungry, and he was going to have to find a place to sleep. As the sun set and the dark chill of night surrounded him, Mordecai realized that the Harborside was the best place to find the people who might have what he needed. Stepping into the Harborside, the guys didn't greet him with quite the same level of enthusiasm. A few fishermen nodded, then stepped aside, looking toward the back. In the back corner of the barroom, passed out and curled up in a ball under a table, with Dingo by his side, was Flip.

"Oh, shit. Why hasn't anybody helped him?" Mordecai said to the guy closest to him. When no one answered, Mordecai walked over to the table. "C'mon, Dingo," Mordecai said as he tried to pick up Flip. His friend's unconscious dead weight was hard to pull out from under the table. The crowd of onlookers watched his efforts with some amusement, and then another pair of hands helped grab Flip. It was Tiger. "Hey, man, what the fuck happened to him?" Mordecai asked.

"I guess he's just hammered," Tiger answered. "Walked in here not too long ago looking kind of fucked up and just started pounding the sauce."

"Really," Mordecai said. He realized that Flip was using booze to compensate for smack. He had never really known Flip to drink hard because he was always kind of a lightweight with the booze. He got drunk so easy, usually after just a few beers, that he preferred getting high. If he was hitting the bottle, it was because the lack of heroin was killing him. Mordecai hoped that maybe Flip's getting drunk was a good thing because it meant he was getting off the shit. "Let's take him back to his boat. We can't leave him like this."

With Dingo following, Tiger and Mordecai half-carried, half-dragged Flip the several hundred yards from the bar to the slip where the *Dogpound* was berthed. It was awkward, but they got him aboard and put him in his bunk down below. His sternman was nowhere to be seen. The night was cold, but the winter sleeping bag had worked for Flip so far, so Mordecai figured he would be all right.

"You think he's gonna be okay like that?" Tiger asked as he and Mordecai walked back to the Harborside.

"Yeah, he's pretty rugged. I'll stay on the boat with him tonight, just to be sure. Say, Tiger, you fishin' tomorrow?"

"Yeah, why?"

"What time you going?"

"Usual time. Five, I guess,"

"Would you do me a big favor and come by the *Dogpound* and wake me up before you leave? I don't want to miss the boat."

"No, you don't," said Tiger, clapping Mordecai on the back as they headed back in the bar.

Chapter 18
Sacajawea

After having a meal of baked tautog, that one of the local boats had provided the restaurant, Mordecai walked back to the *Dogpound* and went below. Dingo was curled up with Flip, who was snoring. She looked up at Mordecai then lowered her head on to Flip's chest to continue her sentinel over her master. Mordecai wondered if either had eaten. Between the two bunks mounted forward in the bow was the diesel engine. Mordecai climbed into the empty bunk and zipped the sleeping bag up around him, but it was no warmer than the air temperature, which was about forty degrees. He could see his breath billowing above in clouds. Gradually, his body heat radiated throughout the bag and allowed him to sleep.

Someone was shaking him, and Mordecai swam up from the depths of slumber to see Tiger standing next to him. "Five AM, Mr. Van Winkle. Time to catch the fishes," Tiger announced.

"Oh … yeah, thanks," Mordecai said. He unzipped the bag and climbed out.

"Where's your buddy?" Tiger asked.

Mordecai looked over at the other bunk and saw it was empty. "Geez, I don't know. He was here with his dog when I came back last night."

"Does he know that your sinking?"

"Huh?" Mordecai swung his feet out of the bunk only to have them splash in a foot of water that was coming up around the diesel engine. "Fuck! Where the fuck is he?" Mordecai said, pulling his wet feet up on to the bunk. He grabbed his boots, which thankfully were up above the rising water. "I hope he knows about this, and he's not here because he's out getting another pump or something." Mordecai nodded to himself. "Yeah, that's what its' gotta be. The truck's gone."

Tiger's eyebrows shot up. "Where the hell is he gonna find another pump at five in the morning? And why wouldn't he fire up the boat and get the ones he's got working? There is more than one pump on this thing, right?"

Mordecai just shrugged and felt a pang of guilt. He hoped Flip was on top of the situation; he had a boat to catch. Walking along the docks with Tiger, Mordecai saw both the *Sacajawea* and *Decisive* were running, and the captains were talking in the darkness. Andy, the kid with the beefed up truck, was standing on the dock.

"Well, well, I guess he can show up," Andy said with a grin as he recognized Mordecai.

"Hey, Andy," said Tiger. He stepped past him and hopped across the *Sacajawea* to the *Decisive.*

"We're feeling chipper this morning, I trust?" asked Andy.

"Always," replied Tiger.

"You're not the one we were concerned about."

"Why? You comin' with us, Andy?" Mordecai asked.

"Nope. I just showed up in case you didn't. Now I can go back to bed. We'll be doing some gear work later. Here." He handed Mordecai a brown paper bag. "It's your lunch. I hope you like marshmallow munchy treats, 'cause I do. That was gonna be my lunch if you didn't show. I'm not gonna to need it now."

"Hey, thanks, Andy. I totally forgot to pack a lunch." Mordecai took the bag and stepped from the dock to the *Sacajawea.*

"No worries." Andy let go of the lines holding the boat to the dock. The *Decisive* had already untied and was heading for the channel. Andy dropped the stern line on the back deck, then threw the bow line to Mordecai, who began coiling it as he noticed Tiger doing on the *Decisive*. The *Sacajawea* followed the *Decisive* through the harbor until the first can that marked the channel. There was a rumble of horsepower and a plume of dark diesel exhaust as the *Decisive* throttled up to its cruising speed. The boat gracefully stepped up on a plane and exited the harbor. A moment later, the *Sacajawea* also throttled up, and Mordecai felt the surge of power. Standing on the back deck, he heard the whine of the turbo that fed horsepower to the bellowing diesel. The exhaust above roared from the stack, and the vibration of power resonated through the boat. It was still dark, but Mordecai could tell by the rush of air that swirled around him that they were speeding across the water as the *Sacajawea* also exited the harbor. It was exhilarating. He had never moved across water this fast before, and he was absolutely enthralled by speed, as if he was powerful and going somewhere.

The boat flew past the first can, and the amusement park receded into the distance, as if driving by it on a highway. On the opposite side of the inlet, the ponies on Assateague Island momentarily interrupted their grazing to watch the two fiberglass hot rods roar past. Mordecai headed up forward to the wheelhouse. Mark was at the helm, sitting in a folding lawn chair and looking at the radar screen. The other sternman, Wayne, sat in another lawn chair, reading a book. Mordecai thought that Wayne and Mark had a New England look to them—as if they could have been the cover of an L.L. Bean catalog. They had an easygoing manner that almost gave the impression they were out pleasure-boating rather than trying to make a living.

"There's a bunk up forward on the starboard side if you want to lie down," Wayne said over the roar of the diesel. Mordecai didn't see another lawn chair, and so he went below and slipped into the bunk.

Mordecai found the ride was not the same as the *Desire*. The side-to-side roll of the *Desire* was replaced by a moderate amount of impact as the bow slammed through waves. Lying in the bunk, he felt his back taking a mild beating.

There was more slamming, but the boat got there a lot quicker. In just under two hours, the men were on deck, with skins on, and grabbing the first high-flyer and hauling gear. With practiced ease, Mark wrapped the line around the hauler, and the first set had fish. The second, third, and fourth sets also had fish. Wayne and Mordecai alternated picking and flaking, with the flaker coming up to the table to help pick when he caught up with the flaking. Wayne showed Mordecai how they set up the lines when setting the gear out. The *Sacajawea* set gear with a different method from the way it had been done on the *Desire.* The setting bar on the *Sacajawea* had a bar that ran about a foot off the deck, just forward of the base of the setting bar. Mordecai watched carefully, not wanting to make the same mistake he had the first time he set out gear from the *Desire*. Flip wasn't there to save him this time, and he wanted to show he was serious about his job.

Around eleven o'clock, Mordecai was flaking the net and pulling it down the table when an uncracked bottle of beer came back in the net. Mark turned from the hauler and smiled with a beer in his hand. Mordecai could see that Wayne was having one, too. The hauler stopped for a moment, and Mordecai twisted the cap, hoisted the bottle toward Mark and Wayne in a toast, and took a long pull. The cold, familiar fizz tumbled down his throat and left a creamy beer aftertaste that he could equate to nothing other than happiness. Mordecai was feeling positive about working on the water and knew he would love fishing with these guys; he wanted the job. It reminded him of how much fun he had mossing with Flip when they were twelve. He looked around at the *Sacajawea,* how she was set up, clean, and painted white. If he could stay working with Mark and Wayne on the *Sacajawea,* he could see a way to saving for a down payment on a boat. He wondered how Flip was making out with the *Dogpound.* If Flip still wanted to go in on a boat, how would he feel about a forty-two–foot Bruno if they could find one for sale? Would Flip save the money? Would he shake the addiction? Then something cold and hard landed on his conscience. *Would he live long enough too?*

They returned to the harbor that afternoon with close to ten thousand pounds. After unloading, Mark told Mordecai there was a shower in the building where they unloaded fish. If he used the shower, Mordecai was welcome stay on the boat with Mark. Wayne split a hotel room with a friend. Mordecai was happy about being done so early and was grateful for a hot shower and his new position. He was walking into the building for a shower when he passed a plastic fish vat with a jagged edge protruding from a corner. A seam on the side of his jeans snagged on it and made a small tear. Mordecai felt a sting of heat in his thigh from the cut, but what bothered him more was the tear in the jeans. A small drop of blood fell through the gap in the cloth. His father had bought him those jeans. He felt it was punishment for having been a quitter again. But he had also begun anew, again. He walked over to the department store and bought needles and thread. And later that afternoon, Mordecai re-sowed the seam on his jeans, patching what had been torn.

Chapter 19
Volleyball

In mid-April, the days were getting longer with some warm, sunny afternoons. As young men, Mordecai and his new friends found it was too nice outside to justify sitting in a bar. Students on spring break arrived to populate the bars and hotels, so one afternoon Mordecai and a group of sternmen walked over to a department store to buy shorts, cheap sandals, and T-shirts for the warmer weather. Mordecai asked Flip how he'd made out with the *Dogpound.* Flip said that it was all set, but Mordecai couldn't help but wonder if it had been sabotage.

They walked back to the hotel and changed into the summer clothes, then headed over the bridge. The group of friends were walking down the beach when they spotted five athletic-looking girls coming down the beach toward them. They were wearing sweatshirts and jerseys, and they stopped at a volleyball net. John gave them a smile and a smooth greeting as the two separate groups came together.

"So, you ladies out for some volleyball?" John asked.

"Yeah, we're not that good, though," said a pretty brunette with a smirk. She had the greenest eyes Mordecai had ever seen, but there was something behind those eyes that attracted him more, and he recognized it immediately: confidence.

"How 'bout a round, then?" asked John.

"No, thanks," she said.

"Aw, c'mon. Be a sport. We walked all the way here and realized we forgot our ball," explained John. "We'll go easy on you." The girls looked at each other. One said to the others, "One game?" They agreed, and the two groups spread out on the sand with the net dividing them, fishermen against college girls. As the girls peeled off sweatshirts, Mordecai noticed the toned bodies. He was in the back row next to Tiger, and they crouched over with their hands on their knees, in a stance they thought would be the posture of a volleyball player returning a serve.

"Hey, Tiger," Mordecai said discreetly. "You seein' what I'm seein'?"

"Yeah, they're hot." His face looked like he was opening a treasure chest. "Check out the one with green eyes."

"I think they've done this before."

"So we won't play for money," Tiger said with a shrug. "She could beat me any time," he said, looking over the net. "Whip me, spank me, tie me up, tie me down."

"You guys promise—if you lose, you go away?" said Green Eyes, smiling as she began the serve.

"What the fuck?" said Tiger as he straightened up.

"Yeah, yeah, that's fine," John said to the girls. He held up his hand behind him to signal to Tiger to just go with the flow. "But if we win, you come have drinks with us."

"You're on," said a blonde in the front row, and the ball was in play. The ball volleyed back and forth for a while, just keeping in play, when one of the girls spiked it into the sand in an empty spot between Tiger and Mordecai. Mordecai was vague on the rules of volleyball, and it didn't seem like any of the guys were experts either, but they were in decent shape from gillnetting and not about to let a bunch of girls beat them. When the ball went back in play, the girls set each other up expertly and returned volleys with a practiced ease that appeared to conserve energy. After the girls scored a couple more points and the fishermen had none, sternmen started diving for the ball and sometimes crashed into each other in desperate attempts to keep the ball in play. Before long, the men were covered in sweat, breathing hard, and losing. Mordecai pulled off his T-shirt and threw it in the sand, ready to give it his all. At one point, Andy lunged for the ball and missed, instead whacking Flip in the head.

"Dude!" Flip protested.

"Sorry, Flip!" said Andy. The girls were laughing and even looked a little embarrassed for the boys. Mordecai tried to cover his laughter. Flip just shook his head and picked up the ball, throwing it back to the girls.

"Forget about it, dude," he said, shaking his head. The girls laughed at the uncoordinated antics, but Mordecai saw Green Eyes look at Flip as though she were impressed that he was good-natured about taking a whack in the head.

The ball went back in play and now the fishermen were really going for it, trying to score a point to avoid a complete blowout, but the girls scored another one. Mordecai decided it wasn't the best strategy to have the shortest guy in the front row, so he switched places with Flip, although he wasn't much taller. When the ball went back in play, they volleyed back and forth a few times and then the girls set up for another spike. The ball was hit straight up in front of the net; a girl from the back charged and leaped at least two feet out of the sand to smash the ball over the net. The ball shot over the net like a cruise missile, hitting Tiger square in the forehead. It bounced straight up, still in play, and Flip set up John, who tapped it over the net. At this point Mordecai gave in to laughter at Tiger's dumbfounded expression. Mordecai was laughing hard when he sensed a body floating through the air on the other side of the net. As he turned to look up, he heard a hand smack the ball, and his face imploded from the tip of his nose. Mordecai hit the sand on hands and knees.

He groaned as blood gushed out of his splattered nose. He stayed on all fours, letting blood stream into the sand. Dazed, he wasn't sure what just happened. Green Eyes came over with the T-shirt he had discarded and said gently, "Here, honey, tilt your head back." She applied the balled up T-shirt to the bridge of his nose, placed his hand there, and said, "Pinch lightly."

For a moment, Mordecai was the kid on the beach, seven years old, with a bloody nose after getting whacked by another kid's pail of sand, and his mother was tending to the injured nose. The gentle touch and the girl's soothing voice brought him back to the present, where he found himself on his knees, looking up at the caring, sensitive face of the girl with green eyes. She gently stroked the side of his face once and then stepped back, leaving him with the T-shirt against his nose. "Just hold it there, like that," she said.

After a few minutes, the bleeding subsided, and everyone agreed that although his nose was swollen, it didn't look broken. John asked if the girls would join them for a drink, but the girls said they weren't old enough. The men thanked them for the game and walked back over the bridge to west Ocean City and the Harborside. Mark and Jan were there at the bar.

"What the hell happened to you guys?" asked Jan, noticing that they were covered in sand and that Mordecai was wearing a bloody T-shirt.

"We got beat up by a bunch of young chicks," answered Tiger.

"I guess so," said Mark. "Mordecai, did you even get a lick in?"

"I wish," Mordecai answered as he looked across the bar to the mirror behind it. The black eye that he got from Wolf had faded but was replaced by two lighter ones and a fat nose. "What the hell am I gonna tell people?" he muttered, and they all started laughing.

Flip said that the girl with green eyes had told him that the girls were all on the volleyball team at a Canadian university.

"Somebody should've asked out that girl," Mordecai said in a nasal tone, while pressing ice to his nose.

"Yeah, me," said Tiger.

"You'd have to wrestle me for her, dude," responded Flip.

"Here's to the girl with the green eyes," said Tiger, and they raised beers.

"Say, did anybody get her name?" Andy asked.

"Brianna," said Flip into his mug of draft. He polished it off and headed for the door.

"Son of a bitch," said Tiger. "You don't suppose he … naw!"

They never found out if Flip had a rendezvous with Brianna that night, and Mordecai didn't know that he wouldn't see his friend again for ten years. Mordecai resumed fishing with Mark and Wayne the next day. It became clear that the catches were steadily dropping off. The haul slowed to about four thousand pounds. They hauled all four sets and loaded each one on. Mark looked pensive for a moment, then decided to set the nets back for another try. The men went through the routine, setting the gear back. Then Mordecai and Wayne scrubbed the boat while Mark headed them west. *Sacajawea* arrived back in the harbor in mid-afternoon and unloaded. Mordecai had barely made it into the Harborside before he heard the news: the *Dogpound* had been impounded. Mordecai learned that Flip had showed up later that morning with two other guys no one knew. These other two were burnouts who had been hanging around, and Mordecai was disheartened to learn that Flip was gravitating toward that element.

They got the boat started up and were steaming through the harbor for a day of fishing. The widely held opinion was that someone must have dimed him out because he never even got out of the harbor before the cops stopped him. The Maryland Maritime State Police found three fucked-up guys, with outstanding warrants for two of them. All three were arrested and the boat was seized. The rumor was that an amount of heroin was also found. Mordecai remembered what Tony Amato had said; it seemed like ages ago: "What some of these guys get into can take over their lives." The dream of buying a boat with Flip was just that now. But Mordecai wasn't as disappointed by watching his dream of buying a boat slip away as he was by watching his friend fall farther into the abyss. Mordecai made phone calls to the local and state police, trying to find what it would take to get his friend out of jail. But since Mordecai was not a family member, getting information was difficult.

Later that evening, Mark came into the Harborside and told Mordecai that Flip needed a lawyer but that he'd be back in Massachusetts in front of a judge before anything could be done for him. Mordecai came to see that this was probably the truth. Mark also told him that the two of them would steam out the next day, haul the gear, and leave it on the boat. Wayne was going back to Chatham on another boat to resume clamming at home. "I miss my wife." Wayne told Mordecai on the steam home. "You can make more money single handed." They'd unload the fish and the following day, Mark and Mordecai would take the *Sacajawea* to Point Pleasant, New Jersey. "The fish are heading north," Wayne said. "And you need to be there ahead of them."

Mordecai was melancholic over leaving Ocean City. He hadn't saved much money and was left with no plan, other than to keep fishing. Still, he didn't want to let go of the dream that they would hit a big school of fish; that Flip would show up and they'd get a boat together; and that this summer, the two of them would be dogfishing in Massachusetts Bay. Although most of the boats and crews that were transient would likely also be in Point Pleasant, Mordecai knew he would miss the Harborside and some of the locals, as well as steaming past wild ponies grazing on the beach. He realized that he would be leaving a home—and leaving before he had accomplished what he came there to do. He also felt like he was leaving a man behind. Although Flip had undoubtedly been hauled back to Massachusetts to face a judge, Mordecai felt anger at having failed to pull his friend through. He finally came to realize that anger was another level of helplessness that accompanied witnessing a friend self-destruct. And he had to acknowledge the *self* part of that. Wanting to help a friend was one thing, but the friend had to want to help himself.

The next day, Mark and Mordecai on the *Sacajawea* steamed out and started hauling the gear "single-handed"—the term for a gill-net operation using just one sternman. There was more work per man but the share increased from 15 percent to 22.5 percent. The logic behind this math was that the captain and single sternman were splitting the work and the share of pay that would otherwise be the other sternman's. Mordecai worked in the stern, pulling the net back and flaking it off the table. Most gill-net operations had the sternman pulling the net over a bar suspended above the back end of the table, just before the net pen in the stern. This created a little more tension on the net and gave the sternman a better angle to work the twists and knots out of the net. The complication was that there were still plenty of fish coming back in the net that prevented the net from going over the bar, so he found it easier to work off the table. It was difficult at first, but Mordecai gradually developed a feel for how to do it. There were five, ten net sets in the water, and the last set was the most difficult. With four sets already packed in the stern, Mordecai had to stand on top of the pile of net that reached the table, so he was working on fish and net down by his ankles. After getting through the last set and having packed all the gear on, they steamed west for their last night in Ocean City. Most of the other traveling boats were low in the water with fish and nets on. The owners of the Harborside, Chip and Lou, threw a big party, and everyone got drunk. Mordecai hugged all the girls that tended bar and got their addresses, promising to write. Later that night he said Good-byes and stumbled back to the boat.

The next morning, the diesel rumbled to life a little after sunrise, and Mordecai rose to throw off the lines for the last trip out of Ocean City. The morning sun sparkled on the waves that caressed the beach, the creamy white foam retreated slowly back toward surging sea. Mordecai pulled the visor of his ball cap down low over his eyes to block the glare. The ponies moved gently through the dune grass, and Mordecai thought of Flip and his idealic notion of harmony among those ponies, on that beach, and how far removed from that existence he must have been at that moment. Mordecai inhaled the air and imagery of the beautiful morning and wished Flip could have seen it. He wished he could have taken one last walk along the beach and stared at the ponies. Yet there was the realization that of the two of them, Mordecai was lucky to be where he was, and part of him would always be on that beach. For some reason, steaming through the inlet and gazing at the ponies one last time, he felt the urge to wave. He stood on the back deck and watched the sands of Assateague retreat into the distance. When the bright sand was just a speck on the western horizon, he went forward to his bunk.

He didn't sleep for very long. Restlessly turning in his bunk, his hand found the tattered edges of an old newspaper that had slipped between the mattress and sleeping bag. It was a local DelMarVa newspaper and had an article that caught his eye about the Mattaponi Indians, who were the first residents of Assateague Island and hid in its bays and swamps when European greed for land and the white man's diseases drove them from their homes. His heart became overwhelmed with a great sympathy.

They arrived in the waters off of Point Pleasant later that afternoon and readied to set out the gear. This was a new experience for Mordecai, as he had never tension set before. Wayne had always handled the setting, while he cut and iced the monkfish that came up with the dogfish. He was a little unsure of himself, as the setting system was more intricate than just letting the net pull off the pile and over a spreader bar into the sea. With tension setting, the net was run up over a bar in the stern, usually about five feet off the deck, and then down to another bar at the base of the spreader bar. The sternman stood in the area between the two bars, conscious of not being on the net that was going out. He wore a raincoat and let the net run under his armpit while applying tension with his hands. The purpose was to create tension on the spreader bar to get a really good spread out of the net. This took some of the chore out of flaking when the net was being hauled. The sternman didn't have to concentrate on every little knot or tangle in the mesh and could focus on the fish. It also helped take out the twists that prevented the net from fishing. If the net tangled on the sternman and he was unable to free himself, he'd be pulled under the tension bar, up over the spreader bar, and be thrown into the water. Chances were that he'd be maimed before he even hit the water. Knowing his own propensity for absent-mindedness, Mordecai became immediately aware of where the ends were and set up everything properly. Mark said he would run along slowly to give Mordecai more reaction time if things started to go wrong. As the net ran through his hands, Mordecai thought of running it between his legs for better tension; his hands were getting tired from pulling against the net. Then he thought of all the sport-fishing hooks and lures he had picked out of nets in his time gillnetting, and he realized that now would be a bad time to find out he'd missed one. Still, getting skewered in the hands or armpit by an errant fish hook would probably be better than in the groin.

Mark kept his word about running slowly, and they successfully set out the gear. Mordecai hosed down the boat of the algae slime that was always present on the nets and that went flying everywhere when setting. It coated everything in a layer that resembled thick pea soup. When the last set had been run out, Mordecai used the deck hose to spray down the net bin. Then he stood on the picking table and held onto the overhead that came to his chest. He looked around at the expanse of sun on water around him. As the light chop splashed against the fiberglass of the boat, Mordecai realized he had accomplished another aspect of fishing that he hadn't done before. He also felt something in him that he hadn't had months ago, when he left home. It was confidence.

Chapter 20
Point Pleasant

Point Pleasant, New Jersey, had a boardwalk on the beach with the assortment of East Coast shoreline attractions, motels, and a small amusement park that resembled a moderately scaled-down version of Ocean City. After tying up the boat to an aging pier in the very back of the harbor, Mordecai decided to throw some laundry in a duffel bag and head off on foot to explore the new town; he also hoped to find a Laundromat. Walking down the street that led from the dock toward the seaside businesses along the boardwalk, Mordecai spied Tiger, also with a duffel bag over his shoulder. Tiger had been to Point Pleasant before, and he showed Mordecai where the laundry was, as well as pointing out the Broadway Bar and Grill, where the fish folk hung out. They threw their laundry in washers and then walked down the boardwalk. "This place is all right, but I never get the feel here that I do in Ocean City," Tiger said.

"Why is that?"

"I don't know exactly. Just never feels like home, but some place in between."

"Where are you from originally, anyway?" Mordecai asked.

"Not really from anywhere. Parents moved around a lot. Guess I'm from all over."

"What do you call home now?"

"The *Decisive*, mostly." Tiger looked around. "This is someplace I'm just passing through. Kinda like everything else." With their laundry done, they walked to the bar. It was sunny and warm, and the two sternmen took their time, casually strolling and looking at the few girls who had come out to lie on towels on the beach. Mordecai relaxed in the sunshine. For the moment, he was without a care in the world and happy to have found someone he knew in this unfamiliar place. From what he could see so far, there was no reason why Point Pleasant shouldn't be as fun as Ocean City. Tiger was quiet, and Mordecai assumed he felt the same. The

Broadway was similar to the Harborside, situated on the water, with simple wood floors. Gillnetters from all over the East Coast congregated there, some of whom Mordecai had met before and some who had been in Point Pleasant since November. People introduced themselves, asked where he was from, and which boat he was on, and they bought him beers and shots. Mark had settled up his earnings from Ocean City, in cash, the night before they left, and Mordecai was happy to buy a few rounds. With new boats arriving and people becoming acquainted and reacquainted, the night took on a festive atmosphere. Everyone anticipated the arrival of spring, and an end to a long, arduous yet prosperous migration. After he'd met everybody and had a couple beers, Mordecai saw Tiger sitting at the bar by himself, staring into a mug of draft beer.

"Whatcha doin', man?" Mordecai asked casually as he sat down on the stool next to him.

"Just passin' time; waitin' to go home. I still want to make money, but I don't want to spend too much time here. I haven't seen my girl since before Thanksgiving. When I get home I'm gonna get a new truck—no, maybe a decent used truck. Yeah, and a Harley. Then we're gonna take a ride somewhere, maybe up to Nova Scotia, Cape Breton. I heard it's nice up there in the summer." He stroked the condensation where the frost had melted on the mug. "I can't wait."

"You talk to her lately?"

"No. Not lately. I've called and left messages, but she hasn't been calling back. I don't understand; she's usually pretty good about that." He looked enviously at one of the guys they both knew from Ocean City; he had his arms around his wife. "Hope everything's all right." His tone suggested that things probably weren't all right and that the trip to Nova Scotia was as likely as Mordecai's ambition of getting a boat with Flip.

"I'm sure things will work out fine, Tiger."

"You think so?" he asked.

"Sure. You've just been away for a while. You'll reconnect when you get home."

"I hope so, man," he replied, staring back into the glass. Mordecai didn't have the heart to tell him that he suspected what Tiger probably suspected himself—that she'd moved on with someone else. Mordecai just wanted to lift his spirits for whatever time this journey had left. Tiger didn't have much of an appetite that night, but the two sternmen ordered food. Mordecai had one of the best cheeseburgers he'd ever eaten, and then he decided to take a walk over to the beach. Tiger said he'd kill another beer and head home later.

The cool spring night was damp with sea air as Mordecai stepped off the boardwalk and into the sand. He kicked off his shoes and socks and carried them toward the surf that was foaming against the beach. He rolled up his pants and stepped into the cold Atlantic, letting it flow around his feet and ankles. The moon was bright in the sky as it towed the tide along in its course. Mordecai thought of the nets five miles offshore and how they were fishing at that moment and suddenly, he felt connected—physically, spiritually, culturally—to his existence as a fisherman. He realized that wherever he was, if he could touch the ocean, part of him would always be home.

On the walk back to the hotel he thought of the men who were reunited with families and was reminded of a story he had read in a local paper back in Ocean City. The story was of William Birch, one of the first white settlers to try to eke out an existence on Assateague Island with his family before the Revolutionary War. At that time, there was plenty of wild game, fish, oysters, and crab, as well as cattle and wild hogs. All a family needed to do was build shelter, catch an ox, fashion a plow, and till a small plot of soil. With a small farm, available wild game, and proceeds from the woolen garments Mrs. Birch sold on the mainland, the family subsisted quite happily for a time.

The bays and coves around Assateague were convenient for pirates. One day, William Birch set out to work his field and never returned. Mrs. Birch never heard from him or of his fate, and for months she was alone with her young son on the island. Her husband had hollowed out a log as a makeshift canoe, called a punk, which they'd used to ferry to the mainland and nearby Chincoteague for supplies. At the close of the Revolutionary War, she set out with her son for the mainland in the punk to sell her woolen garments. They were poling along when they saw a man with a long beard, long hair, and ragged clothes walking along the shore. It was William Birch. He'd been captured by British troops, who took him to their ship, where he was held prisoner. At the war's end, they set him adrift on a raft near where they'd picked him up, and he came ashore just north of his home. The account related that the family was overjoyed to be reunited and hugged and cried for a long time.

As Mordecai thought of the story and of Tiger, who was longing for his girl, he realized that he wasn't homesick. In fact, he wished they were heading south instead of north. He was following the migratory pattern of a fish that were following the dictates of nature. Mark was undoubtedly going to head to his home and family in Chatham, and Mordecai would have to decide what he was going to do. North or south, he felt there was no one waiting for him.

At sunrise, Mark and Mordecai walked from their hotel room down to the wharf. Another fisherman friend of his would be driving Mark's truck up from Ocean City. Mark fired up the Cat 3306 and let it warm at an idle. Mordecai went up on the bow and watched the sky fill with morning light. When they got underway, Mark idled through the harbor, careful not to throw a wake, and Mordecai saw there was a fleet of boats using the harbor. As they came to the inlet, with its breakwater made of massive stone blocks, Mark gradually gave the boat more throttle until the *Sacajawea* was up to her cruising speed of fourteen knots. The boat was motoring through the channel between the breakwaters when Mordecai saw Mark working the wheel from side to side. When the boat didn't respond, he pulled the throttle back as the boat began a slow, arcing turn toward the breakwater. Mark slipped the transmission lever into neutral and muttered, "Son of a motherfuckin' bitch. I think we just lost our rudder." Mark walked to the stern and opened the hatch in the deck to the lazarette. "Fuck! It's gone!" he exclaimed. "Rudder post must've snapped and fallen out. Guess I should just be thankful it didn't go in the wheel." Mordecai was impressed that Mark could find something to be thankful for at such a moment.

They sat in the channel a few minutes, and then the *Decisive* pulled up alongside. The captains didn't even need to communicate. Mark told Mordecai to go up on the bow and grab the towline that Tiger was readying in the stern of the *Decisive.* Jan had seen Mark suddenly stop in the channel and knew that something was amiss. When they didn't get underway again, Jan knew they would require a tow back to the wharf. It was an unspoken agreement among mariners to help out their fellow fishermen.

Mordecai caught the heavy rope that Tiger threw him, wrapped his end around the cleat on the bow, and they began the short tow back to where they'd started. Mark and Mordecai tied up at the wharf and said thanks to the men on the *Decisive* as they again headed for open sea and a day of fishing. "You got the day off, Mordecai," said Mark. "I gotta find someone who can haul us out and fix this rudder."

"You sure you don't need me?"

"Positive."

Mordecai was a little disappointed that he wasn't needed to help fix the rudder. He wanted to learn and contribute, but he knew, as Mark probably did, that he didn't know anything about fixing boats and would probably be in the way. So he decided to check out the downtown of Point Pleasant. He walked back to the hotel and changed out of his fishing boots and into sneakers. After a twenty-minute walk, he was in the heart of downtown, where he found a diner and went in for some breakfast. At the counter, a friendly waitress brought him some coffee and took his order. Mordecai was delighted to find that the paper placemats were also history fact sheets of Point Pleasant.

Point Pleasant, he learned, was right in the middle of the Jersey coast. It was first noted by Robert Juct on Henry Hudson's 1609 expedition aboard the ship *Half Moon.* Juet noted in his journal that it "was a very good land to fall with and a pleasant land to see." It wasn't until 1811 that the first building in the area, Uncle Jakey's Tavern, was erected; it catered to hunters and fishermen. After the Civil War, a disabled veteran by the name of Roderick Clark built the first resort, and resort development then became the trend. Mordecai wondered how it was that the little jewel of his hometown, Scituate, had escaped this trend for so long.

Mordecai thought of the Assateague Indians, William Birch, and all the folks he had met. He saw a pattern that was sometimes a part of nature, sometimes human nature, and he wondered if it was crazy to think either could be controlled.

After two uneventful weeks in Point Pleasant, they brought the boat back to Mark's hometown of Chatham, Massachusetts. Mordecai stayed on the boat in Chatham and found the days off were a lot different from the communities of Ocean City and Point Pleasant. Chatham was beautiful in its rugged, undeveloped, natural tranquility, but there wasn't really much for Mordecai to walk to. He stayed on the boat most of the time, just reading in his bunk. The guys he met in Chatham took him out to their local watering holes and introduced him to their friends and families. But they were easing into their routines of being home. There was also the inconvenience of the boat's being on a mooring and not in a slip. In a slip, or tied to a dock, he could have just stepped off the boat and onto land. With a mooring, Mordecai had to row a skiff a couple hundred yards to shore, and if Mordecai had the skiff at the boat, Mark had to borrow one to get out to it. Mordecai could see that Mark didn't have room for him at his house, and although Mark offered, Mordecai didn't want to impose when he was getting back with his family.

There wasn't much going on in Chatham for fish at that point in the spring. Mordecai had been thinking about just staying there and figuring out a living situation, but he didn't know how long it might take for the fish to show up. He also had one other thing to resolve. He had thought about calling his parents, but decided there was something he wanted them to see. So one rainy day, he rowed the skiff in, walked to Mark's house, and told him that he needed to go home. Mark wasn't happy about being left with no help. Without a word, he drove Mordecai to the Greyhound station in Hyannis, and Mordecai caught a bus to Boston.

Mordecai felt ridiculous that he'd left by boat and was returning by bus. During the bus ride, he realized that he wasn't going home with any more money than he had left with. He'd left with a vision of steaming back into Scituate harbor with Flip, both of them with wads of cash in their pockets, ready to buy a boat.

After a two-hour bus ride, the Greyhound dropped Mordecai at South Station in Boston. He took the commuter rail to Scituate and walked from the train stop to the harbor. Mordecai sauntered over to the pier, unsure of how he would be received. He could see Wolf's pickup on the pier and knew he and the *Desire* were out fishing.

Tony and Eddie were on the *St. Joseph* and tied to the front of the pier, flaking new nets on for the spring fishing season. Mordecai stood at the edge for a moment and let the May sun warm his body. He could hear Tony teasing a fisherman who was offloading his catch from another boat tied to the pier. "Boy, look at all those fish," Tony joked. "How far you got to go to catch all those?" He imitated the question most frequently asked by tourists who had never seen a fishing boat.

"Thank God for this," replied the other as the totes went up in a sling. "By the end of the winter, I didn't have enough money to buy mayonnaise to mix with a can of tuna."

"Gonna git yerself a big ol' jar mayo now, huh, fella?" added Eddie.

"When the truck comes to the supermarket, tell 'em you want a whole pallet of mayo," Tony said as the two of them began a round of belly laughter.

"Does anybody know who a guy can talk to about getting a job around here?" Mordecai called down to the *St. Joseph*.

Tony looked up and saw Mordecai on the pier. "Well … did you make your fortune?"

Mordecai grinned. "Actually, I don't have any more money than the last time I saw you." Mordecai saw Tony smile. "Do you guys need any help?"

"Why? You need a job?" asked Ed.

"I'm unemployed at the moment."

Tony and Ed laughed. "Yeah, we saw that Wolfy came back without ya," laughed Tony.

"What happened to Flip?" asked Ed.

"I don't even know where to begin answering that one, Ed." Tony looked at Ed, then up at Mordecai.

"Well, if you want a job, we'll take you."

Mordecai climbed down the ladder, stepped on to the *St. Joseph* and began flaking the net with the joy of one who has found his way home.

When the re-united crew of the *St Joseph* finished flaking nets, Tony steamed the boat over to her mooring. Ed and Mordecai climbed the ladder to the front of the pier. At the top Ed asked,

"Can I give you a ride anywhere, fellah?" Mordecai thought about where he wanted to go and what he needed to do.

"No. I think I'll take a walk, Ed. But thanks. I got something I need to think about."

"Suit yourself." Ed dug for the keys to his truck. "We're getting a nice run of flounder so be ready for a long day and pack a lunch."

"As always."

"And don't forget one for him, too." Ed laughed while jerking his thumb over his shoulder towards the *St Joseph.* They both laughed at the old joke.

"I'll have to remember to pick up one of those oversize Snickers bars." Mordecai added. Both men walked away still laughing.

Mordecai headed down *Front St*, past the liquor stores, banks and the grocery where he had quit the last time he made this walk. It had only been a year but he felt a lifetimes worth of experience had been crammed into it. He wondered how his parents would receive him. There was only one way to find out. Mordecai walked through the harbor, toward St Mary's at the far end. As he approached the sub shop that stood next to the *Satuit Brook,* walking out, was Kerri Cole. He waved. "Hello, Kerri."

"Hey, Mordecai. How are you, home from school?"

"Home, anyway." He looked at the car she was walking toward, a new corvette. "Snazzy car. Where did you get that?"

"It's my boyfriends'. He's on the football team at Boston College."

"Oh. That's nice of him to let you use it"

"It's really cool. His parents bought it for him, they're *so rich.* We have so much fun in it. He has the coolest friends and we go to the best parties."

"That's great"

"What are you driving?"

"I'm not"

"Can I give you a ride anywhere?"

Mordecai looked over at St. Mary's and saw his father's Buick parked off of the street.

"No, I think I'm gonna walk. But thanks Kerri."

At St Mary's he had a choice of two routes he could take. *Stockbridge road* and *Kent Street* both would deliver him to his destination. He . *Kent Street* ran to the left of St. Mary's and by the grassy courtyard of the Church. In the center of the courtyard was the statue of St Joseph. In the courtyard, was a man kneeling at the feet of the patron saint of fathers, workers and travelers, with his head bowed in reverent prayer or deep thought. As he drew abreast of that figure, Mordecai recognized his father. Mordecai stopped walking and stood motionless. Again, he was unsure how he would be received. His father, kneeling, was also silent and with no motion. There was a slight motion from the man kneeling, and Mordecai watched as his father, with head bowed, made the sign of the cross. There was a little stone wall that separated the grass lawn of the church courtyard and the street that Mordecai stepped over as he said, "Hi Dad."

Richard Young turned, "Mordecai,"startled, unaware he was being watched. "Where have you been? We haven't seen you." He stood and faced Mordecai. "Your mother has been worried."

"I've been away for awhile."

"Are you still fishing on the St Joseph?"

"I'm back on the St Joseph now." Mordecai looked at his father. "How about you; still teaching?"

"I left teaching when the administration was offering incentives for teachers with seniority to retire. They can pay a kid just out of college half of what I cost. I've been unemployed since September."

"And so, praying to St Joseph."

"The patron Saint of fathers', that they may be providers." Richard Young appraised his son. "You knew that."

"Well, I was an altar boy."

"Actually, I came to chew him out a little. I haven't had much luck with the job search and I believe good friends can do that with each other." Mordecai thought about his situation. He was alive. Maybe St Joseph came through for his father in a way his father didn't know.

"How's Mom?"

"Well, why don't you come see for yourself?" The two men began walking toward the car parked on the edge of the street.

“Still got the old Buick”, Mordecai said.
“Yep. Still running strong. Think I’ll hold on to her.”

Epilogue
Requiem for *St. Joseph*

G. K. Chesterton once wrote that there are two ways to find your way home. One is to leave and completely circle the globe until you come upon it again; the other is to never leave. Mordecai had not accomplished what he set out to do when he left Scituate, but he felt there had been some accomplishment in surviving the experience.

Mordecai never did see Mark, Wayne, Tiger, Andy, Fred Good, or any of the Chatham fishermen from that trip again. About ten years later, while working on various gillnetters that could fish outside of the closed-to-fishing Massachusetts Bay, Mordecai saw a white, forty-two–foot Bruno as it passed the tip of the cape, and he wondered if it was Mark on the *Sacajawea.*

In 2006, faced with crippling restrictions and closures that only allowed him to fish forty-four days a year, as well as catch limits that made the economic reality of fishing a boat like the *St. Joseph* impossible, Tony sold the *St. Joseph* to another fisherman who wanted it for the permits. Eddie had left fishing and had taken a full-time job in a custodial position with the public schools in Scituate. When Ed left, Tony had the boat hauled out while he considered his options. Mordecai had been filling in on various boats and going to night school for journalism. The *St. Joseph* sat in the field at Eddie's for over a year, and her mechanizations had frozen completely with corrosion. It was obvious to everyone familiar with the vessel that her fishing days were over. In May 2007, the new owner had the *St. Joseph* hauled away to be stripped of usable parts and demolished. On June 14, the anniversary of Henry Mancini's death, Tony received a call from the Coast Guard. The electronic position indicating radio beacon, or EPIRB, was going off. The EPIRB electronic device, attached to all fishing boats, sent a radio distress signal to the Coast Guard if it sensed the boat had sunk, or if it was manually set off by a crew member. The radio signal broadcast information about the location of the beacon, the size and type of boat, and how many crew were aboard. The Coast Guard dispatcher informed Tony that the EPIRB was going off twenty feet underground, in a landfill in Camden, Maine.

As for his old friend Flip, Mordecai had heard that he made bail and had left the *Dogpound* in Maryland for the owner to retrieve, but that was the last he had heard of him. Mordecai didn't hear anything about where Flip was for ten years, but he always hoped that someday he would manage to find his way home again, too.

In March 2008, after filling in on various boats that worked around the closures and working odd jobs, Mordecai received a phone call from a local fisherman who was looking for one other sternman to fill his crew. Mordecai arrived at five the next morning to find the boat at the back float dock. As he walked along in the single-digit temperature toward the dark silhouette of the boat, Mordecai wondered who the other crewman would be. A figure coiling line in the stern said, "Hey, dude." Mordecai was speechless. Although he could barely see him, he knew, at long last, that his friend Flip had come home. The two stood facing each other, neither knowing where to start. Then Flip broke across the barrier of years and gave Mordecai a big hug. Mordecai could see that the years had taken a toll on his friend. He looked older than his years, with his hair gone gray at the temples and dark creases around his eyes. But Mordecai was happy to have his friend back and to be going fishing with him. As they went through the day, Mordecai learned that Flip had lost his father to cancer, gotten married and divorced, lived in different places all over the country, and had fought a losing battle with heroine, ultimately landing in prison for a year. But he had no regrets of the year in jail. "It's what it took to get me to quit and straighten out," he told Mordecai as they headed for the mooring from the fish pier after unloading a fair day's catch. Flip was happy to be home, helping out his mother, and Mordecai felt that Flip's mother was undoubtedly happy to have her son home.

The sun was setting, and the air held the warming promise of a coming spring. "I think the biggest reward to coming home is the chance to work at getting my self-esteem back," Flip said. Mordecai smiled at this as he leaned back against the rail. The setting sun reflected off the water and warmed him, and he basked in the glow of a friend.

Made in the USA
Charleston, SC
18 September 2013